WINTER STAR

CASSANDRA ELIZZABETH

KISSING CAMELS PUBLISHING

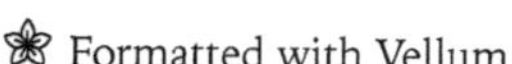 Formatted with Vellum

Dedication

Let's get lost in the frost.
Sure, it's cold here.
But I've got an 8 foot Yeti to keep you warm.

Author's Note

When I was twenty-one, I went on the adventure of a lifetime—including an out-of-body experience in a small temple in Varanasi and trekking through a Himalayan mountain town that still lives in my soul. I came home, dreaming in Hindi, but a piece of me has always remained there, sipping chai on the ghats of the Ganges river with the sun glinting off my glass bangle bracelets.

So when I sat down to write a Yeti romance, I knew exactly where I wanted to return. This story gave me the excuse to not only revisit that incredible time in my life, but to imagine what might happen if something ancient and beautiful was waiting in the dark to claim me and hold me there forever.

Yeti season started with *Yeti or Knot,* a spicy, monster romance novella that I wrote in less than two months. I had so much fun with it, but couldn't keep it short enough for the group release that inspired it. So instead, I wrote an origin story, *Chosen by the Yeti,* and then developed *Yeti or Knot* in a full novel. Eryon wanted his voice heard, and who am I to deny an eight foot Yeti anything he wants.

This story contains graphic sexual content (with the Yeti),

including: knotting, primal play, sensory deprivation, size difference, squirting, ass play, just the tip, and breeding kink. You'll also find one cave (instead of one bed), accidental mating, a cinnamon roll monster, on page violence, and one unhinged cheating ex. There are also references to loss of a parent and genetic disease. If you prefer a bulleted format, read on.

The following is a content note for the epilogue so if you want it to be a surprise, don't read the next sentence. Spoiler: when a mommy human and daddy Yeti love each other very much, the inevitable happens. If you prefer Dahlia & Eryon childless, skip the epilogue. But if you're in for mini-fluff balls, read til the end.

If monster romance, fated mates, exes getting what they deserve, and women in STEM getting absolutely wrecked by gentle giants is your thing—you're in the right cave.

Pour yourself a cup of chai and get lost in the frost with me.

Yeti or Knot, let's do this.

—*Cassandra*

CONTENT WARNINGS

Betrayal and cheating (FMC's fiancé)
Intimate partner violence (wrist-grabbing/controlling behavior
by fiancé)
Violence and peril in survival settings
Death and loss
Gore (animal attacks, blood)
Forced proximity elements
Explicit sexual content, including human/monster intimacy
Size and power imbalance (consensual)
Possessive/protective love interest
Alcohol and drug use or references
Terminal genetic disease

PLAYLIST

AURORA – *Runaway*
Hidden Citizens – *Silent Running*
Puggy & Rochelle Riser – *Out in the Open*
Isabel LaRosa – *Cry for You*
David Kushner – *Breathe In, Breathe Out*
Ruelle – *War of Hearts (Acoustic)*
Jade – *Frozen*
Hozier – *Like Real People Do*
Florence + The Machine – *Cosmic Love*
Katie Garfield – *Who Will Save You*
Hidden Citizens – *I Ran* (cover)
Slipknot – *Vermilion, Pt. 2*
Slipknot – *Snuff*
Lana Del Rey – *Gods & Monsters*
Florence + The Machine – *Never Let Me Go*
AURORA – *Running With the Wolves*
Sleeping At Last – *All Through the Night*
Ruelle – *Where Do We Go From Here*
Hidden Citizens – *Immortalized*

Freya Ridings – *Lost Without You*
Ben Platt – *Grow As We Go*

CHAPTER ONE

DAHLIA

I cradle the small clay cup in my hands, the warmth seeping into my fingers as I edge closer to the fire. I tell myself I should go to bed—rest before the long, grueling trip home tomorrow. But the pull of this bittersweet night keeps me rooted here, savoring the last moments of an incredible, albeit fruitless, journey.

I take the final sip of my chai—the rich, creamy tea that tastes like the essence of this place, its sweetness lingering on my tongue as I half-listen to the other travelers swapping tales. Their voices melt into the background as my gaze drifts over the edge of the woods across the Migaia River.

Moonlight pools like silver on the water, dappling trees in sharp relief against the night. Below the canopy, the forest floor vanishes into inky shadows, breathing secrets in invitation.

I don't know why I can't tear my eyes away. I've seen this same view every night since I arrived, been up and down its banks. But tonight, there's something different. Something alive in the air. It crackles over my skin like electricity before a lightning strike and raises the fine hairs on the back of my neck.

I scan the riverbank, searching for the source, until...*there*. Two luminous eyes lock onto mine, glittering under the moonlight like the icy blue heart of Migshira, the holy glacier at the headwaters of this river.

They are too high for any of the local animals—far above where even a tall man's gaze would reach. Too large, too fierce and knowing to belong to the monkeys that call these trees home. Their gleam cuts through the darkness with an intensity that steals my breath.

Who, or what, is watching me from the shadows?

I freeze, pinned in place, caught like prey ensnared in a hunter's trap. A thrill courses through me, sharp and jagged, mingling fear with something darker, something hotter. My instincts scream at me to run, but my body doesn't move—can't move.

It's not just fear keeping me rooted here; there's a pull in those eyes, a wordless promise of danger and...something else. Something primal and fierce that I long to chase me down and lay claim to me, as illogical as that sounds. Something to disrupt my tightly held control, to piece back together my life that is slowly unraveling at the seams.

Adrift in a sea of loss from my failed research expedition and an uncertain future without the plant I was so desperately searching for, the idea of belonging, of being made whole again calls to my soul. An anchor for this stormy season.

Despair threatens to wash over me, drown me in its dark, icy depths. But I can't give up hope yet. Surely, all cannot be lost. My throat aches as tears prick my eyes. *Not here, not now*, I tell myself, surprised by the emotion that stare has pulled from the dark recesses of my soul. Shocked at how easily it cracks my carefully controlled facade to wrench me open, bare my secrets.

As if there is also a promise, a comfort that I finally could be free if I only gave myself over.

I blink hard, breaking the spell. When I open my eyes, the darkness has swallowed the mysterious sight. They may be gone, but the pull remains, and oh, how I want to surrender myself to those shadows. How I long for the release from these self-imposed constraints. How I wish to be as wild as these mountains.

I glance down at the clay cup in my hands, tilting it toward the firelight. The liquid swirls innocently. Just tea, none of the local *bhang*. I had tried the edible cannabis only once when I had first arrived. After all, what kind of ethnobotanist would I be if I didn't partake in the ceremonial and social use of a native plant?

The fire burned brighter that night as we sipped our laced *lassi* drinks. I wanted a second one, but luckily, my friend and host, Sita, stopped me at one. A few hours later, I was relaxed enough to want to dance under the stars on the hard-packed dirt surrounding the firepit.

I stuck to what I had learned early on in my field research— listen to the locals. As Sita steered me to my room and away from my impromptu dance floor, I was thankful for her guid- ance. A second drink and I might have hallucinated.

Tonight's vivid vision must be my mind playing tricks on me, exhaustion casting imaginary eyes where there aren't any. The yearning to belong must just be my heart aching for my fiancé, Ben, back home. He is my anchor, not some imagined, myste- rious pull from the dark woods. I just need to get home and go back to serious, scientific Dahlia Wilde. Although as Ben liked to point out, Wilde had always seemed like an oxymoron for a science nerd like me.

The past few days had been brutal as I pushed myself to find the elusive plant this whole trip had been for—*Silene vitalis*. A tiny flower with a big possibility to save lives. My life. And it had been for naught.

I had always loved plants, and the summers I spent working in a greenhouse taught me they made it easier for me to interact with people. So, when I stumbled upon a niche career where I could marry the two, I was thrilled. What I hadn't known then was that my unusual choice would turn out to be my only chance at running down a cure for the disease that took my mother. An inborn error of metabolism that would cause an accumulation of fatal proteins to turn toxic over time.

There is no known cure or treatment, no hope on the horizon. So, I took matters into my own hands and empowered myself the only way I knew how: I took my grief over losing my mother in the middle of college, and I buried my nose deeper into books as I lost myself in the library.

I analyzed botanical medicines, natural cures, and dusty tomes of plant extracts, seeking an antidote to the protein. I don't know why I thought I, Dahlia Wilde, would find some miracle cure when all the doctors and scientists had failed. But I didn't have a choice. Because my mother had passed that same damn gene down to me.

So, I scanned every database, exhausted every dusty library stack, and hounded every botanist I could get to talk to me until I found one promising compound in a handwritten journal. I traced it down like a determined bloodhound until finally, I hit paydirt, digging through some nice lady's great uncle's dusty attic bins where I found a single preserved specimen.

When I lifted it from its resting place, undisturbed for years and forgotten by the world, the setting sun streamed through the grimy window, casting the specimen in a golden glow. Time had reduced most of the plant to a withered, lifeless brown, but one petal—just one—defied its fate.

It gleamed with an almost unnatural brilliance, a luminous, iridescent, blue violet that mirrored the striking eye color my mother had passed down to me, along with this cursed disease. From the moment I first stumbled upon a mention of this plant back in the library, I knew the coloring they described was no coincidence. But there were no words to do it justice, it was mesmerizing.

Seeing it in my hands, tangible, solidified my resolve—I, too, would defy my fate. Like the lone petal that refused to fade, I would be the first to survive this legacy of death. The *Silene vitalis* was the answer, and I would track it down.

The journal had listed a vague, general location deep in the Himalayan mountains with a hand drawn map. It would be like finding a needle in a haystack. But what choice did I have?

Back in the lab, the mass spectrometry had analyzed the only viable fragment from the shimmering petal preserved by sheer luck, or maybe fate. My hands had trembled as I prepared the sample, scarcely daring to breathe. The slightest mishap could ruin the only sample in existence, and thereby, the only Dahlia Wilde in existence.

Using a sterilized mortar and pestle, I ground it into a fine powder and then soaked it for hours in methanol. As I filtered the liquid until it ran clear, I felt like I was walking a tightrope— one wrong step and I'd lose everything. With a whispered prayer, I injected the final extract into the mass spectrometer.

I counted the beats of my heart while I waited for the results to load, each thud echoing the weight of my hope, my hard work, my *life*, hanging in the balance. As the machine's readout flickered to life, a graph blooming in jagged peaks against a black screen, I held my breath as if my exhale would make the image vanish. Each peak held its own story, its position on the x-axis marking its mass-to-charge ratio while the height declared its abundance.

My eyes locked on a towering spike at m/z 152.1—a match to the theoretical mass of the compound I was hunting. A smaller peak at 198.3 confirmed the presence of a secondary compound, hinting at the medicinal properties I needed.

In the corner, the software cross-referenced the data with its molecular library. The text glowed faintly, *C12H10O3*, followed by the name: Silenol. Below it, a 2D molecular structure appeared, its lines and rings promising salvation.

I exhaled a shaky breath. It wasn't just hope anymore. It was proof. I read it, then read it again, my vision swimming as tears blurred the screen. I was right. I was *fucking* right!

Risking that one shimmering petal had been worth the gamble. The plant's unique chemical profile confirmed my theory—a potential cure, real and tangible, blooming before my eyes. The weight of it crashed over me, my forehead sinking to the desk as I let the tears finally fall.

It wasn't just overwhelming joy—it was something deeper, sharper, and infinitely more complicated. A fierce exhilaration tangled with a grief so raw it left me aching inside. The knowledge that I had been right, that I had proven it, was a triumph I had dreamed of.

But the burn in my chest expanded in the shadow of the hollow victory because I hadn't found it in time to save my mother. The cure sat before me like a promise kept too late, a bittersweet triumph that came with its own kind of failure.

The juxtaposition tore at me, the euphoria of discovery and the devastation of loss hopelessly tangled into a gordian knot of emotion. A sob broke loose, harsh and ragged, and I let it. Because no amount of progress, no groundbreaking discovery, could undo the aching truth that she was gone.

Beyond my own harsh sobs in the cold and still lab, her voice came to me so clear I jerked my head up to look around.

Onwards and upwards, honey.

I took a deep breath, forcing air through my collapsed lungs and willing the blood to pump again through my broken heart. I moved forward with my discovery because I knew she would never want me to stay locked in the past, would never want me to waste a second chasing down my own cure as I grieved the loss of her.

I took her advice to heart, pushing ever onwards as I wrote grant proposals with fierce determination, convincing my department that this expedition was essential, not just for my doctorate, but for something far greater. Saving lives. Though I suspected the promise of new pharmaceuticals swayed them more than my appeal for humanity.

But I didn't dare tell them it was to save my own life. Ben didn't even know yet. There was just no good way to put words to the magnitude of what I was facing. I promised myself I would tell him, maybe when I finally had the cure in my hands.

And so, here I stand—literally, onwards and upwards—in the village of Migdhari, nestled high in the Himalayan mountains, chasing a plant lost to time. The people are as warm and welcoming as the air is thin and crisp. My journey has taken me up and down treacherous mountain paths, along roaring riverbeds, and crisscrossing terrain as I spoke to anyone who would listen.

I asked yogis meditating in solitude, travelers passing through on pilgrimages, locals with weathered faces, and elders whose families had lived here for generations. But no one knew of the star-shaped, blue-violet flower I hunted for.

Every once in a while, I thought maybe I saw a flicker in someone's eyes, as if they had heard of the plant, but weren't willing to share their knowledge. But maybe that was what I wanted to see—a glimmer of hope where there was none. Even with Sita, whose own family had deep roots here, translating and paving the way, we still had come up empty handed.

My last set of labs showed the toxic protein in my blood is just now starting to increase. I'm not out of sand in the hourglass of my life quite yet, but I am out of time here in India. I need to go home and regroup. The idea of retracing my footsteps through the years of research that had led me here is daunting, but what choice do I have? I have to do so, and fast.

Maybe the journals I had read and the research I had painstakingly done were wrong. Just one mountain range over, hell just one town over, would make all the difference in my ability to find it. Handwritten notes certainly ran the risk of being inaccurate. Or maybe I really am blinded by my own impartiality. But I let it go. I can't solve this problem tonight, and I can't search anymore.

Although I still have a few months left on my visa, I am out of research funds, and my flight home leaves tomorrow. The only silver lining is getting home to Ben. He was guarded when I explained my grand plan and cautioned me to not be overly optimistic, but I know as soon as I'm in his arms, he will help me find a path forward. I've helped him with his work for years, and I know he will help me with mine now.

I understood he couldn't before; first when he was working on his own academic progress and then with all the responsibilities as a new tenure track professor. But surely now, especially when I tell him what lies in the balance, he can carve out the time for me. I can't in good conscience wait for the cure any longer to tell him my future is uncertain. Especially now that we are engaged. I want our future to be built on trust.

A sudden snap of the fire pulls me from my thoughts, the sound sharp and alive in the stillness. The circle of travelers comes back into focus, their laughter rising like sparks into the quiet night. For a moment, I let the peace of the evening wash over me, but it's the question that cuts through it all, drawing me fully from my spiraling thoughts.

"Have you ever seen one?" someone asks, leaning forward with a conspiratorial grin.

"Seen what?" My voice comes out steady, even as my pulse thrums beneath my skin, thinking somehow they had heard about my mission, that someone had seen my flower. Hope flares in my chest that somehow this random traveler had found my elusive plant, and just in the nick of time.

"A Migoi," the man says, his voice dropping to a near whisper, as if one might be lurking just beyond the ring of firelight. "They say their eyes catch the light like stars scattered across the night sky. And sometimes if you're lucky, or unlucky, you'll see them watching. Silent. Waiting."

His words fall like stones in the silence until another traveler breaks the heavy moment with a scoff, waving the comment away. But his words claw their way into my thoughts and refuse to let go. The locals had spoken of such creatures, what I'd call a Yeti, with quiet reverence. I'd dismissed it as folklore, an easy story to weave into the mystique of these mountains.

Stories and plants are my bread and butter as an ethnobotanist. I don't just study plants; I study the way people live alongside them, how they turn leaves and roots into food, ceremony, and, as I hope to, medicine. But now, the idea of the legendary guardians of the mountains and forests worms its way into my mind. Myths, after all, often hold a kernel of truth buried somewhere deep inside.

And if something as massive and elusive as a Yeti could remain hidden here, it means there are places I haven't yet explored in my search. It's humbling to think how much I've missed, how much still hides beyond the edges of the trails I've carefully mapped from my research notes. Because surely, I would have noticed a giant Migoi if it were anywhere near this town or in the surrounding mountains I've crawled over inch by inch. Wouldn't I?

A woman claps a hand on my shoulder, pulling me out of my spiraling thoughts. My face must've given me away—again. The pain of leaving India empty-handed mixed with the far-off stare of someone seriously contemplating the existence of Yetis, likely left me looking torn between heartbreak and madness.

"Don't let those guys spook you," she says with a chuckle,

misinterpreting my expression. "I've traveled the world, and every culture has its tales of watchers—be it the waters, forests, or mountains. Once I was certain I saw the Daughter of the Moon. Have you heard that legend? But it turned out to be nothing more than a white deer, mixed with jet lag and a heavy dose of imagination."

I force a laugh, murmuring in agreement, but I'm already ruminating on where I could have missed both the Yeti and the flowers in the months I'd been here. Searching for logic in lore.

With a huff of frustration at both the situation and my own ridiculous musings, I toss the dregs of my tea into the flames. Liquid hisses into a faint wisp of steam, and my eyes follow the trail as it dissolves into the cooling night air before glancing back across the river—to the spot where I had seen the mysterious silver orbs. That was the one area we hadn't searched. The place Sita had warned me was too treacherous, even for the locals.

Although I can no longer see them, I still feel their heated stare, a weight pressing against my chest, heavy and unyielding. Whoever—or *whatever*—those eyes belong to, it's as if they are still there. Watching. Waiting.

A flush creeps up my neck, and I rise abruptly, murmuring goodnights to the others. No one seems to notice as I retreat toward the safety of my room, the pull of those shadows pressing at my back, insistent and unshakable. I tell myself it's just the night chill, but the feeling lingers, prickling along my skin long after I've stepped away from the firelight.

Away from the fire, the mountain air and darkness conspire against me, whispering secrets of danger into my ear to hurry me along. The uneven stone path forces me to tread carefully, but every scrape of my boots against the rocks seems too loud, too exposed. I quicken my steps, the memory of those luminous eyes haunting me—piercing and inescapable—more unnerving than the risk of a twisted ankle.

What was it someone had said? *"Eyes like stars in the dark?"* The image gnaws at me, the description matching exactly. Could there really be Yetis in these mountains—Migoi lurking in the forests beyond the river?

A rustle to my right snaps my nerves taut, every instinct screaming at me to move faster. The memory of those fierce eyes flickers in my mind, and I realize how foolish I'd been to think I wanted whatever it was to chase me, to claim me. Out here, alone and vulnerable in the dark, I recognize the absurdity of that reckless fantasy.

Another sharp noise breaks the quiet of the night, but I don't dare look back. By the time I reach my door, my hands are shaking, the key slipping against the lock. It takes a few fumbled tries before the mechanism clicks, the sound slicing through the stillness like salvation.

I slip inside and press my back into the door, drawing in ragged breaths as my heart pounds. From the safety of the locked room, a nervous giggle escapes me, and I roll my eyes at my own foolishness. I'd let myself be consumed by a fireside tale. But the break in focus was welcome compared to the devastation I now face.

The thick quilt on the bed promises comfort, its weight a soothing barrier against whatever lies outside. Still, my thoughts swirl like the impending snow, refusing to settle. The unease clings to me, my mind replaying the sight of those eyes and the dark promise that danced in them. Could it have been exhaustion playing tricks on me? Or maybe desperation?

Three months of chasing down an elusive plant. Three months away from home and Ben, only to return empty-handed and out of options. No plant means no research, no progress, no doctorate, and little time left to find another solution.

Failure. The word lodges in my throat, thick and viscous. I had failed to save my mom, and now I may very well fail to save myself. But failure isn't an option.

My hands still shake as I pull the blanket higher, trying to chase away the cold reality of defeat. So much time, so much effort, so many long days. I wonder if Ben will be as upset as I am. Or worse, what if he's disappointed in me? Or won't help me after all?

The thought tightens something in my chest, but I reassure myself that he loves me. The unease must be the lingering thought of those damn eyes. Silly really, when they were nothing more than a trick of the firelight, a phantom born of fireside chats and exhaustion. And even if something is out there, it's not like it can follow me home tomorrow. And I don't think I'll ever be back here.

With my heart ticking like the death knell that awaits me without the damned *Silene vitalis*, sleep claims me.

CHAPTER TWO

ERYON - EARLIER

Despite the pull of my Winter Star—my name for this divine creature—I force myself to stay hidden in the woods. Even at this distance, I can see her moving about the guesthouse. I watch her pull her coat tight against the cold, her fragile human body shivering as she races from the warm fire to her warm sanctuary, her feet slipping on the icy, rocky path.

I pity this female with her clumsy movements and lack of adaptive evolution—she hardly has enough hair to even keep her head warm. Despite the weakness of her flesh, I can sense in her a quiet, determined strength. Tonight, though, the tightness around her eyes betrays her smile, and her heartbreak rides to me on the Northern winds where it wraps around my own heart like an icy vise.

I've studied her for months now and can read her face as easily as the clouds that will soon bring the winter snows. So, though she tries to hide her infinite sadness, tries to be strong and independent, I can see her suffering. She hasn't always been like this.

The change is so drastic compared to when I had first watched her crisscross the mountain paths and surrounding towns like a determined, stubborn little goat. Those stolen glances had provided me with more happiness than I've known in many, many years.

I remember the first time I saw her, an unexpected surprise when I had stumbled upon her from behind. One glance at her rounded bottom peeking out from beneath a bright berry purple coat as she bent over, digging in the dirt, demanded my attention. I stood there, admiring the view, while she squatted down and examined something more closely.

When she turned her head to call someone over, the autumn sun bathed her face in golden light as if she were a divine offering birthed from the season itself. My heart pounded like a *tabla* drum, each beat reverberating through my chest like a prayer. Her hair shimmered with all the colors I've ever seen the sun kiss the earth—the golden glow of a spring sunrise, the rich red of the ruby flowers that shimmered during the monsoons, and the deep chestnut hues of autumn leaves just before they surrender to the ground.

Each kaleidoscope curl was like a living thing, playfully catching the light as if inviting me to sink my hands into its glorious mass—to wrap them around my fingers and tug just until she gasped in pleasure. Vividly, I could imagine her kneeling before me, the sharp contrast of her small head held between my large palms as I claimed her mouth, plunging my length in and out between those full lips.

I wanted to bury my face in those curls as we lost ourselves in each other, wind them around my fingers in the lazy dawn, feel them cascade over my flesh as she laid in my arms. A thousand visions of the fiery ringlets danced in my mind, each more sinful than the last.

Watching her, I forgot the centuries of solitude that had dulled my frozen heart. All that remained was her, bending over those flowers, utterly oblivious to the way she had just cracked the thick wall of ice around the poor dead organ that lived in my chest.

I wanted her—no, I *needed* her, as surely as I needed my next breath of mountain air. She should have looked out of place, a stranger in this land. But instead, she looked like shelter in the storm, warmth in the frigid cold of winter, a light in the darkness of my lonely existence. Perhaps my heart wasn't so dead after all.

I was so enthralled by my fantasies of her that an audible groan escaped me, drawing her gaze over her shoulder toward the trees where I was hidden. I froze—not in fear of being discovered, I almost wanted her to see me, but because of her eyes.

Her perfect, round bottom had caught my attention, her hair had my imagination running wild with desire, but those eyes— they pierced my soul and threw my entire world off its axis.

As she started to look back down to the little plant at her feet, I made another small noise, on purpose this time, just to see her eyes once more. I wasn't done looking my fill. I don't know if I ever will be.

I had never seen a human with eyes this color, the exact shade of the little star shaped flower that only grew in my caves. We called it winter star, named for its shape and the season of its bloom. Thus, her name was born—my Winter Star.

Humans are nothing new to me. After all, I've protected the balance of nature for centuries, and humans are part of that balance—sometimes a source of creation, often a force of destruction, but always part of the harmony. I had seen many of them over the centuries, but I had never cared about what they looked like.

But this human—she called to me in a way wholly unexpected. I wanted to know everything about her. Not just see her but *understand* her. Not just marvel at the flame in her hair and the flower in her eyes, but to drink in the essence of who she is. I wanted to watch the night sky reflected in her gaze, to see if their hue shifted with the first light of dawn. Or better yet, to see if they deepened into the rich, endless blue of twilight when she lost herself to me in pleasure as I devoured her.

And yet, beneath that primal desire was something deeper. Something raw. Fragile. Once, I had known a love bond where my soul sang in harmony with another's. And I had lost her—not to nature or time, but to human greed. To their hunger for domination over the world and all its gifts.

I had vowed never to mate again, certain I would never experience love again, that all my hopes and dreams were buried with my family. But now—now my heart roared to life, thrumming with a rhythm I'd thought long silenced. It was both exhilarating and terrifying.

Why had fate led me to this woman of all creatures? A human, the very kind that had torn my world apart before. And yet how could I deny this pull? This thread that wound itself around me and bound me to her? It felt as though the stars themselves had carved this path, weaving her into my life in defiance of my fears. Or perhaps even in spite of them. Was this the balance?

I had so many questions for her—where she had come from, what was she doing? But I didn't need to ask where she was going. That, I already knew. She was coming with me.

As confident as I was in my assertion, a shadow of doubt lingered in the back of my mind, whispering warnings. Did I dare trust her? Could I risk the pain of losing again? My brain rapid fired rational questions, but my heart beat steadily on *mine, mine, mine*. My soul throbbed with the knowledge that she had to feel this, too.

When she scanned the woods, searching for the source of the noise I purposely made, I held my breath, motionless. When her eyes passed over me, I felt them as if she were running her fingertips over my flesh. I knew she couldn't see me, but I could feel the ripple of her awareness, as though some primal instinct stirred within her. As if my soul called to hers and not only had it heard, but it answered, *Here. I am here.*

Her gaze returned again to the exact spot where I stood, her brow furrowed as though sensing something just beyond her reach. I knew her soul would respond in kind. After a few heavy beats, she stood and gave herself a small shake, as if trying to cast off my hold on her and went to find her friend. But even as she walked away, I felt her awareness linger, and for the rest of the day, her curious gaze searched the trees for me.

I was curious about her, too. Unlike the others, this little human hadn't come for yoga or a pilgrimage. She seemed to be here for the earth itself—to study the plants and the land. I could tell she was looking for something specific and couldn't help but wonder not just what she searched for, but why.

Unlike so many who passed through these mountains, even those who called themselves pilgrims, she walked as though she belonged here, as though the earth itself welcomed her soft footfalls. Countless times, her fingers brushed the plants and trees with a reverence I had never seen in a human.

When I saw her delicate fingers stroking the broad leaf of a low bush, a growl escaped me at the thought of those same hands brushing against my flesh—an aching need to be worshipped by her. To have those same fingers buried deep in my fur or gripped tight around my aching member, which had been hard at the sight of her all day.

I couldn't recall the last time I had physical contact with another living creature, but guessed it was easily over a hundred years ago, ever since—I stopped myself, shoving the memories back into the shadowy recesses of my long memory where they belonged. It was too painful to examine them in the light of day.

The sun played in her curls, casting shadows and light like

the rippling river as she searched. All day, I watched her, unable to look away. When evening came, I followed her to make sure she reached the small town safely. I knew of the guide who accompanied her—a member of a family I once saved during a cruel winter when they ran out of fuel.

But I didn't trust anyone to get her home without my oversight. I had learned long ago that when humans are a force of destruction, they could rival the devastation wrought by the goddess Kali herself. And I couldn't let her be subject to her own kind.

Once the two women were safely back home, I crossed back over the river, the icy water biting at my legs, and lingered at the edge of the woods. From my hidden vantage point, I watched as my Winter Star emerged to sit by the fire, its warm glow reflecting in her eyes.

We repeated this process for months, me trailing after her like a lost pup during the day and then making sure she got home safely in the evenings. As the days grew colder and her determination grew fiercer, I grew to feel as if I knew her. I could read the angle of her smile and the tilt of her head. Her excitement was evident in the way she made that little hand gesture, and her fatigue showed in the way she put both hands on her hips and stretched her back.

Eventually, from overheard snippets of her conversation, I learned that she was looking for a specific plant with a name I had never heard. I watched her talk to anyone she could find with a ready smile and hope shining in her eyes.

But with each passing day, her light dimmed, and I sensed her time here was drawing to a close. She pushed herself harder and longer, exhaustion etching lines into her face as she raced against a sun that set a little earlier each day. The mountain waits for no one. The loss of hope seemed to tug at her curls, as if even they mourned.

I tried to convince myself this had just been a diversion—a

novelty, a fleeting encounter with a bright, little human who stirred long-forgotten feelings in my heart and body. But the lie was bitter in my mouth.

And tonight, that bitterness deepens when I sense she's leaving tomorrow. Though she goes through her usual night-time routine, each task is a little slower, a little more deliberate —as if she's committing every moment to memory, savoring the last of it. As if she doesn't want to leave not just her search, but this place—my home. And in that moment, I can't help but wish it was me she didn't want to leave. *Me*, that she had been searching for all along.

As she sits by the fire and carefully schools her face, she cannot hide the heartbreak that bleeds so freely from her chest it sneaks across the river like fog to wind its fingers into me, scrabbling at my heart like the icy northern winds.

I want to go to her, wrap her up in my great strong arms, shield her from the world with my body. I want to give her comfort and reassurance that whatever she is so sad about doesn't matter. Whisper into her tiny, round hairless ear that everything will be okay if only the two of us face it together. We can hide away for all time in my caves and lose ourselves in each other.

But I cannot run to her, cannot take on the darkness with her. Because she is a human, and I—I am not.

The truth settles in my chest, a cold, aching weight with the destructive force of an avalanche. She belongs to the world of the rising sun, to the warmth of firelight, to the land of others like her. And I—I am made of shadow and stone, of cold wind and endless silence. There is no place for me in her life beyond this fleeting moment, this strange crossing of fates.

I ache to go after her. To tell her she doesn't have to leave. That she could stay here, with me, in this wild place where infinite stars prick across the velvet tapestry of night and the North winds sing through the trees. Where there is austere beauty in rock and snow, and great discovery within the silence. Where we can just be two souls, lost to the world but found in each other.

But I know better. The pull of her world with its speed and technology is too strong, her journey not one I can share. No matter how much my soul protests, how much this thread between us tugs my soul to hers, I cannot be what she needs. I am a Migoi, a monster, a legend. I am tied to this place and this sacred duty, my dharma, to protect and balance.

And so, I let her go.

I close my eyes and release my worry for her out into the universe, as if unburdening it will keep her safe. The mountains around me stand steadfast and unchanging, their peaks holding back the coming light of dawn as if cradling this moment in the sky's velvet embrace. I focus on them, on their ancient wisdom, and I ask them to watch over her. To pass their quiet comfort into her soul.

I imagine her footsteps on the trail ahead, her heart heavy but determined. I hope she feels the mountains' strength beneath her feet, grounding her. Hears their whispers in the wind, reminding her she is not alone. I hope she carries the wildness of this place with her always, even as she returns to a world that will stamp it out and endeavor to erase the magic touch of these peaks.

The ache does not leave me, but I accept it. It is the price of knowing her, even for so brief a time. Yes, she is human, and I am not—but in some strange, impossible way, we are still bound. And perhaps that is enough. It has to be, because it is all I have.

I watch the horizon where she will disappear, willing the thread between us to hold fast. Even as she goes, I vow that I will remember her, always, and choke down the exquisite pain that comes with her loss with a deep thanks and grateful heart.

The heartache was worth having her be mine, even if only for a little while. Even if she will never know.

In my eagerness to protect her, even from herself—to be just the smallest bit closer to her and shoulder her burden—I had unconsciously stepped right up to the edge of the trees. When her eyes flick up from the fire to meet mine, I freeze, shocked that she has seen me from this great distance.

Shooting a glance at the sky, I realize the full moon and starry expanse must have reflected back at her in my luminous eyes, glinting with a bright silver sure to draw her attention. The weight of her stare sinks into my soul, stripping it bare, bringing my pounding heart painfully to the surface, leaving me exposed and vulnerable. My adaptations to the harsh environment I call home can't save me now. I have no defenses against her.

The shock and awe that accompany the rare instance I am seen are there, but above it rises a stronger current—so powerful it's almost tangible, like the warming bite of *rakshi*, the moonshine of the mountains. Heat, desire, and raw primal need floods my soul and pulses through my veins when our eyes meet. I see it reflected back at me in her gaze—she feels it, too.

Stunned, I stumble back, retreating into the welcoming, dark safety of the forest, watching as she runs off to her room, alone. I stand sentinel as the moon tracks across the sky and stars blink out of existence. As the sun rises, bathing the land in its golden glow—reminiscent of her curls that have captured my heart—I remain, desperate for one last look at the human who calls to me.

In the early hours, my nightlong vigil is rewarded when she emerges with several bags to say her goodbyes. The unshed tears only make her eyes more luminescent, my beautiful Winter Star. They call her Dahlia, but she has been named for the wrong flower. She is *my flower*.

This is it. She looks over her shoulder, directly across the river to where I stand hidden in the shadows. My heart leaps with the hope that she will come to me, drawn by this connection. But she simply turns back around and climbs into the vehicle.

This beautiful creature, who didn't just capture my attention but breathed life back into my frozen heart, is gone. With a sigh so deep, it rattles the leaves around me, I turn and head back to my home. Alone again.

CHAPTER THREE

DAHLIA

The next morning, I make my way down the mountain, leaving behind the serene loneliness and crisp, clean air of the Himalayas. As I descend into Delhi, the bustling chaos consumes me.

The noise, the heat, the relentless press of people—after the quiet majesty of the mountains, the city feels claustrophobic. Even the airport, with its harsh fluorescent lighting and stale recirculated air, offers a small reprieve from the unrelenting sensory overload as I tuck myself away into a corner at my gate.

I type a quick text to Ben, telling him how excited I am to see him. My thumbs hover over the screen for a moment, lingering on the unspoken distance that's grown between us. We haven't talked much during my time away, but I brush the thought aside, chalking it up to mismatched time zones and busy schedules. Instead of hitting send, I lock the home screen, reassuring myself that everything will be just as it was once we're face to face again.

I pull out my laptop, thinking I might get some work done,

but the blank screen stares back at me, mocking. Without the plant, there's no point. The data I need, the keystone of my research, is still out there somewhere, just as elusive as the hope I chased through the mountains no matter how many leads I had followed. Disappointment can wait until later.

Sighing, I stow the computer back in my carry on and scroll through the hundreds of photos on my phone instead. Faces and landscapes flash across the screen: Sita, my guide turned friend, laughing at something I said; her father, Tenzig, the welcoming host of the guesthouse I called home; the jagged peaks of the Himalayas piercing endless blue skies; and, of course, the plants —so many plants.

I love India. The warmth of the people, the spicy food, the tiny cups of chai served in clay cups. Somehow, this vibrant, foreign land felt more like home than I ever expected. But as I sit in the airport, watching the last sunset I'll witness here, a bittersweet ache pulls at my chest.

The exotic country held me spellbound, but my real home calls to me now, its pull quieter but no less insistent. I think of the familiar comforts waiting for me: my small desk in the ethnobotany department, the quiet hum of the research lab, and the dusty, welcoming scent of the university library.

And, more than anything, I miss my fiancé. We've both been so focused on our careers, and Ben on climbing the academic ladder, that we promised to prioritize our relationship when I returned. The thought of seeing him is like a compass, pulling me back to true north.

Ben's career had taken off while I stayed in the background. His first semester teaching had been wonderful, and I had fun helping him grade papers and plan lessons. We had both sacrificed so much to achieve our dreams and lay the solid foundation for a life together. By mutual agreement, we pushed his career forward first, knowing mine would then follow.

Now it was my turn to prove my worth in our field. But I'm

not sure how my failure will impact my funding and finishing my doctorate. Botany is already a small department, and specializing in ethnobotany, the study of not just plants but the relationship between them and people, is truly niche.

Disappointment burns in my throat, and my chest tightens in what is becoming a familiar feeling. I am older than most of the other doctoral candidates. Supporting Ben was a choice I made with love and conviction, but now I can't help but wonder if I had gambled away too much time. If maybe I should have directed some of my energy and efforts into myself.

No. I shake my head, forcing the doubt away. We followed our plan, and he is brilliant. Together, we'll figure this out. I just need to get home to him. That's all this melancholy is—exhaustion, defeat, the weight of too many goodbyes. India isn't my home. The Pacific Northwest is. Our little house in the suburbs, minutes from the university, is where I belong.

When boarding is announced, I close the pictures with the finality of turning the last page of this chapter of my life; a grand adventure before settling into marriage and finding my way forward. But as I rise to join the line, that hollow feeling doesn't dissipate. It clings to me, insistent, a whisper of everything I've left undiscovered—not just the plant, but also those damn silver eyes.

On the flight home, the cabin lights dim and brighten in a rhythm I no longer understand, marking a passage of time that feels meaningless. Between eating what I think is at least three dinners, I drift in and out of restless sleep, the hours blurring together as I anxiously await our arrival.

But even in sleep, there's no escape. That gaze haunts me, unrelenting, always watching, always pulling. It doesn't just linger at the edges of my mind—it wraps around me, as though it's a part of me now, impossible to sever. A puzzle that I can't help but want the solution to. A lingering heat that doesn't dissipate even with the distance.

I press my forehead against the cool airplane window, hoping to anchor myself in the here and now. The endless darkness beyond offers no comfort, no answers. And yet, the feeling doesn't fade. If anything, it grows stronger the farther I go, the connection pulling tighter with every mile until the tension thrums under my skin.

The clouds stretch below like a vast, empty ocean, but the thought surfaces unbidden—maybe I was never meant to leave. Maybe some part of me is still there, bound to that place, to that silver stare.

The idea steals my breath as awareness pricks the back of my neck, as if someone still stares. Watching. Waiting for me. I force myself to pull away from the window, but even as I close my eyes, I know the truth I'm not ready to face yet—some ties are too strong to break, no matter how vast the ocean.

Countless hours later, after a blur of stumbling through customs and baggage claim, the taxi pulls up in front of my house. The driver helps me wrestle my luggage out of the trunk, and I mutter my thanks, my mind already on what awaits me inside.

I try to leave thoughts of India behind and focus on the here and now. Reconnecting with Ben. Grounding myself in reality. Casting off the cloak of fanciful thinking and mysterious eyes. I shove my feelings down, determined to get back to serious, scientific Dahlia and focus on what matters—the next steps in finding the plant and, with it, the cure. That's the only thing I can afford to concentrate on right now.

Every step down the walkway to my front porch feels heavier than it should, as though I'm dragging the weight of my old life behind me. The familiar sight of my house, warm and welcoming, should comfort me. Instead, a strange melancholy grips my heart.

I thought I'd be happier to come home. I've been looking forward to seeing Ben for weeks. Sure, I was disappointed when he told me he couldn't pick me up at the airport, but I understood. He's busy. And after three months apart, what's another hour or so?

I imagine the reunion ahead of me—wrapping my arms around him and basking in the familiarity of our years together. But the warmth that should flood me at the thought doesn't come.

Instead, my stomach knots. Maybe it's just jet lag or the nerves of being away so long. Maybe it's the faint pull of India lingering at the edges of my mind—the mountains, the friends I made, the steaming chai, and, yes, those eyes that won't seem to let me go.

Even with an ocean between us, I feel their magnetic pull, an invisible thread tightening around my heart. Watching. Waiting with an intensity I can't ignore. Leaving wasn't enough—maybe it never could have been. Whatever calls me back isn't done with me yet.

The pull toward that place is relentless, but I firmly tell myself it doesn't matter. I'm here now. This is where I belong. Ben is my anchor. That hasn't changed. That can't have changed. Not when I'm drowning in this sea of uncertainty.

I stop at the door and drop my bags onto the stoop, wrangling my keys out of my backpack pocket when I find the door locked. I frown, surprised that Ben didn't leave it open for me when he knew I was coming home.

The small knot in my stomach tightens. It's silly—I tell myself it's nothing. I'm being ridiculous. But my hand lingers in front of the doorknob for a moment longer than it should, hesitation prickling at the back of my mind. Something feels… off.

I tell myself it's just the residual fog of travel, the emotional whiplash of arriving home after so long away as I slip the key into the lock and turn it. The door swings open, and instead of stepping into its warm embrace, I feel like I'm being swallowed by the gaping maw of the unknown.

"Hello?" I call as I make my way inside, dropping my bags in the foyer.

I wonder at the lack of a response. He had to know I was coming home today. At least I think he did. Flying backwards over the international date line never made sense to me, especially as challenged as I am with time. I very well may have told him the wrong day.

Shrugging off my jacket and kicking off my shoes, I make my way through the living room and down the hall. At the sound of the water running, a smile spreads across my face.

Of course, he wanted to freshen up for me. I walk down the hall, excitement quickening my steps at the thought of surprising him. Until the faint murmur of voices gives me pause. Shrugging it off as one of the many podcasts Ben is always listening to, I continue to the bedroom where I toss my travel-wrinkled clothes into the hamper and grab my robe.

The red velvet is soft in my grip, and I smile at the memory of receiving the Valentine's Day present, back when we still exchanged gifts. My smile falls as I try to recall the last time Ben gave me something like this.

No matter, we are together again, and that's all that matters. I shake my head as I walk past the rumpled bed, just like it always is when I'm gone. Somehow, the unchanging sight steadies me. I was always the one to make it, not Ben. All is as it should be.

I step into the bathroom, steam billowing out at me. My skin pebbles at the cool air from the bedroom at my back and the humid heat from the shower at my front. I hang my robe on the back of the door, set my phone down on the counter, and step forward to pull back the curtain to surprise him when a distinctly female moan cuts through the steam.

My face screws up in concentration as my hand hovers in front of the curtain, trying to figure out what Ben could be listening to that would sound like that. He doesn't like fiction.

"Oh, fuck yeah, just like that," Ben groans.

My stomach bottoms out as I realize this isn't a podcast, and he sure as shit isn't in the shower in anticipation of me coming home. With dawning horror, it hits me. He's in there with someone else.

I stumble backwards, silently take my robe off the hook and slip back out the door where I jerk my robe on, my nakedness making me feel even more vulnerable and raw. I glance around the bedroom, searching for clues to help me piece together the life that is falling apart right now. Should I have seen this coming?

Looking around in bewilderment, I notice minute details I hadn't seen in my excitement of surprising him. The pictures of us are missing from their usual spots on the dresser, and the slippers on the floor next to the bed are most definitely not mine.

Walking over to his side of the bed, I can't stop myself from peeking into his trashcan and seeing the discarded condom wrappers it contains. I double over, the sight a visceral punch to the gut.

Ben is cheating on me. The irrefutable evidence is staring me in the face.

Questions race through my mind—how long has this been happening? With who? And most of all, why? I'd given him years of my life. I've gone above and beyond to be supportive, even going so far as to write papers and lessons for him. I'd offered, no begged, to be more adventurous in the bedroom.

Hell, I'd molded myself to his exact specifications with the exception of my petite, curvy build. No matter what I did, I couldn't change that. I tried. I really had. Everything within my control that I could do to be a great partner, I had done.

And what had Ben done? Taken. Always taking, without giving anything in return—except taking me for granted. It had all been about him—his wants, his needs, his desires. What a fool I had been. What a fucking fool.

I stand there frozen, the weight of his betrayal crashing down on me. The lies. The years I'd wasted on him. After my failure to find the plant, I had thought if I could just make it home, to him, I would be able to figure out a path forward. I could do it with his help.

But now, I have nothing. *Nothing.*

My chest implodes in on itself until it's all I can do to force air in and out of my lungs as the truth guts me. But the more I think about it—the deception, the audacity—the heaviness begins to shift into something hotter. Sharper.

Rage hits as fast and furious as the monsoon rains, propelling me into action as I storm out of the bedroom. In the kitchen, I reach under the sink for the cleaning bucket and carry it to the ice cube maker—the one he had to have because he likes the nuggets. I fill the bucket with as much ice as I can and top it off with cold water.

Lugging the heavy load, I creep back into the bathroom and cautiously climb up to stand on the toilet. I'm exhausted from traveling, heartbroken from my failed research expedition, and blindsided by the abysmal end of my relationship.

But rage pumps through my veins, and the taste of revenge is sweet in my mouth, urging me to lift the heavy bucket as high as I can at the edge of the curtain.

I'm precariously balanced but when I hear the filthy words he's spewing—words he refused to use with me when I wanted to spice things up—it gives me the extra burst I need to dump the ice water over their heads.

A maniacal giggle escapes me as the mystery woman shrieks and Ben bellows, "What the fuck?"

He rips back the curtain to reveal a woman kneeling at his feet with his now limp dick in her hand as I drop the bucket to the floor and say, "You're right, that nugget ice is where it's at."

"Jesus, Dolly. I thought you were coming home tomorrow," he barks, wiping the icy water from his face and cranking the faucet handle so hard I'm surprised it doesn't snap off in his hand.

And there it is. My failure to understand dates and times has serendipitously saved me from a doomed marriage. I snap, "Yeah, that pesky international date line is totally to blame for you putting your dick in someone else's mouth. Did you trip over it and fall?"

My eyes drift to the younger woman and I snort. "Really, Ben? Is she your TA or your student? Could you be any more cliché? Get the fuck out, you worthless piece of shit."

I glare down at them from my porcelain pedestal, listening to Ben sputter as icy water drips off him and the other woman.

"I'm not fucking leaving. This is my house, too," he says, his voice rising.

I spot my phone on the bathroom counter where I'd set it earlier and step down, snatch it up, and unlock it with a flick of my thumb. I hold it up and snap a picture of them.

"Ben, I just flew halfway around the world. I didn't find the damn plant. Instead, I come home to find you cheating on me. I've got nothing left to lose. Do you really want to fuck with me right now? I am one second away from sending this pic to the dean and destroying you. Get. The. *Fuck*. Out."

His face pales as the weight of my words sinks in. He steps out of the shower, grabbing his robe off the back of the door and throwing it on.

The younger woman—Felicia, I think her name is, as I vaguely recall meeting her once—looks back and forth between us, following the conversation like an obscene tennis match.

I turn my withering stare on her and say, "You, too. Get the fuck out of my house. You think he's not going to cheat on you, sweetheart? I got news for you. Cheaters cheat."

She shrinks back, covering herself in embarrassment and reaches for a towel.

I throw out a hand over them and say, "Oh, no. You can drip your shame right out the front door for all I care. Don't you dare fucking touch my towels. Get. Out."

Am I being cruel? Harsh? Maybe. But I have no fucks left to give. I'm filled with a grim satisfaction as she runs from the bathroom, leaving a trail of wet footprints in her wake while I am left to clean up not only the puddles they left behind, but the wreckage of my heart.

CHAPTER FOUR

I take the same towel I refused to let her use and carelessly toss it onto the floor to sop up the mess. Staring with detached fascination at the fabric as it slowly darkens, I jump when I hear the front door slam, followed by the screech of tires as they speed away in Ben's sports car. I hope the leather seats get water stains.

I should have known that fancy sports car wasn't about us—it was about impressing other women. He called it *our car*, the one we'd use to look polished, successful, the perfect couple. But every time we drove separately, it was *his car*, leaving me with my old sedan. I convinced myself it was fair, that we were a team. Now I see it for what it really was—another lie to keep me small so he could shine. Not anymore.

I rip off my robe, the Valentine's gift that now feels like a cruel joke, and march to the hall bathroom. There's no way I'm stepping into the other defiled shower ever again. I stuff the robe into the small trash can, where it overflows in a heap of betrayal.

I crank the water as hot as I can stand it and step in. The heat beats against my skin, but it can't touch the cold that has settled in my marrow. It clings to my core, pulling at memories of the icy winds in the Himalayas, the bite of the air that burned and invigorated all at once. The water cascades over me, but nothing washes away the hollow ache that echoes in the space where my hope used to live.

I sit down hard under the steaming water and wrap my arms around my knees in a futile attempt to staunch the bleeding of my hemorrhaging heart. I thought I would be coming home to the safety and reassurance of my carefully curated life and loving relationship. That Ben would help me navigate these uncertain waters and figure out my next steps.

Hope swirls down the drain. Without him, I don't know how I'm going to continue my research or even finish my degree with both of us in the same damn department. If the world of botany is small, ethnobotany is a microcosm. And my small section is under his purview as the tenure-track botany professor.

Sure, I have a picture that might be enough to get him in trouble. But in the male-dominated world of academia, all it would probably earn him is a slap on the wrist with a sly wink and a quiet warning to be more discreet next time.

But even worse, I don't have the plant. The doctorate was part of it, yes, but the real reason was something far more personal. Ben knew I believed that the enzymes in the Silene vitalis held potential for treating the disease that killed my mother. What he didn't know, what I had never told him, was that I have the same gene. I could barely even admit it to myself.

At last, the cooling water prompts me to climb out into the steamy bathroom. The humidity grips my lungs, so I throw open the window and stick my head out. I watch wistfully as steam swirls past me and escapes out into the dark night, wishing I could float away with it.

Pulling in deep breaths of the cool night air, I decide I'll allow myself this night to have an epic pity party. I'll ugly cry until I'm empty and then tomorrow, I'll turn on my logical brain and figure out a path forward. Without Ben.

But for tonight, I'll shut down analytical, logical Dahlia and just allow myself to wallow in misery. I reach for my favorite robe, but when I see it stuffed into the trash, the tears start up all over again. Breaking my own rule about using the decorative guest bath towels, I grab two and wrap my hair and body, then trudge back to my closet to find the rattiest, most comfortable sweats I own.

When I open my sock drawer to grab my fuzzy slipper socks, my breath catches. All of the pictures of us—the snapshots I lovingly framed and arranged just so on our shared dresser—are stuffed inside, hidden away as if they were nothing. Key moments of Ben and me frozen in the timeline of our life together, forever immortalized, shoved in here as if they don't matter. As if they never mattered.

As if *I* never mattered.

I grab the entire stack and flip through them, recognizing a pattern. One I hadn't noticed before. They all highlight him and his achievements. I've continually helped him move forward, prioritizing his successes above my own—his lab work, his research, his doctorate, his appointment as a professor.

Hell, even our engagement and marriage were scheduled to accommodate his academic calendar. I would have married him years ago. Thanks the gods for small favors.

In each one, he looks at the camera while I gaze at him adoringly. I feel so damn stupid. Everything was about him, and I blindly followed along.

When I reach the photo from our engagement party, my stomach twists. Standing in the crowd of our university colleagues, Ben's friends really, I see *her*. Felicia stands at the fringe, lips pressed tight, fists clenched at her sides. How did I not see it? How long has this been happening? Months? Years?

But now that I've seen it, it's so damn obvious. She's been there all along in the sidewings. Or maybe she's been center stage. I thought Ben and I were equally devoted not just to each other, but also to our work and shared future. But now I see the truth: it was painfully one-sided.

I gather the pictures to my chest and storm out to the backyard, grabbing the gas for the mower and the fireplace lighter from the garage along the way. The fire pit is already stacked with wood, and I give it a generous soaking of the accelerant, a maniacal grin splitting my face.

I hold up our engagement photo, studying the frozen moment of fake happiness under the fading twilight. For one ridiculous second, I almost pull it back, the weight of what we'd built together tugging at my hand. But then I remember the look on his face when I caught him in the shower—wide-eyed, not with guilt, but with surprise that he'd been caught. Not a trace of shame. Not a shred of remorse.

Not even a fucking apology.

With finality, I light the corner of the frame, my satisfaction growing as hot orange flames lick up the cardboard backing. I toss it into the pit and flames shoot up into the sky with a satisfying whoosh as the fire roars to life, and for the first time in weeks, so do I.

"Yeah! Take that, fucker!" I whoop into the night, pumping my fist as adrenaline surges through my veins and the fire burns brighter—just like me.

I'm done feeling hopeless. I don't need Ben to help me figure this out—he never helped me. I've been the one researching, planning, and holding everything together. The realization hits me like a tidal wave, resolve and independence surging through me with a force I can't ignore.

I march back inside, dumping out a basket of laundry onto the floor and filling it with his things. His favorite hat. The photo albums I spent hours making for his milestones. His collection of journals he'd been published in. And with a wicked smile, I raid his underwear drawer.

Grabbing handfuls, I toss his absurdly expensive briefs into the basket, barely able to keep from laughing. Who spends this much on underwear? They're just another reminder of how pretentious he is, how everything about him screams self-importance.

As I walk through the kitchen on my way back outside, I throw a bag of chips on top, a tub of ice cream with a spoon, and the bottle of expensive tequila he had been saving for a "special occasion." After all, I think this qualifies.

Flopping into one of the Adirondack chairs that surround the firepit, I try to get comfortable for my conflagration celebration, but I hate them. I've always hated these stupid chairs. Ben is the one who had loved them because they looked "perfect," but I found them awkward and impossible to get out of with my petite height.

I wrestle my way out of it, turn around, pick it up, and hurl it out into the yard for all I'm worth. What my throw lacks in distance, it makes up for in satisfaction when the dumb thing breaks with a crack as it bounces on the lawn.

"Stupid chair," I mutter, brushing my hands off like I'm dusting off his pretentiousness.

I grab a folding chair and a sleeping bag from the garage instead and stomp back to the firepit. It's easier to sit in, but nothing about this night feels comfortable. The fire is starting to die down, so I start feeding it my pilfered items as I steadily make my way through the tub of ice cream, the bag of chips, and Ben's expensive tequila.

"Cheers, fucker," I mutter, raising it in mock toast to the fire before taking a swig straight from the bottle. I sputter and cough, but choke it down, welcoming the heat that follows in its wake.

Repeating the process—swig, toss, swig, toss—I'm surprised

to find just how quickly the laundry basket, and the tequila, empties.

Despite my best efforts—the fiery revenge, the snacks, the booze—the hollow ache inside me refuses to burn away. The throbbing emptiness spills over, carving hot, salty tracks down my cheeks. I shove another spoonful of ice cream into my mouth and chase it with another swig of tequila.

The flames are starting to die down, flickering lower and lower as the last bits of Ben's life disintegrate. For the first time since walking into that bathroom, I feel the weight of it all hit me.

This was my life, too. Carefully built, brick by brick, around someone who never gave me a second thought. Everything I burned tonight wasn't just his—it was the version of me that bent over backward to keep him happy. I spent years making myself small so he could take up more space.

Never again.

Pulling the blanket tighter around my shoulders, I let my fuzzy gaze drift to the edge of the woods. Even though I'm half a world away, I find myself scanning for those silver eyes again. Their absence triggers an ache within me—irrational, impossible, and yet so visceral.

A desperate, relentless need to see them again curls in my gut, even in this drunken, grief-slicked haze. There is nothing left for me here. The life I built is gone. And if I don't find that plant, things will only get worse.

The flickering embers bring me back to that last night in India, to the firepit where I sat, staring across the river at those silvery, luminescent eyes in the woods. Whatever is pulling me back to that place isn't finished with me yet.

I sway slightly in the folding chair, the tequila bottle dangling from my fingertips. The fire has burned down to glowing coals, their deep red glow mesmerizing. I lean forward, my drunken mind fixated on the way the embers shift and shimmer, as if they're whispering something I can't quite hear.

Just like the wood, everything I'd built with Ben had been reduced to this—ashes and dust. I huff out a bitter laugh and lift the bottle to take another swig, surprised at how light it feels.

Frowning, I peer into the neck like it might hold some secret answer, but instead all I see is the last dregs sloshing in the bottom. With a shrug, I let it drop to the ground, the remaining liquor trickling out in a thin stream.

"One for me, and one for my homies," I slur, the words tumbling out before I can stop myself.

The tequila buzz makes me think of that song. Or at least, I think it's a song. I dig my phone out of my sweatshirt pocket, debating if it's lyrics or maybe a movie quote. My thumb hovers over the display as I squint at my lock screen—a selfie I snapped in front of the guesthouse back in Migdhari. Behind me are the woods, dark and endless, where I saw those damn eyes.

The memory tugs at something deep inside me, sharp and insistent. It sparks a wild energy I can't contain. The solution floats to me like a whisper on the crackle of the fire. For once, I don't overthink. I've always been a planner, the one with lists and backup plans. But not tonight. Tonight, I'm done thinking. It's time to act and damn the consequences.

After all, that's what everyone else does. Why not me?

"Do it Dah–*hiccup*–lia," I say, cheering myself on as I giggle at hiccuping my own name, and open the app without a second thought.

CHAPTER FIVE

I walk the criss-crossing tunnels, my footsteps hollow in the silence, my breath a whisper against the stone. The air is thick with memory, the shadows stretching long with ghosts.

The light that one small human brought into my life—brighter than fire, wilder than any storm—has only made the darkness sharper. The loneliness deeper. The cold, more cutting.

I should not have let myself bask in her light, but I couldn't stop following her, a moth to her flame. For centuries, I have been stone and silence, ice and duty. She is fire, burning through the cold, thawing things within me that should remain frozen. I shouldn't have allowed her to thaw my icy heart. But the warmth felt too good to stop.

So, I seek the one thing that endures, the only thing time cannot take—my past, carved into stone, preserved in the silence of the mountain. The beginning greets me first. These are the oldest carvings, the stories passed from claw to claw, from parent to child. The tale of our kind, immortalized in rock.

I know every line by heart, as familiar as my own hands. I

have traced these stories a thousand times, let my fingers follow the rise and fall of each carefully drawn stroke. They used to bring me comfort, but tonight, they are a dirge, a deep wail of my soul.

I move forward, past the birth of my kind, the moon goddess and her daughter, and the teachings of my ancestors. Past the carvings of generations before me, of duties fulfilled, of lives that had purpose. The further I go, the fewer the images become. The lonelier they become.

Until at last, I reach the ones I carved myself.

My life, drawn in the stone. I stop, eyes shut tight, chest caving in. My breath catches as my throat closes around the weight of what I already know I will see—the simple lines that could never do justice to my greatest joy.

My touch finds them even without my sight, a trembling finger ghosting over the delicate curves of the figures before me. The strong, steady form of my mate. The smaller, fragile one nestled between us. They were not only my greatest joy, but they are also my deepest failure.

I drop my hand. I am unworthy to touch even the drawings of them.

The wind outside howls through the mountain, sending a faint, keening whistle through the tunnels. I let it carry through me, stripping me bare, breaking apart the walls I have spent centuries fortifying.

I have told myself, time and again, that my dharma is enough. That my duty will keep me whole, that I exist for the mountain and all within its shadow, for their protection.

But here, in the darkness, with the ghosts of my past carved before me—I know the truth. The mountain cannot hold my grief. Even if it swallowed me whole, even if I let the earth and stone take me, even if I buried myself beneath ice and time—it would not be enough. I turn from the walls, from my past, from my failure.

And I flee.

I run, fast and hard, feet slamming against the cold hard stone as the muscle of my legs burn with the exertion. But no matter how fast I run, the wailing winds chase me like ghosts and I cannot outrun the pain. Lungs bursting, I push myself faster through the tunnels, through the cold, but I still cannot escape the weight of history pressing down on me.

So I escape to the place where I keep one of the few things that can help me on the nights like this. I wipe away the thick dust on the old, fragile bottle with unsteady fingers. *Rakshi*, the moonshine of the mountains, is strong enough to warm even my kind. Strong enough to burn the past away.

I should not wash away their memory like this. But I do. Because once again, I am weak. My freshly thawed heart brings the long dead feelings bubbling back to the surface. The reminder of all that I have lost then, and all that I have lost again with her departure, is too much for even a monster to bear.

The first sip burns, but it is nothing compared to the ache in my chest. Nothing compared to the quiet, gnawing hollowness of nothing. So, I drink again. And again. And again.

At last my feet carry me to the secret springs without thought, without direction. I sink into the heat of the water, but it does nothing to comfort me tonight. I tilt my head back, watching the stars wheel overhead, the slow, endless churn of time indifferent to the things it has stolen from me.

I pick the bottle up, surprised to find it half empty. The world blurs at the edges, and I welcome the haze, welcome the slow erosion of thought, of pain, of them, of her.

But then—I see the flowers, just starting to bloom with the coming of winter. The tiny, star-shaped blossoms clustered at the edge of the spring. Small. Unassuming. Born of cold and stone and impossibility. I stare at them, my mind thick with drink, with memory. They bloom here and nowhere else. A secret, a gift, a thing meant only for the mountain.

My chest tightens as I stare at the color—her color. Violet-blue, like the shimmer of her eyes in the firelight. My Winter Star.

I tip the bottle back again for another swallow, desperate to chase away the aching, desperate pull in my gut, the cruel flicker of feelings that press sharp against my ribs. But it does not work. She lingers in the darkness, in my mind, in my bones. A phantom that will not leave.

I cannot look at the damned flower and not think of what it has cost me. *Everything.* The past rises up to meet me, and I slam my eyes shut, as if that alone could prevent the memories that wash over me.

But they come anyway to drown me in their devastating embrace. A weight in my arms. Warm. Small. So impossibly small. The snowling's fur was softer than the spring breeze, his tiny hands curling instinctively around my finger.

I had never known fear the way I did then.

Not in the fulfillment of my dharma. Not in the unknown. But in that moment—staring down at the fragile, precious life I had been entrusted with—I had been terrified. I was enormous, built for protecting, for destroying. How could I ever hope to hold something so delicate without breaking it?

But when his tiny silver eyes blinked up at me, a mirror of my own, when his chest rose and fell in perfect, steady breaths, I had known—I would die for him. I would kill for him. I would burn the world to ash before I let anything take him from me.

But I had.

I let him slip through my fingers like melting snow. The memory of that last breath slams into me with the force of an avalanche, and suddenly I am roaring, teeth bared to the sky, furious with the gods, with fate, with myself.

I slam my hands down against the banks, claws scraping

stone, as I scrabble for purchase on the earth, trying to anchor myself in an ocean of rage. They took everything from me. I have nothing.

I grab the bottle, drinking it dry, but the burn in my throat is nothing compared to the ache in my chest. I am alone. I am always alone. And the mountain has always been with me.

The *rakshi* swirls in my blood, turning my thoughts sluggish. My head tilts back against the stone, my eyes slipping closed as I exhale, long and slow. My hands slowly release their death grip on the ground beside me. The warm waters courses over my flesh like a lover's hands, and I realize I am drunk.

Drunk on grief. Drunk on memories. Drunk on the ghosts I cannot lay to rest. I surrender to the pull of unconsciousness, my body finally going still. Maybe I will drown and be free. But until then, I dream. Not of loss. Not of pain.

I dream of a fire in the distance. A woman sitting beside it, her wild curls reflecting the light, her gaze sharp and knowing as she stares across the dark. Watching me. Waiting for me. As if she has always known I was there. As if she is not afraid.

As if, for the first time in over a hundred years—I am no longer alone.

CHAPTER SIX

DAHLIA

With a loud groan, I grab my head, as if holding it together will stop it from exploding. My eyes slam shut, but the weak morning sun still presses against my lids, unrelenting. The sleeping bag is tangled around my legs like a boa constrictor, and I wince as I finally manage to kick it off, shivering as the chilly air hits me.

I roll onto my hands and knees, the world tilting unpleasantly as I push myself upright. Blinking blearily, I take in the firepit. Twisted, charred metal frames and smoldering ash are all that remain of last night's fire—that and this wicked hangover.

My body aches from sleeping on the hard ground, and my mouth feels like I ate an entire bag of cotton balls. The mere thought of eating anything sends my stomach churning dangerously.

Shading my eyes against the watery light, I take in the wreckage around me—a broken Adirondack chair, a melted tub of ice cream, and a very empty bottle of tequila littering the ground.

With a groan, I scrub my hands over my face, then rake them back through my hair to twist it into a knot. My fingers snag on something, and I pull free the missing ice cream spoon tangled in my curls. Of course.

Shaking my head, I grab the empty container and tequila bottle. On my way inside, a whiff of last night's mint chocolate chip wafts up from the melted tub. My stomach clenches hard, and I barely make it to the bushes before emptying its contents.

Still gagging slightly, I head for the guest bath once again. Rummaging under the sink, I pull out a spare toothbrush and the extra toiletries I keep there. The spicy cinnamon of the toothpaste is a welcome change, chasing away the lingering taste of mint, tequila, and regret.

Stepping into the shower, I let out a sigh at the luxury of indoor plumbing. The steaming water cascades down my back, soothing the tight muscles from sleeping outside on the hard ground—or okay, fine, from passing out.

My thoughts wander as the heat works its magic. This is worlds away from the buckets we used to bathe in the Himalayas. There, the water was ice-cold, a shock to the system no matter how much you braced yourself. Here, it feels indulgent, almost too easy—just a twist of a knob and out it comes. So simple, yet so unappreciated.

I wash the sticky ice cream residue from my hair and take the time to shave. The sweet-smelling steam wraps around me, and for a moment, I'm tempted to stay here. To hide in the warmth of the shower, letting the return to indoor plumbing and indulgent body products shield me from the mess waiting beyond the curtain.

But something stronger pulls me forward. I've wasted enough time sacrificing for Ben and his success. That's over now. From here on out, my needs and wants come first. I'm going to make myself the priority for a change.

With one last deep breath of the humid air scented with

flowery body wash, I shut off the water and head out to face my new life, starting with unpacking my bags and doing laundry. While I wait for the washer and dryer to run their cycles, I stand in the kitchen and choke down some tea and toast, missing the sweet chai of India.

Rain begins to fall, soft and steady, as I watch out the kitchen window. My gaze drifts to the edge of the woods, my eyes scanning the shadows between the trees. I don't know what I'm expecting to see—maybe a flash of silver. Maybe nothing. But the pull is still there, tugging at me, refusing to let go.

The buzzing of the dryer jolts me back to the present. I fold my clothes and carry them down the hall, but my steps falter halfway to the bedroom I shared with Ben. The idea of tucking my clothes away in that closet, in this space we filled together, feels like admitting this is still my life. But it's not. It can't be. Not anymore.

Although I don't want to settle back into this house that holds the ghost of my relationship with Ben, I also don't know where else to go. All of my friends are "our" friends. As I run through the list of people I could call to cry to, help me move, or let me crash on their couch for a few nights, the realization hits me—I don't have anyone.

The friends I had from college drifted away as I poured all my energy into Ben. And now I can't help but wonder if that was intentional on his part. I was the only child of a single mom, lost to our rare hereditary disease. It had been so easy for him to become my entire world. And now that he's gone, I really am alone.

The thought brings me to a standstill. For a moment, I consider finding another bottle or burning something else, but instead, I let the jetlag layered over a hangover pull me toward the guest room. Dropping the basket to the floor to deal with later, I curl up on the bed, set my phone to silent and escape into the comforting embrace of sleep.

When I wake, the sun is setting, painting the room in muted hues. I grope for my phone on the side table, squinting at the bright backlight cutting through the gloom of dusk. I'm shocked at not just how long I slept, but the flood of notifications of missed calls, voicemails, and text messages from Ben.

Not ready to hear his voice, I exhale a heavy sigh and swipe to open the messages instead. They're exactly what I expect—excuses and lies. Not a heartfelt apology in sight. My chest tightens, but I refuse to let him get to me. I lock the screen and head back to the kitchen, a loud growl from my stomach reminding me the toast I ate earlier was a lifetime ago.

I pop a frozen pizza into the oven and lean against the counter, pulling my phone out of my pocket to start searching for another place to live while I wait. Another notification pops up, not from Ben, but from the same airline I just flew home on.

I frown down at the screen, confusion prickling at the edges of my tired mind.

Time to check in for your flight tomorrow.

A flight? My stomach flips as I try to piece it together. What flight?

Opening the notification, I see an odd error. I think about calling the airline but quickly decide against spending hours on the phone. Instead, I switch to my banking app where I confirm there's no glitch on the airline's end. Last night, in a tequila-fueled haze, I bought a nonrefundable, one-way ticket back to India.

And it leaves in less than twenty-four hours.

Well, this is interesting. I tell myself I must have bought it because I need to keep searching for that elusive plant. That I'm not entertaining the idea of flying back around the world because of the pull I still feel or the thought of catching another glimpse of those silver eyes.

No, this is about survival. My survival. I need that flower.

But as I stare down at my phone, another question surfaces,

sharper and harder to ignore. Am I really running toward something? Or am I just running away from the emptiness here?

I could stay. Piece my life back together. Figure out where I'm going academically. Sell the house. Mourn the loss of my relationship. Slowly tease my life apart from Ben's. The practical choice stretches before me, logical and predictable.

The kind of choice Ben's 'Dolly' would make. He loved to call me Dolly Mild—a play on my last name. The nickname always grated on me, even when I forced myself to smile through it. It made me feel small. Diminished. A version of me Ben could mold to fit his life, control like a marionette. But I'm not her—not anymore.

I'm not Dolly Mild. I'm Dahlia. Dahlia *fucking* Wilde. Untamed as my name.

And Dahlia isn't going to fall into line, picking up the pieces after being cast aside. She sure as hell isn't going to stay here, walking back into the department with her tail tucked between her legs. As the decision cements itself in my mind, something else rises within me—something thrilling and unfamiliar.

A bubbling sense of freedom. And it feels good. The house, Ben, my degree—all of it can wait. Because honestly? I don't know if any of it really matters anymore. Or honestly, that I even care.

"Good thing I didn't put everything away," I mutter under my breath, the decision already made.

Pulling up the airline app again, I hit *check-in* and blink in surprise. Apparently, drunken me had splurged on a first-class ticket for the return trip. A flicker of pride warms my chest as I say with a wry grin, "Good girl, Dahlia."

Sitting down with my sad frozen pizza dinner, I grab a pen and start a list of everything I need to do to pause my life here and head back to the other side of the world.

I decide to take only what I can't live without, stashing it in a storage unit rather than leaving it here for Ben to destroy. After all, once he realizes I've burned a few of his prized possessions, I doubt he'll feel very charitable toward mine.

Then again, my time in the mountains has taught me how little I actually need. Most of the stuff I accumulated with Ben feels like dead weight anyway—his taste, his priorities, his life. I don't want any of it.

I repack my travel gear, cutting out the items I hadn't really needed last time and adjusting for the change in seasons. The last of my warmer layers fits neatly into the bag, and I step back to admire how streamlined it is now. It's not just the bag, though—I feel a quiet sense of pride at how much I've learned.

Like how to rely on myself in ways I never thought possible. I was resourceful—more than I'd ever given myself credit for. Back here, Ben had been the center of everything. Out there? It was just me. And I managed. More than that—I thrived.

Anything I can easily buy there stays behind, leaving my backpack a model of efficiency. From the house, I restock my first aid kit with essentials and toss a few snacks into my carry-on, just enough to get me through the long trip ahead.

With tomorrow planned and my bags packed, I check and recheck my list, restless. The guest bed, already rumpled from my earlier nap, doesn't call to me the way it should despite how tired I am. This house, this life—it feels like a stranger's.

I stop in front of my neatly zipped backpack, the sight filling me with an unexpected pang of finality. I've pared my life down to what can fit inside it, shedding everything else like a snake discarding old skin. But it's not just things I'm leaving behind—it's an entire version of myself.

The house feels heavy around me, its silence pressing in. Every corner holds echoes of the life I thought I was building with Ben, and for the first time, I realize how much of myself I sacrificed to fill this space.

I tried so hard to make this house feel like a home, to shape myself around him and his needs. Now, all I can feel is the echoing emptiness of our lie of a relationship. The thought makes my chest ache, a dull throb that no amount of planning or packing can erase.

Eventually, I climb back under the covers, forcing myself to lie still even as my thoughts spin with everything I've lost and everything I hope is waiting for me on the other side of the world. Sleep comes slowly, fractured and fleeting.

When I finally slip into dreams, they pull me back to the woods. The air is sharp, the scent of pine and woodsmoke thick in my lungs. Shadows ripple across the ground, cast by the flicker of the firepit. And beyond the flames, those silver eyes gleam, waiting, pulling, calling me back.

I wake before dawn, my pulse racing with the memory of them. The pull is sharp, visceral, impossible to ignore. Somewhere deep inside, I feel it settle—the truth I've been resisting.

My heart never left India.

CHAPTER SEVEN

DAHLIA

I lie in bed watching the rising sun chase away the shadows until I finally get up and shuffle into the kitchen, bleary-eyed but brimming with restless energy, and make myself a French press coffee—probably the last good cup I'll have for quite some time. The rich aroma fills the air, grounding me for a moment, but not enough to ease the knot in my chest.

I sip it slowly, savoring the rich brew while also anticipating the switch to the sweet scalding chai of India. Cup in hand, I head to the garage where Ben's pathologically organized storage containers line the shelves, each neatly labeled in his precise block handwriting. For a moment, I just stare at them, their rigid perfection grating against the chaos he's stirred within me and my life.

"What's good for the goose," I say aloud to the garage as I dump several of them onto the floor, sending tools, cords, and who-knows-what scattering into a haphazard pile, "is good for the gander."

A petty thrill zips through me, imagining his reaction to the mess. Welcome to my world, Benny boy. Grabbing the empty tubs, I walk through the house and start packing up my own things—what little I actually care to keep.

Maybe I'm numb, a robot going through the motions, or maybe I truly don't care anymore, but the small pile I end up with feels unimpressive. A few of my favorite kitchen gadgets, most of my clothes, a couple of sentimental keepsakes. One box of academia—copies of my published works, a handful of notes. And several boxes of books, too many to justify but too precious to leave behind.

Packing my car to the brim takes effort, but it means only two trips to the storage shed to get everything moved. Despite renting the smallest one, my belongings barely take up half the space.

Pride at my lack of consumerism wars with disappointment as I stare at the shoebox unit. Is this really it? Is this all I have to represent my life? The thought stings, and not because I care about material things, but because of what it says about me. If I'd met my academic goals, maybe my lack of achievement wouldn't burn quite so much.

What do I have to show for my thirty-odd years on this planet?

A few tubs of random belongings. A failed relationship. No family. No doctorate. An unsuccessful research expedition. A bruised ego. A broken heart. And no cure.

When I think about my life in these terms, it's not just bleak. It's downright depressing.

But then, as I lean against the car, staring at the mess Ben has made of my life—the pieces he left me to pick up, the years I can't get back—another saying of my mom's rises unbidden in my mind.

Sometimes, honey, the only place left to go is up.

The words settle over me, their warmth a stark contrast to the emptiness within. I close my eyes, letting them wrap around me. Maybe she was right. Maybe this is rock bottom. But rock bottom, for all its jagged edges and shadows, is also a starting point. And that means there's only one direction left to go.

With that comes a freedom as I realize I have nothing to lose, and the weight of a thousand expectations lifts off my shoulders. Endless possibility unfurls in front of me. The entire world is open to me now. I can go anywhere, do anything. I am free. Free to forge my own path, free to return to my hunt for the plant, free to do whatever *I* want.

I vow I'm not going to let this disease take my life before it *takes* my life. I am going to go live. I *am* free. And it feels incredible. I close the door and step back, staring at the padlock like it's sealing away not just my things, but my old life. My old thought patterns that held me hostage.

"I am fucking free," I yell, pumping my fist in the air.

"I beg your pardon," comes a haughty voice behind me.

A startled gasp escapes me as I spin around to the parking lot. An elderly woman clings to her husband's arm, shrinking into him. I'd been so lost in thought, I hadn't even heard their footsteps approach. Her face is frozen in horror, while her husband barely hides a smirk.

"I said what I said." I shrug and walk away, leaving the storage unit, and my old life, locked away behind me. I'm done caring about the judgement of others. I head back to the house for one last pass—one last goodbye—before I chase down the *Silene vitalis* and whatever time I have left to live.

My mood is short lived, the burst of euphoria curdling into a pool of disgust in my gut as I round the bend to see Ben's car in the driveway. I grip the steering wheel, pulse hammering with irritation as I pull in next to it. I should have known he wouldn't just slink off quietly.

Guarded, I step inside to find him sitting on the couch, elbows on his knees, head bowed. The perfect picture of shame and remorse. But I know it's all just an illusion now. His head snaps up at the sound of the door.

"Dolly, please," he whines. "I didn't mean to hurt you."

A week ago, those words would have found purchase in my heart. But now? They barely graze the surface. There's no anger, no sadness in me—just a quiet, eerie nothingness. I've already chartered a new course, one that has no place for regret, especially about him.

Ben stands and crosses the room, arms outstretched like I'm supposed to fall into them. When he reaches for my hands, I step back, voice sharp as a blade.

"Don't call me Dolly. And don't fucking touch me," I bark.

"Okay, okay." He raises his hands like I'm the unreasonable one.

"Dahlia," he amends, offering the name like a peace offering. He exhales shakily, as if this is hard for him. Him!

"It was one night. I was weak and lonely without you. We'd never been apart for so long before." His voice trembles—just slightly. The perfect balance of remorse and vulnerability.

But now I know, it's a performance. Our years together have taught me to read his micro expressions. I watch him closely, and there it is—the tell. His fingers spin his ring on his right hand. His left eyebrow twitches upward.

I've seen this exact expression before. When he schmoozed trustees for funding. When he convinced donors to cut a check. When he humored students who weren't pretty enough to warrant his real attention. And now, he's doing it to me.

Curious, I play along. "Why, Ben?" I whisper, tilting my head just slightly. Widening my eyes in feigned wonder. "Why should I forgive you?"

He relaxes, thinking he's won me over, and I use the moment to edge back toward the door. There's nothing here I need. Nothing worth fighting over. And the hair on the back of my neck is standing on end, prickling with the instinct to run.

Ben's voice softens, taking on that coaxing tone he uses when he wants something, as he steps toward me. "Dahlia, we've been together for years. We have too much history to throw it all away over a silly mistake that meant nothing."

The word silly sinks into my stomach like a stone, leaving emotions rippling in its wake. Incredulity. Hurt. Betrayal. All my logical thoughts about putting myself first collapse in on themselves, a house of cards knocked down by a tsunami of emotion.

He gestures between us, narrowing his eyes. "It's you I love. You I've devoted my life to." His lips press into a thin line, voice lowering. "I've sacrificed so much for you. For us. Think of our work. Think of the lab. The department."

I retreat another step, feeling the transition from carpet to linoleum as my back nears the entryway at the door. Think of *what*? I gave him years of my love, and he's making it sound like our relationship was some kind of contractual agreement. As if we were business partners and our love was nothing more than a footnote. Like I owe him something. Like I owe the freaking university something.

What about me? What am I owed?

He must see my hesitation because his mask drops, face hardening. "We're so close, Dahlia. So close to everything we wanted. Let's go back—together. I know I can help you find the plant. You just needed me. I should have gone with you from the beginning."

My blood chills. Help me find the plant?

He hadn't wanted to go. He dismissed my theories as wishful thinking, suggesting I was allowing my bias and grief over my mother's death to color my research. He had no interest in trekking through the Himalayas, sleeping in guesthouses, or bathing with buckets of cold water.

So why does he suddenly care now?

His voice drops, turning smooth. "The university funding wasn't enough for your expedition. If you really want to find your plant, help other people like your mom, we need investors. There are far bigger players out there. People who pay for innovation."

Foreboding skates down my spine as his words echo in my mind. I think back to the hushed conversations at the university, the ones Ben always brushed off when I tried to ask him about them. The rumors that pharmaceutical companies had been sniffing around, quietly pressuring researchers to sell early findings before they became public knowledge.

I remember the way Ben used to roll his eyes at the idea, scoffing that real scientists didn't chase corporate money. That staying in academia kept the research pure.

But now when there's money on the table for him? Suddenly, he cares. The nausea in my gut has nothing to do with last night's tequila. This was never about us. Never about me.

Ben isn't here because he lost me—he's here because he wants in.

I'm piecing it together, but I don't have all the information yet. And he sees it—the moment I falter, my mind racing through the possibilities. He knows I'm on the cusp of figuring out something important, something he doesn't want me to know without being on his side first.

Ben takes a slow step forward, voice smooth, cajoling. "Come on, Dolly." His voice rolling over that damn wretched nickname leaves an oil slick over my heart. Although he keeps his voice controlled, I see the flash of anger in his eyes. "Let's be smart about this."

I shift my weight, fingers tightening around the door handle.

My instincts scream go, go, go, as right on cue, he lunges and snags my free wrist.

"Ben," I gasp, shocked that he would lay his hands on me.

In response, he tightens his grip, grinding the bones together. Not hard enough to break them, but enough to make his point. Enough to remind me that, for all his carefully constructed charm, power and control have always been what he wanted most.

It explains his annoyance with the board and donors, with the students, and now with me. I know he thinks I'm weak. He's made vaguely disguised insults before about my size and strength, insinuating I just needed to exercise more. Have more will power.

But the months spent hiking and breathing the high-altitude air of the mountains have made me stronger. Faster. And I am angry. So angry. It bubbles up through the uncertainty like lava, filling the cracks of my broken heart. I become rage, vengeance, and it fuels me into action.

My fingers tighten around the door handle behind me, and I channel my feelings into reclaiming my own power, throwing it open—right into his face. A satisfying thunk precedes a rather unmanly screech.

Ben wails, clutching his face as blood streams between his fingers, "My nose! You broke my fucking nose!"

"It's Dahlia, asshole," I call over my shoulder as I whirl on my heel, sprinting for my car. As much as I'd love to stick around to admire my handiwork, all that matters is getting out of here and away from him.

Jumping in, I slap the locks down and yank the gear shift into reverse. The tires screech as I tear out of the driveway, the car bouncing as I clip the curb before slamming it into drive and flooring it. My hands shake as I grip the wheel, my staccato heartbeat thunders in my ears as I retreat.

He doesn't follow, yet I can't seem to stop checking in the

rearview mirror every few seconds, never slowing down. Not until I get back to the storage facility where I'll leave my car for long-term storage do I finally ease off the gas. I pull into the lot, shove the gear into park, and fumble for my phone. My hands are still shaking, making it harder than it should be to tap through the app and order a car to pick me up.

My eyes flick between the arrival time on the app and the entrance to the lot. Waiting for the glare of headlights, the screech of tires. For Ben to somehow find me, come flying in, block my way, and throw out one last desperate plea. Or lay a hand on me again. I should have done more than break the bastard's nose.

But no car comes flying around the bend. Several long minutes later, a car approaches at a reasonable pace matching the one listed on my phone. Only then do I get out and grab my bags, slide into the back seat, and clutch them tight as the driver confirms, "Heading to the airport?"

I hesitate for half a second, my gaze flicking to the lot entrance once more. I swallow hard, forcing my voice to be steady. "Yeah. Thanks."

As the car pulls away, I let my head fall back against the seat and exhale, slow and steady. For years, Ben was my anchor. But anchors don't just hold you steady. They keep you in the same place. Stagnant. Unmoving.

And I've finally cut myself free.

CHAPTER EIGHT

DAHLIA

Despite being physically and emotionally drained, I can't sleep. Every creak of the plane, every rustle of movement in the cabin yanks me back to full alertness, as if the adrenaline hasn't left my system. The caffeine from the two lattes I definitely shouldn't have sucked down churns with the stress still coursing through my body, leaving me hollow and shaky.

I push my food around on the tray but can't force anything down even with the upgraded first-class fare. I flip through books on my phone, but the words blur together. Even an audiobook can't hold my attention—every shift of fabric, every muted cough, every click of a seatbelt latch pulls me back to full alertness.

The miles stretch behind me, but the tension thrumming through my body like a live wire refuses to fade. I can't shake the feeling that I haven't seen the last of Ben. I know him too well. He won't let this go.

I stare blankly out the plane's window, my mind sifting backward through the years. Trying to pinpoint the moment I stopped being his partner and became something else. Something smaller, as if I were nothing more than a disposable commodity. A paper napkin, used, crumbled, and carelessly tossed aside.

Had he ever really loved me? Or had I only ever been useful? Just another pawn to move in whatever game he is playing at.

I curse myself for being so naive, so damn trusting. Just handing over everything, never questioning if he deserved it. But in my defense, I was in love. He was my whole universe. Everything I did—every sacrifice, every compromise—had been for Ben.

Now, out from under his thumb, the truth sharpens into focus. The changes over the years had been so subtle, so insidious, that I hadn't even noticed. Like the proverbial frog in boiling water, I never realized I was being conditioned—slowly, deliberately—until I was drowning in his version of who I should be. Shoving myself into a mold that just didn't quite fit, no matter how uncomfortable it was.

Never again.

Not only had I put Ben's needs above mine, but I had put his wants above my needs. That is not love. That is not a partnership. And now, the end result is staring me in the face—I'm alone. Truly, utterly alone.

No one is coming to take care of me. There is no white knight.

And that's okay. It's time I take care of myself. It's time I put my own wants and needs first. Hell, if I take half as good care of myself as I did of him I'll be in great shape. And what better way to start than by chasing down the future I almost let slip away?

By the time I step off the second plane, retrieve my luggage, and meet the jeep I hired during my layover, a quiet confidence settles over me. I'm back. This time, on my own terms. No research agenda for the department, no timelines for a dissertation. I have one goal and one goal only. Secure the plant and extract the cure so I can survive.

The ten-hour drive ahead feels like both an eternity and a blink—too long for the restless energy swirling in my mind, but not long enough to prepare for everything that awaits me.

For the first few hours, I bury myself in my handwritten notes and maps, combing through every page for something I might have missed—a misplaced marking, an overlooked clue. I attempt to upload my new theories to my online research files, but the truck jolts over the winding mountain road, making typing impossible. I eventually give up, and switch to jotting down the swirling thoughts in my mind while bracing myself against the door as the driver expertly weaves through the switchbacks.

When we finally stop for lunch and a bathroom break at a roadside *dhaba,* or food stand, I practically tumble out of the jeep, rubbing my numb backside. The scent of sizzling spices and fresh bread hits me first, followed by the comforting warmth of the food stall's tandoori oven.

The hot *aloo gobi*—a fragrant mix of potatoes and cauliflower coated in a rich, spiced sauce—welcomes me back to the flavors I've missed. I tear off a piece of *paratha,* a seasoned flatbread, using it to scoop up the curry, the familiar heat spreading through my belly. A final bite of tangy mango pickle puckers my lips, its tartness a perfect contrast to the rich flavor combination.

As I sip my steaming chai, warmth seeps into my fingers, reminding me of the last time I held a clay cup like this. Then, the night had been crisp, the fire crackling, and beyond its flickering glow, a pair of luminous eyes watched me from the dark. A tendril of fear mixed with something hotter curls down my spine at the memory, and I still can't help but wonder, who—or what—did they belong to?

Part of me hopes to see them again. The other part knows I

can't afford the distraction. Winter is closing in fast, and once the snows settle in, my search will be over. I don't even know when the plant will reemerge—early spring? Late summer? Next year? But I'm running out of time.

At least I'd had the foresight to keep Ben away from the small savings my mother had tucked away for me. After she died, I'd been blindsided to learn she had somehow managed to set aside a little nest egg—scraped together, no doubt, from the things she denied herself.

The discovery had been a gut punch. All those years I'd complained about secondhand clothes and off-brand sneakers, never realizing what it must have cost her to make sure I had even that.

Every Christmas, there were presents under the tree—even when I knew money was tight. But I can't remember a single time she bought something nice for herself. She must have made so many quiet sacrifices—things she went without, needs she pushed aside—all so I'd have something to fall back on.

And now, I have no choice but to use it.

I've missed her every day since she's been gone—but never have I wished she was here more than in this moment. I can't help but wonder what it was like for her to also know her time was running out and wish for her guidance. Ask her all the questions I didn't think to ask when I was caught up in the business of caring for her, and the horror of watching her die from a disease that had no treatment. No cure.

Although I cannot turn to her, I hope I can still depend on Sita, my guide turned friend. I need her help not just to help navigate, translate, and smooth the way, but because I can't face this final summit for survival alone.

We load back into the jeep, and I force my thoughts away from my fears. Instead, I manifest success. I picture myself trekking through the rugged terrain, scanning for the heart shaped leaves and small iridescent flowers, their delicate shimmer nearly lost in the vastness of the mountains.

A ray of watery sunlight pierces the winter sky, glinting off something just ahead—just like in the attic back home. My breath catches as I rush forward, heart pounding. I drop to my knees, hands trembling as I cradle the fragile blossom, the culmination of everything I've been searching for. Its luminescent blue-violet matches my own unusual eye color, another gift from my mother.

Somewhere in the distance, an engine rumbles, creeping into the edges of my awareness like a half-formed thought. The sound feels out of place in this serene place, splintering the dream as the jeep jolts to a stop.

My head snaps up, disoriented, my heart still racing like I had actually been kneeling there at my discovery. The vision dissolves, fading like a fogged breath in the cold morning air. I blink against the sudden shift in reality, realizing that I must have drifted off—stress and back-to-back travel finally catching up with me despite the rough roads.

With a groan, I stretch and climb out of the jeep, my muscles stiff from the long, winding journey. The crisp mountain air bites at my skin, but despite the ache in my body, something inside me feels lighter. It almost feels like coming home.

Only a few days have passed since I stood in this very spot, waving goodbye to this little guesthouse. But it feels like a lifetime ago—a different world, a different woman. I've returned back to Migdhari, but I am forever changed.

I follow the familiar worn path to the main lobby, the bells above the door tinkling softly as a wave of incense curls around me in greeting. The owner looks up, his mouth falling open in surprise before his expression melts into a warm smile, deepening the weathered lines on his face.

"Dahlia-ji! I thought you had returned home." Tenzig hurries over and presses his hands together with a slight bow. "Namaste."

"Namaste," I reply, mirroring the gesture. A sad smile tugs at my lips. "I did."

He studies me for a moment, then nods as if he understands something I don't yet have words for.

"The mountains have called you back," he says simply. "So, you must answer."

There's no judgment in his tone. No question, no expectation. Just an acceptance I hadn't realized I needed. As if flying half way around the globe and back is the most normal thing in the world.

"You are tired," he continues, already turning toward the hallway. "Come, come. I will show you to your room."

I follow him, grateful for the kindness. His hospitality is a balm to my raw, aching heart. When he opens the door to my room, a wave of relief washes over me. It's the same one I stayed in before and nothing has changed. It is a simple space with a single bed, a chest of drawers, and a small desk. Modest. Practical. But as I step inside, I realize it feels more like home than the house I so hastily abandoned.

"Come to the lounge when you are ready for tea," he says before departing.

I take my time unpacking, placing each item carefully, as if this is more than a temporary stop in a sea of uncertainty. Then I sink onto the bed, gaze drifting to the window, where the river glimmers in the fading light.

Last time, at Sita's insistence, I had searched only this side of the water. But now, my eyes keep straying to the dense line of trees on the far bank. There's something about them—something vast and unknowable—that calls to me from their shadowy depths.

A beckoning. A challenge or a promise, I don't know. But this time, I intend to answer. If the Migoi is real, who knows what else those forests are hiding? Tomorrow, I'll ask Sita if she can guide me again—this time, I'll insist on crossing the river.

Tonight, though, even as exhaustion tugs at me, I bypass the comfort of my waiting bed and head to the lounge to meet Tenzig and the promised chai.

I slip outside, following the narrow path. No matter how tightly I pull my coat around me, the wind still finds a way in, threading icy fingers beneath my hood and along the hem of my parka. Even this short walk confirms it—winter isn't just creeping in. It's arrived.

The moment I step into the lounge, warmth envelops me, chasing the chill from my bones. I sink into a seat by the fireplace, stretching my hands toward the flames.

Tenzig settles across from me, silent and steady as ever, and passes me a small steaming cup of chai.

I wrap my fingers around it, letting the heat seep in. Sitting next to the fire, sipping the sweet tea of the mountains, I feel a tiny crack form in the permafrost encasing my heart. Coming here was the right decision.

At last, I break the comfortable silence. "Tenzig, do you know if Sita is available to guide me again? I really trust her."

His gaze, which had drifted to me while I spoke, slides back to the fire. For a moment, his face is unreadable, the firelight carving deep shadows into his features. "I believe so," he says finally. "She will be here in the morning. You can discuss your plans with her then." A pause. "You have come back for the plant?"

I nod, eyes fixed on the flickering flames. Although his words both earlier and now acknowledge my search for the plant, his tone almost hints that he knows it isn't just the plant drawing me back.

The memory of the eyes I saw beyond the firepit is stronger than ever now, a ghost pressing against the edges of my mind. The sensation is so vivid, so tangible, that for a split second, I swear I can feel it again—a gaze, distant yet piercing, sliding over my skin.

Watching.

Waiting.

A trickle of unease should creep down my spine at not just the thought but the absolute intuition of being watched. Instead, something warmer slides through me—like a lover's touch, slow and certain. It curls low in my belly, a pulse of warmth that has no business being there right now.

This is the kind of gaze that promises not just warmth, but visceral heat. Possession. Something primal and all-consuming like a wildfire.

But that's ridiculous. I'm safely tucked away inside. .

And yet—

The unexpected desire that pools in my stomach is a stark reminder of just how long it's been—not just since I've had sex, but since I've had intimacy. A real connection. Back when Ben and I first got together, our sex life had been what I assumed most people had—good enough, slotted into the rare moments when our schedules allowed.

But then, little by little, something shifted. Every attempt I made to bring us closer, to spark something deeper, was met with dismissal. So, I stopped trying.

We were already slipping into a pattern of less and less, and I didn't want to rock the boat. And when we did happen to connect physically, it was mechanical—going through the motions, his mind elsewhere.

Now, I know where. It wasn't just the sex, nor even the passion slipping away, but the intimacy. The knowing of another's soul.

The thought of him whispering filthy promises to someone else—offering her the passion he withheld from me—sends a hot rush of anger to my cheeks.

I deserve more. Better. I deserve someone who won't just

tolerate my desires but will ignite them. Someone who will meet me fully—mind, body, and soul. Not that I expect to find that here, high in the Himalayan mountains.

But maybe—once I locate the plant, make it back home, extract its medicinal properties, save my life, write my paper, and defend my dissertation if I have a university to go back to— then, just maybe, I can think about building a healthier relationship. One built on passion and partnership, not convenience and compromise.

Who was I kidding? That was a lifetime away, hanging on a thousand ifs—if I found the plant, if I lived long enough to turn it into a cure, if I somehow found someone who actually saw me. Yeah. Totally realistic odds.

A voice saying my name pulls me from my spiraling thoughts. I blink, realizing Tenzig has been calling me—probably more than once.

"I'm sorry, it's been such a long day," I say, rubbing my temples.

He just gives me a kind smile, his eyes full of understanding. "Rest, Dahlia-ji. The mountains will still be standing here tomorrow, just as they have for millions of years."

I nod, murmuring my thanks before standing. The warmth of the fire clings to me as I step outside, but the cold is waiting. It slips beneath my coat, winding around me, sharp and unrelenting. Tearing away any heat or comfort with its scrabbling skeletal fingers.

I pull my parka tighter and walk faster, my boots crunching softly against the frozen ground. My breath curls in front of me, vanishing into the night. Each step feels heavier than the last, the weight of everything I'm up against pressing down on me with suffocating weight.

I was so sure when I left. So certain I was meant to come back here and continue my search. But now, standing on the edge of what could either be an amazing discovery or abject failure, doubt creeps in, quiet but persistent. I am one woman. A PhD student attempting her own research with no resources now. The odds aren't in my favor.

They never were.

I shove the thoughts aside and focus on my feet. One step. Then another. Just keep moving. By the time I reach my room, doubt and exhaustion are bone deep. I barely manage to kick off my shoes before collapsing onto the mattress, dragging the heavy quilt over me. The moment my head hits the pillow, the tension in my body finally gives way.

Sleep claims me before I can worry about tomorrow. Whatever waits—whether it's the plant, the truth, or something I can't yet name—will come soon enough. But tonight, exhaustion wins.

CHAPTER NINE

Even though I knew she was gone, I kept returning to keep watch over the guesthouse.

She is a thorn buried deep in my skin, a wound I cannot leave alone. I press against it again and again, unable to stop myself from seeking the sting if only to reassure myself that it is there. That she was real.

I have seen other travelers leave these mountains, only to return months or even years later. Some are called back by unfinished business, others by something they cannot name. So it's not impossible that she could also return. Hope is a dangerous thing, but I cannot seem to let it go.

And yet, my heart tells me the truth. If she had only been leaving for a few days, she would not have cried like that. She would not have held herself like the first fragile snowflake waiting to be blown away by the North wind.

Still, I can't seem to stop keeping watch.

It is my duty to maintain the great balance, to protect the mountains, the forests, and the life within them. It is the dharma of my kind—to preserve the delicate thread that binds this world together, given to us at birth by the creator. Every year, this task grows harder as more humans arrive, their hearts disconnected from the land, their hands taking without reverence.

But I endure because the land endures. The mountains stand sentinel, silent and unyielding. Even when grief hollowed me out, when I wanted to let the balance crumble around me, I held firm. I did not give in. I found peace in my purpose, beauty in the world around me once more.

But she is different than the others. Her presence does not disrupt the balance. It hums in tune with it, vibrating along unseen threads of fate. A force beyond even my understanding. And no matter how I try to return to my duty, I cannot stop seeking her.

Every night, I keep vigil across the river, my body still as stone, my senses reaching for her. My mind tells me to abandon this place, to leave and return to my home deep in the mountains. But something deeper—something older—keeps me rooted.

It is more than instinct. More than duty.

It is the same ancient force that moves the tides and shifts the earth beneath our feet. The same force that pulls birds to migrate home. That tells the trees when to shed their leaves and the flowers when to bloom again.

It is something I have felt only once before in all my years. And I know better than to ignore it.

For days, I sit in stillness, meditating on her memory as if my devotion alone could summon her back to me. And then— like a prayer answered by the earth itself—she returns.

I feel her before I see her—a shift in the breath of the mountain, a ripple in the silence that speaks of change. A tremor, subtle but certain, like the first breath before an avalanche.

The wind carries her scent, curling through the trees, whispering through the stone. It reaches for me before my eyes confirm what my heart already knows. She is here. Something that does not belong to these mountains yet somehow belongs to me.

The moment I see her, something inside me snaps taut.

She stumbles slightly as she climbs out of the jeep, exhaustion weighing her down. The golden light catches in her wild curls, and my fingers twitch with the urge to bury my hands in them. Dark shadows smudge the skin beneath her eyes, but her lips are set in that determined line I remember. The lips I couldn't stop imagining wrapped around me.

She has changed.

She was always strong, but now, I see the cracks. Not broken, but reforged. There is something sharper in her now. A woman who has lost things she will never get back. A woman who has learned what it means to be alone.

She has suffered.

And I feel that suffering as if it were my own. A low growl rumbles deep in my chest before I can stop it. My fingers curl into my palms, claws biting into my flesh.

Who hurt you, Winter Star?

The fury burns low and deep, a heat that coils in my gut like embers waiting to be stoked. My beast snarls within me, demanding retribution, but I force it back, barely restraining the need to act. Not yet.

I move closer, as near as I dare without revealing myself again, watching as she makes her way toward the main house. Her movements are stiff, careful. As though carrying something invisible but unbearably heavy.

When the door closes behind her, I do not hesitate. Nothing matters outside of her. The river is freezing, but I do not feel it. The current roars around me, but it is nothing compared to the storm inside my chest as I make my way across the river to her.

Within moments, my great strides eat up the distance and I

am at the guesthouse, pressing close to the outside wall, the stone biting through the damp fur of my coat. I hold still, listening—waiting. Cursing the wall that separates us while at the same time thankful because without it, she would already be in my arms.

And then, I hear her soft, muffled voice. I cannot make out the words, but I feel them—the raw edges of something she does not let others see. A wound still bleeding beneath the surface. I brace my hands against the stone wall and drop my head, fighting to steady my ragged breathing at the mere thought of her pain.

I inhale deeply, catching her scent through the wood and stone. The moment it hits me, my body tightens, heat surging through my core. My rage turns to feral desire.

She smells like the first whisper of sun upon the earth in spring—full of hope and promise. Like the first bloom after winter signaling new life. She smells like home.

The urge to go to her, to comfort, to protect, and claim, rises like a tidal wave. I force every muscle in my body into submission, forcing myself to stay still. Caging the beast rising inside of me, desperate to get to her. Threatening to break down the walls, the mountains, anything that stands between us.

My head knows this is not the time, but my heart, oh my heart, how it disagrees. And my body...my body knows what she is the most.

She is back, called to my mountain kingdom where all is under my protection. And now, that includes her. I realize whatever she faced during her absence, it has left her even more fragile than before. And yet, beneath the fragility, I sense that same quiet strength that drew me to her the first time I saw her.

She is the first snowflake that falls. Beautiful. Unique. And just like every piece of this world, down to a single snowflake, she is here for a purpose. And I cannot help but feel that purpose is tied to me in ways I don't yet understand. She has come back to these mountains. To my home.

I close my eyes, exhaling slowly, centering myself. I cannot act on this impulse. Not now. And though I don't yet know why, I do know one thing with absolute certainty—I will not let her walk this path alone.

No one will harm her again. No one will take her from me. Not now. Not ever. I swear it to the river, the wind, and the mountain itself. I swear it to my Sruhnar, my Winter Star.

CHAPTER TEN

DAHLIA

I had every intention of waking early to meet with Sita. But my body, finally allowed to relax in a safe space, betrays me.

When I roll over, stretching the knots from my neck, my room is flooded with the warm amber glow of the sun. Dust motes swirl in the golden light, defying gravity as they dance through the air.

I follow the path of one as it loops and whirls in beautiful chaos—so at odds with my rigid world of science and research. How I long to be like that dust mote, free from the laws of physics, from the constraints that bind me to reality—dancing to my own tune.

The tiny speck drifts along the sunbeam, pulling my gaze toward my travel clock. The amber glow shifts from mesmerizing to alarming as realization sets in. I slept the entire day away.

A wave of frustration crashes through me. My timeline is already razor-thin, and I've just lost precious hours. Each passing day feels like grains of sand slipping through my fingers —each one bringing me closer to the inevitable.

"Damn it, Dahlia," I curse myself out loud and throw back the heavy quilt, shivering as the cool mountain air seeps into my sleep-warmed skin. I jerk on another layer, grab my jacket, and hastily lace up my boots before hurrying out the door.

I rush to the lounge to look for Sita and apologize for my lateness, but Tenzig directs me to the outdoor fire pit. I step onto the stone pathway, my breath curling in the crisp evening air as I head in search of my friend.

A new group of travelers has gathered around the fire, likely the last of the season before winter locks the mountains in ice and snow. They huddle close to the fire's flickering warmth, steaming cups of chai cradled in their hands, soaking in the final days of tolerable weather.

Sita moves among them, effortless and friendly, refilling cups and exchanging easy conversation.

I curse my timing. The fire pit isn't the place for private conversations, but I've already wasted an entire day, and every lost hour stretches like an eternity—each one stealing precious daylight, each one bringing the snowline lower down the mountain.

Anxiety simmers beneath my skin as I hover at the edge of the firelight, waiting for a chance to speak with her. As if sensing my impatience, Sita finishes serving and takes a seat, beckoning to me to join her.

Sitting down, I say, "Sita, I'm so sorry I slept the day away."

Her brown eyes glimmer with quiet understanding as she waves off my apology. Lips curving into a soft smile, she says, "Please, do not apologize for the rest you so clearly needed. I didn't think to ever see you again, *didi*. I was thrilled when my father said you had returned but also worried that you were back so soon."

The word didi, or sister, eases some of the tension in my

chest. Sita has been more than a guide. She's been my friend, supporting me through the relentless cycle of hope and disappointment—each lead turning into a dead end, every inch of the rugged mountain terrain yielding nothing—she has been there, helping me weather it all.

Still, I can't shake my urgency. "Honestly, I didn't expect to be back ever, much less in a few days. But here I am. We *must* find the plant, Sita."

Her smile dims slightly as she locks her warm brown eyes on mine, sympathy bleeding through her gaze. She knows—she's always known. I had confided in her why I was so desperate, and she had matched it with relentless determination, scouring the mountains by my side, chasing every lead, no matter how thin. She had been just as crushed as I was when I left for home empty-handed.

Sita is steady, unwavering—a force as certain as the sunrise over these peaks. But I hadn't missed the unshed tears shimmering in her eyes when she hugged me goodbye. She had believed it was for the last time.

I glance toward the river and the darkened stretch of forest beyond. "I feel like we need to search there," I point. "Across the river."

The change in her expression is instant. Her hand lifts automatically, catching mine and lowering it. Then, with a swift flick of her fingers, she traces a small symbol in the air. A gesture I don't recognize.

"Dahlia," she says carefully. "I know how badly you need this plant. But we must not cross the sacred waters of Migaia."

I frown. "Why not? We've searched everywhere else."

She shakes her head slowly, her fingers curling in her lap. "It is not...safe."

Sita has guided me through treacherous terrain before, fearlessly scaling ridges and navigating dense brush without hesitation. She is not someone who scares easily.

But this—this is something else. This seems more like reverence. A deep, abiding caution rather than fear.

It's not the first time she's held back information from me, either. While we searched, she often translated when speaking with locals—yogis, elders, people whose wisdom was passed down through generations. They shared ancestral knowledge, pointed us toward possibilities, helped us rule out false leads.

But there were times—like now—when their answers had been too vague, or Sita had hesitated before passing along their words. Not because she didn't want to help—she did. She wanted me to find the plant just as much as I did. But more than that, I think she wanted to protect me. Even if it was from myself.

I don't push her. Not yet. Instead, we sit in silence, watching the fire burn down to embers until the cold creeps in, chasing away the last traces of heat. The night settles in around us, the warmth of the dying fire no longer enough to hold back the mountain chill. One by one, the travelers retreat to their rooms, until only one man remains.

Sita excuses herself to place hot water bottles in my bed, extra warmth against the chill of the night. The thick quilts and insulation will help keep the room warm enough, but I'm not going to say no to the added comfort.

Left alone, I offer a shy smile at the man which he takes as an invitation to join me. While he starts up some small talk in a delightful British accent, I find myself unable to focus on what he is saying, distracted by the weight of eyes on my back again.

Instead of the hot caress of a lingering gaze I experienced the last time I was here, tonight a different kind of heated look emanates from the woods behind me. Not sensual but watchful and possessive. Territorial even.

I glance over my shoulder, expecting to see someone from the guesthouse—but there's nothing. My eyes search the rapidly darkening night, but there is no movement in the trees. Not even luminous eyes in the darkness.

Despite not finding a source of the sensation, my skin still prickles with awareness. Shrugging off the feeling as lingering stress from Ben, I try to politely direct my attention back to the fellow traveler.

"Something wrong?" the man asks, tilting his head at my clear distraction.

"I thought I heard something," I murmur in excuse.

He leans around me to look, balancing with a hand on my knee, saying, "I didn't hear anything."

I freeze. Not because I feel threatened, but because I don't know how to read this casual touch. I've been with Ben for so long that I can't tell if this man is flirting or just friendly. I look down at his hand on my knee and then back up to meet his eyes. He leans in, flashing a teasing smile—and the forest explodes.

A thunderous crash shatters the quiet night. Branches snap and the fire shoots sparks into the sky with a crackle as if it, too, is alarmed. The sudden noise is followed by an even more unnerving silence. Even the river has hushed its rushing waters.

We lurch to our feet, the man stumbling back in alarm as I step closer to scan across the river, eyes roving over the darkened woods where the sound came from. My heart hammers against my ribs as I search the darkness. I can't see anything, but my heart tells me—something is out there.

"Well, I definitely heard that," he chuckles nervously, rubbing his arms. "Probably just a monkey or something, yeah?" He offers a lopsided grin, but there's an edge to it, like he's trying to convince himself as much as me. "Anyway, I think that's my cue for bed."

"Yes," I choke out, throat dry, unable to tear my eyes away from the search. "I think you're right."

He hesitates for half a second, glancing toward the tree line.

Then, with a stiff nod at me and then at Sita as she approaches, he turns and heads toward his room, quickening his pace the farther he gets from the fire.

"Everything okay?" Sita asks, watching him retreat. When he disappears into the guesthouse, she turns back to me, her gaze flicking between my face and the darkened tree line.

"Sita, there was a huge crash over there," I explain, pointing off in the direction the sound had come from.

Her reaction is immediate. She grabs my hand and all but drags me toward my room. Once inside, she closes the door and leans against it, her expression unreadable.

"Sita, what is going on?" I ask, heart pounding at her reaction on the heels of the night's events.

She gestures to the bed, and we sit together. Her gaze flicks to the small window overlooking the forest, her expression solemn. "Didi, there is a reason we have not searched those woods. What you heard—it's not unusual here."

A chill skates down my spine. "What do you mean?"

She hesitates, then lowers her voice to a conspiratorial whisper. "The mountains have their own secrets, Dahlia. We call it the Migoi."

"I heard that myth around the campfire. We call them Yetis back home, or Bigfoot."

I can't help the slight chuckle over the Bigfoot memes and car stickers back home, but the memory of that strange heat prickling my back, followed by the crash in the woods when that man touched my knee and leaned in, has my nerves still on edge.

Sita presses her palms together, her expression turning solemn as she looks at me over her steepled fingers.

"The Migoi is not like the stories you hear in the West. It is not just a beast that wanders the mountains. It is a spirit, too. A guardian." Her voice lowers. "Sometimes, they help. Sometimes, they send warnings. Other times..." Her voice trails off as she averts her eyes.

She glances toward the window again. "The crash you heard —it may have been a warning."

Her words settle deep in my chest. I glance toward the window and out at the forest beyond. If the Migoi is real—what was tonight? A warning for what?

I chew my bottom lip thoughtfully and reply, "Or just an animal."

"Maybe," she allows. "But the forest you pointed to—it's not a good idea."

I lean forward. "So, you believe they're real?"

She meets my gaze again, her voice dropping back to a whisper. "When winter comes, almost everyone leaves. But my family has always stayed. We've seen the tracks in the snow, the broken branches—signs of something too big to be a man. When we have enough, we leave offerings. When we have no choice, we enter the woods with caution."

With a far off look in her eyes, she turns her face to the window and continues. "One year, an early storm swept in—stronger than anything we had seen before. It buried the roads, sealed us inside, and lasted so long we burned through what little firewood we had. We thought we would freeze to death. The day we ran out, we opened the door to find wood stacked in a huge pile."

She blinks away the memories and meets my eyes again intently. "No mere man could have stacked that much wood overnight. I listen to the mountains, to the earth. And I respect the Migoi."

Her words hang in the air, and for a moment, I think back to the crash we heard, the strange tension I felt. "But why would it warn us—or worse?"

She shrugs, but there's a flicker of concern in her expression. "Maybe it wasn't a warning. Maybe it was just passing through.

But the forest you pointed to—it's still not a good idea even without the Migoi. There are other dangers—the harsh terrain, unpredictable weather, wild animals, and sometimes avalanches. I can't guide you over there like I have here."

I swallow hard, realizing the weight of her words and say softly, "Sita, it's the only place we haven't searched. And you know I can't leave again without that plant."

She watches me for a long moment. Then, with a sigh, she pats my hand. "We will go up to the ashram before the snows come. We will speak with the elders again. We will listen to the mountain." She squeezes my fingers. "Now, sleep. We'll leave at first light."

I nod, but as she slips out the door, a strange restlessness clings to me. I should be exhausted, but sleep doesn't come easily. The room is warm, safe, wrapped in thick walls and heavy quilts. But my thoughts are still outside, in the dark, tangled somewhere between the firepit and the shadowed tree line.

Listening. Waiting. For what, I'm not sure. But I can't shake the feeling that something out there is waiting for me, too.

CHAPTER ELEVEN

ERYON - EARLIER

She is back. The refrain echoes in every beat of my heart as I watch from my vantage point across the river. Her presence ripples through the trees, the river, the very bones of the mountain.

And now she appears as a vision before my eyes, wrapped in the golden light of the setting sun.

For one glorious second, time holds her still—immortal, untouchable, a golden statue impervious to the ravages of life and death. But her eyes—shining with that impossible blue-violet iridescence—declare my Winter Star alive. She is no mere statue. No fleeting vision. And oh, how I want to feel the heat of her in my arms.

For she is the promise of warmth, of fire glowing deep within my cave in the heart of winter. Of comfort against the cold loneliness of my existence.

The moment passes, and she moves through the cold, unguarded, her body soft from a world gentler than mine. She pulls her jacket tighter as she hurries toward the fire, her breath curling in the air.

I should leave.

The sight of her sends an ache through my chest, deeper than hunger, sharper than the wind that howls through these peaks, because I am no gentle creature. I swore to myself that I would not seek her out again. That her presence would not stir the things inside me that should remain quiet.

And yet, here I am.

Watching. Waiting. I tell myself it is only to ensure her safety. That I let her go once because she was leaving my mountains, leaving the place where my claim on her held weight. But she has returned, whether by fate or chance, and now that she is here, I will not let her walk this path alone. It is a duty. It is instinct.

It is a lie.

I cannot ensure her safety because I am not safe. She has barely been back a day, and already, I feel the old war between logic and something darker stirring in my blood. I cannot let her pull me from the shadows.

She is not mine, my head warns.

Not yet, my heart snaps back.

A restless growl hums in my chest as I press forward, eyes locked on the distant glow of the guesthouse below. Smoke curls from its chimneys, firelight flickers in the windows, and human voices carry on the wind. Their language is rough, foreign.

But hers—I would know hers anywhere.

Her voice falls gently upon my ears, like the hush of falling snow. And oh, how I long to hear my name fall from her lips in worship. Let it drift over my skin, praising me as I pleasure her. Listen for her to call out for me across our home.

It has been so very long since I have heard the sounds that make up my name from another. The thought spears through me, sharp and unwanted. My gaze lingers on her face, searching for something even I cannot name.

She sits near the fire, her face glowing in the flickering light. There is a shadow to her aura, a weariness that was not there before, but her spirit has not dimmed.

Her friend, the small one she calls Sita, leans in, listening. They share words weighted with meaning, gestures that speak of old pain and new determination.

And then, she smiles. Not at me, but at Sita. A smile that is easy, familiar, given freely.

Seeing her with a measure of happiness should bring me peace. Instead, it twists something in my gut because that warmth is not for me. And I want her smile as much as I want to hear my name fall from her lips.

My greedy eyes take in her every move, and when I see her gesture toward the river, her arm sweeping toward the darkened stretch of forest beyond, my heart stutters.

She points to *my* forest. To the place where the mountain calls to her. To me.

A low, warning rumble builds in my chest. If she crosses into my territory, I do not know if I will be able to stop myself from not just showing myself to her—but claiming her.

Does she know what she is asking? Does she feel it, the way the air changes when she speaks of stepping beyond the boundary?

My heart stutters at the thought of her crossing that line. Into my woods. Into my reach. I imagine it too easily—finding her lost beneath the dark canopy, eyes wide, heart racing, as her breath exits her perfect lips in sharp pants that feather into clouds.

How would she look if I stepped from the shadows? Would she run? Would she scream? Or would those iridescent eyes meet mine with something else?

Curiosity? Recognition? Desire?

I press a clawed hand into the frost-covered earth, grounding myself. She is not mine.

Not yet, my heart whispers again.

The one called Sita leaves, moving toward the guesthouse. She does not see the moment that follows when a stranger, a man, settles beside Dahlia. Not a beast like me. Another human, one she could turn her smile on, too.

I do not know him, but I know he does not belong here with his sharp voice. He is too easy around her. A true male would be on guard, protecting her from the monsters in this wood. Protecting her from me. He does not deserve her smile.

I shift forward, my massive form hidden among the trees. His posture is relaxed, his grin easy, but his movements are measured. Calculated. His hand lands on her knee, his fingers flexing just slightly.

I see the way he leans in, the way he touches her. A small thing. Maybe an innocent thing. And yet, the sight of it sets my blood to a slow, burning simmer. For what man is truly innocent?

I see her stiffen at his touch. She does not want it. Something hot and ugly unfurls inside me. I do not understand it.

No. That is another lie. I understand it too well.

A warning growl rumbles in my throat, a sound that does not belong to these peaceful foothills. But, before I can stop myself, I reach for a thick branch above me—snap.

The crack echoes through the still night like a thunderclap. Exploding like the pain resounding in my heart. A warning, unintentional, yet wholly deliberate.

Even the fire jumps, my anger pulsing through the night like a concussive force. The forest stills, small creatures ducking into their burrows, attuned to the presence of clear and present danger—to me.

She hears me. I know, before she even turns towards the sound, she senses me. Feels my soul calling to hers. I see it in the way she stills, the way she glances over her shoulder toward the tree line, toward the darkness where I stand. Searching.

Her companion startles, laughing uneasily, brushing off the sound as nothing more than a forest creature, or a trick of the wind. A harmless thing.

What a fool he is. I am not harmless. I am the dark of the mountain.

He hesitates. Just for a breath. He glances toward her, toward the empty space beyond the fire. And then he waits. That is the only thing that spares him. Had he left her alone, had he abandoned her to face whatever lurked beyond the firelight, I would not have restrained myself.

I rarely take life, but I am not above enforcing the balance. And a male who would leave a female unprotected in my mountains has no place in them.

He waits for her companion to return, only leaving when Sita arrives. That is why I let him go. For now.

Sita, however, does not hesitate. She knows. She sees Dahlia's reluctance, the way she lingers, searching the darkness. But Sita does not let her stay. She does not waste time scanning the tree line and knows better than to dismiss the sound.

She pulls Dahlia away with quiet urgency, murmuring words I cannot hear. Perhaps a warning or a plea. Wisely, Dahlia listens and follows her to safety. The door closes behind them, sealing them in away from the night. Away from me.

I exhale slowly, rolling my shoulders against the tight coil of my muscles. My claws flex at my sides, resisting the urge to tear something apart in place of the man.

I should leave. And yet, I do not. Not yet. I linger, moving higher into the trees, watching over the place where she sleeps.

The fire burns low, fading away with the voices inside the buildings. The stars whirl overhead in their eternal dance while I count the beats of my heart until the world stills under the hush of night. Only then do I turn away, retreating into the shadows.

She is here, back within reach. But still too far.

Tonight, I let her rest. Tomorrow, I will follow her on her quest. The first steps to forever.

I feel my feet tread over the frozen earth, feel the mountain breathe beneath me, letting it bear witness. A vow spoken in the heart is a vow carved in stone. But what I'm about to do? This is no mere vow. This is the weight of fate itself.

I drag a claw across my palm, a slow, deliberate cut, dark blood welling against the pale frost of my skin. The cold bites deep, and though the sting is sharp, I do not flinch. I let the blood fall, let the land drink it, an offering to something far older than even me and my kind.

I have made a vow like this before. And still, the world took what was mine.

The earth does not bargain. The wind does not return what has been stolen. No matter how tightly I held on, no matter how fiercely I swore to protect—I was not enough. But I will *not* fail again.

I breathe the words into the night, letting them settle into the bones of the mountain, into the roots of the trees, into the frost that is sneaking over my skin in the darkest hour before the dawn. The words do not belong to the language of men. They are older. They are mine.

"Let the land bear witness. Let the cold remember. She is not mine until she chooses. But I am hers. And I will not let her walk this path alone."

Chapter Twelve

Dahlia

The cold wind turns brutal as we make our way up the winding trail to the ashram, cutting through my thick layers like a blade. Even with my coat zipped to my chin and my scarf wrapped tight, the chill seeps in, numbing my fingers inside my gloves. My breath fogs in the thin air, each exhale stolen away by the wind before it can crystallize in the air.

Despite the endurance I have built hiking in these mountains, the altitude still burns my lungs. My thighs ache with exertion as I push to keep pace with Sita, who moves ahead of me with effortless grace, sure-footed as ever. She barely seems winded, but even she keeps glancing toward the thickening clouds above us.

A storm is coming. And we're running out of time.

When we finally arrive, I barely register the relief of being indoors before disappointment more bitter than the weather crushes it.

The ashram is quiet, its stone walls heavy with the weight of old knowledge and prayers. Smoke curls lazily from the wood stove as the warm incense perfumed air wraps around me, but none of it thaws the icy knot in my chest.

After much cajoling from Sita—and my own desperate pleas—one of the yogis finally speaks.

"Yes, we have heard of the plant you seek," he admits at last, his voice carrying the weight of something more than secrecy.

My pulse leaps.

"But it grows in a place that cannot be disturbed."

The words fall like a stone into my stomach. I glance at Sita, but she only lowers her eyes. There will be no arguing this point. No convincing them. I'm surprised they have admitted this much.

No matter, I already know where it is. Fate is pulling me across the river to the forbidden woods like a compass points north.

I press my lips together to keep from shouting my frustration. I knew it. Every instinct in my body tells me the plant is there. And despite the warnings, despite the stories of the Migoi and the dangers that lurk in those untouched forests—I must go.

There's no other choice.

I inhale slowly, forcing calm into my voice. "Let's head back so I can update my notes."

Sita hesitates, glancing toward the window, where the clouds have thickened to an ominous grey, swallowing the last hints of daylight.

"The storm—"

"We'll make it," I cut in, forcing a reassuring smile.

I'm not lying—I do need to update my notes. But the real reason I want to get back tonight is so I can slip away at first light. If the yogis won't tell me the location, and if Sita refuses to cross the river, then I'll have no choice but to do it alone.

And I will.

I refuse to leave these mountains without that plant. I'm not scared of the weather or the terrain. And the stories about the Migoi are just that—stories. The same kind of legend as Bigfoot back home. A bear print stretched in melting snow, a tuft of fur caught on a branch that could belong to anything. The woodpile outside Sita's house? Probably the work of a neighbor, someone who didn't want to draw attention to their charity.

Nothing more than superstition or folklore, I reassure myself. If I sneak out early, I'll have a few hours to explore before needing to return. It's definitely reckless. Probably dangerous. But it's the only plan I have, cobbled together from desperation and the small flickering flame of hope that refuses to die.

Once I get my hands on that plant, everything else will fall into place. I'll worry about anything else after that. After all, it's better to beg forgiveness than ask permission.

I mentally run through what I'll need: my collection kit, some food, my first aid kit, extra layers. I can do this. I *have* to do this.

Sita interrupts my silent checklist, again urging me to stay the night at the ashram, but I shake my head. If we stay, I'll lose another day.

"We'll make it back before the worst of the storm," I insist. "It's all downhill from here, so it will be faster. We have plenty of time to get back. Please, Sita."

I stare at her with imploring eyes, the sting of tears pricking behind my lids. I blink past the shimmer, and one lone tear falls down my cheek.

She studies me for a long moment, her gaze tracking the pitiful drop, then nods with a sigh.

We thank our hosts, and by the time we step outside, the mountain is even colder. The sky has shifted from vast and endless to low and oppressive, a heavy gray shroud hanging over the peaks. The quiet is eerie, a hush that presses in around us like the whole world is holding its breath.

We descend as fast as we can, our boots crunching over frost-hardened earth. But despite our hurry, halfway down the trail, the first flakes begin to fall. My desperation has turned me reckless. Just as we lose sight of the ashram behind us, the snow starts falling in earnest.

At first, it seems harmless—delicate flurries dancing in the wind. But within minutes, the snowfall thickens, transforming the landscape into an eerie, shifting blur of white.

This isn't like the snowstorms I know. This falls like monsoon rain. Thick. Heavy. Consuming.

The path quickly vanishes beneath the rapidly accumulating snow. I push forward faster, heart hammering. We have to make it back before this storm buries us. I match her steps, watching the way she moves. Planting my feet in the footsteps she leaves.

Sita stops and faces me. "Dahlia, we're more than halfway between the ashram and home. I think we should keep going, since downhill will be easier in the snow."

I have never seen her hesitate before. Never seen her uncertain. That chills me even more than the cold surrounding us.

"I'm so sorry I pushed us to go," I apologize.

"No need to apologize, I agreed. Let's focus on getting home as quickly and safely as we can," she says.

She squeezes my arms and gives me a reassuring smile, but I see the concern lining her face. She's lived in these mountains all of her life. She knows we are going to have a hard time, but I can tell she is trying not to scare me.

Eyes locked on the trail ahead, I push forward as fast as I dare, carefully planting each step to avoid twisting an ankle or tumbling on the steep, slippery descent.

Within the hour, the temperature plummets. I stick close to Sita, her vibrant jacket a beacon of color in an otherwise blinding sea of white. The wind bites at my face, forcing me to pull my hood lower in a futile attempt to shield myself from the freezing assault.

My fingers and toes throb with the sharp sting of encroaching numbness. I curl my hands into fists and open them over and over, trying to keep the blood flowing, but every movement seems to happen just a little slower than the last.

The snow swirls so thickly I can barely make out Sita's form just ahead of me. I'm so focused on staring intently at her jacket that my numb foot stumbles, skidding off a hidden rock. I let out a startled yelp and look down as I fight to steady myself. The second it takes to regain my balance is enough—I look back up and realize Sita has vanished into the storm.

She's gone. There's nothing but a shifting, swirling void of white. I blink hard, stepping forward, scanning for any sign of her. But there is nothing but a snowglobe world.

I stop dead, breath freezing in my lungs.

"Sita?" I call out. She was right there. Right there!

But there's no response.

My heart stutters, panic rising, but I force it down, thinking she must be ahead by just a few steps. I hurry forward, expecting her to reappear. But she doesn't.

A sickening realization crashes over me. Not only can I not see Sita, but even the trail has disappeared. The storm has swallowed the world whole.

"Sita!" I yell, my voice carried away instantly by the wind.

I hurry another few feet on where I think the trial should be, but all I find is endless snow. No Sita. I spin in a circle, blinking against the swirling flakes as I search out a flash of color, anything other than this blinding white.

"Sita!" I yell, over and over again.

No answer comes, and now I have myself completely turned around. I have no idea which direction I'm facing, much less if I'm anywhere near the trail.

I'm lost.

The thought slams into me like a blow to the gut. I squeeze

my eyes shut, trying to think through the rising panic. My mother's words filter back to me from when I was a little girl.

If you get lost, stay where you are, someone will come to find you.

Not wanting to get any more turned around than I already am, I stand in one spot, yelling for Sita every few seconds. Within minutes I have to force my hoarse voice through my chattering teeth.

Shivers wrack my body, and I realize I need to get my blood circulating. I simply cannot wait here to be found. At this rate I'll be here until the Spring thaw.

But which way?

I take a few tentative steps, trying to determine if they are going uphill or downhill but the complete whiteout causes an eerie sense of disorientation. I could be heading upside down for all I can tell. In the end, I pick the direction that feels like it slopes down the most, and take slow, cautious steps.

I try to map in my head where on the trail we could be, since I have walked it several times before. But it's impossible—I am well and truly lost. Rubbing my hands together to keep my circulation going, I continue walking—it's my only chance.

Too late, I realize my next step lands on nothing but air. Mom was right. I should have stayed put.

I fall—

And the world falls with me.

A deafening crack splits the silence, followed by a roar that drowns out my scream. The mountain shifts, collapsing in a surge of snow and ice. I tumble with it, battered by an unstoppable tide. I try to shield my head, arms curling over my face, but I'm weightless, helpless, freefalling until a violent thud knocks the air from my lungs.

Silence.

Darkness.

Time stretches as I lay there stunned. My lungs burn, and my body desperately tries to gasp in a breath, fighting for oxygen, but it doesn't come. My pulse pounds in my ears until I choke in a breath as my paralyzed diaphragm finally relaxes.

My arms are locked around my head, my body twisted at an awkward angle. My ribs ache with every ragged inhale. I try to move my legs. Nothing. I try to shift my arms. Nothing.

Oh, shit. I didn't just fall, I triggered a damn avalanche and now—I'm buried alive.

My breath comes too fast, using up what little air I have left. My chest tightens as panic surges, but I can't panic. My mind knows this, but oh, my poor body wants to react instinctually.

With renewed urgency, I try to maneuver my arm further, but the weight pressing down on me is relentless. I can't move. I steady my breathing, fighting against the pounding of my heart and the growing sense of terror welling up inside me.

"C'mon, Dahlia," I whisper to myself. "Fucking think. You're smart. You can do this!"

The pep talk gives me the encouragement to continue to try to make some room around my face, but the small pocket won't be enough air to last very long. I need to balance using up more oxygen with exertion versus trying to get free.

I want to yell for Sita, but I have no idea where she is and that will only waste more precious air. The only sounds I can hear are the frantic beat of my own heart and above that my shaky breathing. I continue wiggling my arm, hoping I can somehow thrust it up and out through the top.

Within minutes, my body becomes impossibly heavy, limbs weighed down by the crushing embrace of the snow. An icy tingling is creeping up my legs from my numb feet. If I don't suffocate, it looks like I'll freeze to death instead. And I don't know which is worse.

Deciding suffocation to be my bigger fear, I slow my breathing, each shallow inhale scraping icy claws against my lungs. The cold feels sharper with every breath, but it's a gamble I'm willing to take. Maybe, just maybe, slowing down will preserve what little oxygen remains in this icy tomb until help arrives. It's a long shot, but it's all I've got.

The silence presses in, a weight of its own. No sound penetrates the thick layers of snow—not the howl of the wind, not the faintest echo of life.

It's as if the world above has ceased to exist. I could be inches from the surface or buried under an endless white void. The stillness is maddening, disorienting.

I focus on the shallow rise and fall of my chest, counting breaths to keep the panic at bay. Time becomes meaningless here in the frozen dark. Minutes, hours—how long have I been trapped?

The snow clings to me, stealing the warmth from my body, and my thoughts start to slip. There's no way to tell if rescue is coming or if the lonely beat of my heart will be the last thing I ever hear.

As the heaviness abates and instead, I float, my life doesn't flash before my eyes. Rather, I see a highlight reel of the highs and lows. I watch as I grow up and head off to college where for the first time in my life, I thrive. Instead of being a nerd, I'm celebrated for my intellect and curiosity.

I see myself, a promising young undergrad, falling in love with Ben. Putting him on a pedestal and thinking he is my soulmate. The friends and fun I had discovered slipping away as he eclipsed everything else in my life.

Stuck here in the snow on the other side of the world, I'm struck again by just how much he was the one riding my coattails. How all of his successes were mine boosting him up. I see with perfect clarity how he used me and took advantage of the love I offered freely.

"You were the smart one, the whole time. Be smart now," I stammer out to myself, teeth chattering.

My mind is slow but drifts through what to do in an avalanche from some book I read long ago. I realize, I don't know what direction I am facing to get out. I work up what little saliva is in my cold mouth, and I spit. It falls straight down into the snow, and I realize I am face down. I never could have punched up.

With a small laugh, I realize I went ass over tin cups down the mountain. The thought triggers a memory, a song. Wildly inappropriate lyrics start coursing through my mind, telling me to back that ass up. I start nodding my head to the beat and try to wriggle my body, booty end first.

It's the only plan I've got. All I can do is hope that it's crazy enough to work. Within minutes, crippling fatigue weighs me down, and with the lack of progress, I debate giving up. Maybe freezing to death won't be that bad after all. Just me and my off-key rendition of this song fading into oblivion.

The thought hits me with brutal clarity—I am going to die here.

I am going to freeze to death alone in this storm, buried beneath the weight of my own recklessness in pursuit of my cure. The ultimate ironic death.

A laugh bubbles up, half-hysterical, but I bite it back. As the song plays on repeat in my mind, I dig down deep and tap into my survival instinct. It is me and my will to live against the avalanche. I channel the fear, the hysteria, the fucking irony into my movements, shaking more and more until I'm twerking my way, ass up, out of the damn snowy tomb.

Suddenly, I feel something shift, and an icy blast hits my rear.

"No, shit, the nineties for the win," I chatter out, half frozen, half hysterical, but wholly grateful.

Delicious icy air flows past my body and floods my lungs, but no matter how much I tell my body that I need just a few more seconds of energy, it will not listen. The wind whispers to just rest, and I nod. Maybe just for a minute; after all, shaking that booty was a lot of work.

"Something, something, back that ass up," I mumble the lyrics I can remember, the words coming slower and slower when someone grabs said ass and pulls.

Sita must have found me after all. Tears leave an icy trail down my face as I cry in relief. This was a close call. Way too close.

I flop gratefully onto my back, staring up into the sky, barely feeling the snowflakes landing on my face. Despite the cold pulsing through my body, I welcome the icy blast of crisp mountain air into my lungs. I let my eyes drift shut, too exhausted to even blink.

"Thank you," I force past my chattering teeth. My words are barely recognizable, no more than a breath drifting away on the wind.

Feeling Sita lean over me, I open my eyes expecting to look up into her familiar smile and warm brown eyes.

My heart stops. My brain misfires, refusing to process what I'm seeing.

Not Sita.

Not even human.

An enormous creature covered in shaggy hair caked with snow leans over me. But it's the eyes that are locked onto mine that has terror colder than the bitter snow sinking into my soul.

The Migoi.

"Fuck," I breathe out on a curse.

The wind howls. The snow rages. And the creature crouches over me, watching. Waiting.

I should be screaming. Running. *Something.* But all I can do is stare.

This situation is going from bad, to really, really bad. I must be going into shock because if I didn't know better, I could swear a flash of amusement flickers in the creature's gaze at my expletive.

I squeeze my eyes shut and inhale, willing the shock-induced hallucinations away. I must have sustained a concussion in the avalanche. Or maybe this is a dream. Or perhaps I really am dead. But when I reopen them, the figure remains.

A towering mass of thick white fur. A legend made flesh. Its eyes—deep-set, silver as glacial ice—lock onto me, unblinking. In the fading light, they almost seem to glow, twin beacons in the snow. A kaleidoscope of frost and pearl, made to withstand the storm and see through the blinding white.

A wave of primal fear crashes over me. My pulse pounds in my ears, loud enough to drown out the howling wind. *Run!* Every instinct I have screams the command, but my body refuses to obey. Too cold. Too weak. Too late.

I swallow hard, forcing my lips to move, my voice barely more than a whisper.

"Uh, hi." The word fogs in the freezing air before vanishing into the wind. "Thanks." I clear my throat, trying to force my voice to continue. "Thank you for saving me. I—I didn't mean to enter your territory. I mean you no harm."

I scramble to convey respect, frantically trying to recall what Sita had said about the mysterious cryptid. The great eyes blink at me, and I take in the immense shaggy white head that takes up my entire field of vision at this close range. Other than its eyes, the facial features are obscured by the white, thick fur that is caked with snow.

The Yeti glances up at the sky and heaves a great sigh.

A shiver wracks my body as the snow accumulates on my exposed face, falling down into the hood of my coat around my neck and ears. I can't figure out which direction this is going to go. I should probably be afraid of this massive creature who could crush me in a single blow. The one Sita warned me about.

Instead, I find myself curious and very, very cold. Another shiver wracks my body, setting my teeth to chattering until I can't control the sound of them clacking together. The noise draws the creature's gaze back to me, alarm flashing through the mystical eyes.

It's head tilts, regarding me as if not quite knowing what to do with this half-frozen human it has stumbled upon. With a huff of what I'm guessing is resignation, it scoops me up out of the snow and pulls me into its very large body.

A yelp of surprise escapes before I can stop it. My pulse stutters, my frozen limbs too weak to resist. I can only hope it is rescuing me and not saving me as a snack for later. I squeak out a muffled thanks into its fur but it sounds more like a question than a statement.

A low grunt rumbles through its chest. Acknowledgment? Dismissal? Before I can decide, its grip tightens, pulling me closer. Heat radiates through its thick fur, sinking into my frozen skin. My shivers lessen, muscles unclenching from their painful spasms. But as circulation returns, fire sparks in my fingers and toes. Please, don't be frostbite.

The storm rages, shrieking around us. The wind should tear through me. The cold should steal what little life I have left.

Instead, the creature shifts its hold, and—impossibly—its fur grows longer, thicker, surrounding me like a living cloak against the elements.

From my warm and safe cocoon, I can't help the soft moan that escapes my lips. Exhausted, my body gives up, my vision tunneling as the void pulls me under. The last thought in my fading mind is absurd.

Sita was right.

I've just been saved by a Yeti.

Chapter Thirteen

Eryon - Earlier

I follow her. Unseen, unheard, unknown. I keep pace above the two women, the forest swallowing my steps and hiding my form.

As if she can sense me, she chances small glances over her shoulder to the tree line. Sometimes her eyes slide over me, and I feel them pulling me forward till I can scarcely resist their call.

But I do. I vowed she would not walk alone, and she doesn't. I trail them to the ashram, then hide outside when they go in. Even with focusing my keen hearing towards its thick walls, all I can hear are muffled voices.

Though I didn't need to hear what they said, because when she emerges, their answer is written in the slump of her shoulders, in the tears sparkling in her lashes like the first frost of winter.

I heard her say the name of the plant she is looking for, *Silene vitalis*, but the foreign word is unknown to me despite my familiarity and understanding of many of the centuries that have passed.

Man's names for the plants of my mountains and forests is not something I ever wasted time on learning. What is the use of a name when knowing the use of the plant itself is what matters.

Knowing when to harvest and how to preserve, what phase of the moon makes the plant's essence more potent or which to leave on someone's doorstep for health. What plants and animals are in harmony, and which need to be balanced to fulfill my sacred duty to the mountains and the forests of my domain. These are the things I concern myself with.

And now, also with her.

As the women stand outside the large wooden doors of the ashram, their voices drift back to me on the wind. I listen as she tells Sita she needs to get back to her notes. But as they come into view, I see the truth in her eyes. The conviction of a woman with nothing left to lose. I've seen it reflected in my own face, and I know—she is going to cross the river. She is going to enter my domain.

And I will not be able to stop her.

The thought unsettles me more than it should. She does not belong there. In fact, she does not belong here at all, and yet she keeps coming back. Pulled to me just as I am to her.

The wind shifts, sending tension coursing through my limbs, my fur prickling with awareness. The sky is heavy, pressing low, thick with something unseen. The trees murmur, uneasy. The scent of the storm curls through the peaks, slow and creeping, until it is all I can smell—all I can feel.

The mountain is changing.

I tighten my pace, scanning the ridges above them, my instincts twisting with unease. She isn't safe. The thought echoes in every beat of my heart—not safe, not safe, not safe.

The first flakes fall, no more than a breath.

She does not heed the warning the mountains whisper. I debate forcing the women to turn back to the safety of the ashram, but they are determined to return to the guest house. My only option to not yet reveal myself but still assure her safety is to ensure their arrival back home.

The wind whips through the trees as the weight of the sky deepens. The flakes move from a delicate flurry to an absolute downpour, a monsoon of white, blinding in its intensity.

Instinct has me moving, as close as I dare to protect them and then—I see it happen. She falters for a moment, and Sita keeps going. I'm close enough to see her spinning in a circle, yelling for her friend. Yet too far away to stop the danger looming ahead.

Instinct has me running, my long legs eating up the distance before my mind can even register I have made the decision. My heart pounds in my chest as I will my Winter Star to stay still until I can get to her.

But the determined thing moves again, chasing her friend, and one wrong step is all it takes.

The ground shifts. And then—she is gone.

The world collapses with her in a deafening blast of snow and ice and rock tearing away from the mountain, roaring down its side, consuming everything in its path, devouring my heart, and ripping it from my chest into its icy maw.

I lunge forward, a snarl ripping from my throat, but I am too far away. Too late. The avalanche takes her. And for the first time in ages, I am powerless. Once again watching as forces beyond my control tear my heart away.

I move.

Faster than I have in years, pushing through the storm, through the chaos, my breath a fire in my chest as I chase my own heart down the side of a mountain that for the first time in my existence, I hate.

As love is ripped once more from my grasp, as hope disappears in the deluge, I curse the earth that swallows her as eagerly as it accepted my blood oath.

I track her scent before the wind can steal it and track it down, heedless of the unstable ground beneath my feet. The mountain does not give back what it takes.

But I will defy it. I call on the creator, the moon goddess, and all the guardians that have come before. I beg for their blessing, throwing myself down at their mercy if only I can hold this sweet flower, my harbinger of Spring, my Winter Star.

If I can only sweep her up into my arms, just once to save her, not for my sake but for hers, it will be a divine miracle.

The storm thickens, an unrelenting force bent on stopping me. Even the wind tries to push me back. The world is nothing but endless white. My hands burn as they tear through the drifts, peeling away the layers of ice and snow and rock that swallowed her whole. My fingertips shred against the debris, my muscles scream—but I do not stop. I cannot. Her oxygen is slipping away; each second lost like grains of sand in an hourglass.

Then—

A sound. Her sweet voice. At first, I think she is calling for help. My brilliant flower is helping me find her. Brow furrowed, I listen harder. She isn't crying for help. I think she is…singing.

A strange, muttered melody drifts up from beneath the snow —soft, cracked with cold, absurdly light for the gravity of her situation.

She is dying. And yet she is singing some terrible song with words that are so strange. She is singing about, if I'm not mistaken, her ass. Although it may also be my favorite part of her, I cannot imagine why on earth she would be singing about it.

A growl rumbles deep in my chest, sharp and incredulous. She defies reason. She is a paradox, a Gordian knot I ache to unravel. Even on the edge of death, she does not understand how fragile she is. Or perhaps she does but simply does not care.

But I do.

I care enough for the both of us. And I will not lose her. I should dig faster. I should tear through the snow until she is safe. But for a single moment, I hesitate and just listen.

I let her have these final notes, because if she is singing, she has enough air, and I need her to know that she is brave and fierce and strong. But I also need her to know that I am here.

I am here for her, and I will not allow those tears in her eyes, will not accept the slump of her shoulders in defeat. I will not allow her to live without whatever plant she so desperately seeks. Yes, she is strong, but she is my strength now, too.

I act.

Her terrible singing allows me to reach her with surgical precision, my hands breaking through to where her body is entombed in the snow. It could have been behind the thickest stone of the mountain and still it would not have stopped me. I would have clawed the earth bloody until it yielded to me.

She is limp in my grasp, her limbs too light, her breath too faint. She is smaller, frailer under all of her mountain gear than I could even have imagined. Her bones feel like a bird's beneath my great hands. I gentle my grip, afraid to leave a mark on her delicate flesh.

I pull her free and watch her lie there in the snow. The flakes swirl over her face, falling down around her ears. I watch one dance in her panting breaths until it finally loops and arcs to land softly on her lips.

Oh, how I want to land there, too. To be the snowflake that dares kiss her lips. But it does not melt. The cold is stealing her from me.

Her eyes flutter open and words fall from her mouth, but I cannot even comprehend them in the enormity of this moment —she and I are finally together.

She sees me. And she should be afraid or even surprised but the only thing I see reflecting back at me in the violet-blue eyes of my Winter Star is like recognizing like. Soul meeting soul.

This may be the first time she is truly seeing me, but she has felt me all along. Despite the storm raging around us, her warmth floods my veins like the summer sun.

Her small pink tongue peeks out, sweeping the lucky snowflake into her mouth as her teeth begin to chatter and she pales even further.

Without thought, I sweep her up and into my body, cloaking her in my thick fur against the raging elements and she thanks me.

Me. She thanks *me*. Not with fear. Not with hesitation. With gratitude.

Her voice, barely more than a whisper against my flesh, reaches through the storm, curling around something deep inside me.

She is not afraid. She only knows that I have saved her.

Something inside me tightens. Something ancient. Something I never thought to have again but has declared itself, established a foothold deep in the mountain of my soul.

I shift her against my chest, cradling her carefully, pressing her into the warmth of my body. Her skin is like ice, but she is soft. So soft. Beneath this ridiculous puffy coat and the jeans that have no place in this snow, I feel her curl around me as if she were carved from my own flesh.

But I should not want this. I should not crave this. My hands are made for shaping the land, for protecting, for killing if I must. Not for holding something so delicate. Not for keeping. I've proved it before, but my heart does not listen.

It screams, *mine*.

The word slides through my mind, unbidden. I crush it down. She is dying. She does not belong to me.

Not yet, my heart says.

I will it with every fiber of my being, and although I am hers, just as I have vowed, she will need to choose me. I honor her far too much for any other way.

The wind howls, wrapping around us like a living thing, but it no longer matters. She is no longer lost.

And neither am I.

I tighten my hold, fitting my body around hers, sheltering her from the storm. And then I turn toward the mountains. Toward safety. Toward the only place she will be truly protected. The storm swallows us whole.

And I carry her home.

CHAPTER FOURTEEN

DAHLIA

I drift in and out of consciousness, pulled between waking and dreaming by the rhythmic sway of movement. I don't know how long I've been here, wrapped in this cocoon of heat and fur, my body cradled against something impossibly warm.

The storm is gone. The wind still howls in the distance, but it no longer pursues us relentlessly. A sure and steady heartbeat pounds beneath my cheek, slow despite the perpetual movement and the strain of carrying me.

My fingers twitch, flexing instinctively, brushing against the thick fur wrapped around me. It's softer than I expected, smooth where it meets skin beneath the dense coat. A fresh wave of heat unfurls in my chest, seeping down, warming places that shouldn't need warming after nearly freezing to death.

I shouldn't feel this safe. I shouldn't feel this *good*. A low sound rumbles through the body beneath me—deep, resonant, *male*. My breath catches, eyes fluttering open as awareness crashes into me. The creature. The Migoi.

He saved me.

Panic should be pulsing through my veins. I should be afraid. But instead, there's only curiosity and a driving need to explore. I slide my hands deeper into the thick fur, fingertips grazing against skin like heated velvet. A shudder rolls through him, and I freeze. His arms tighten around me, a silent response to my touch.

I should stop. I should do a lot of things. But I'm so tired of doing what I should, and the heat is intoxicating. Before I can overthink it, I press my face deeper into the warm fur, nuzzling against it, seeking more of the delicious warmth and that velvety skin.

Another rumble. This time, unmistakably pleased.

A rush of something wicked pulses through me, and my thighs press together instinctively. My cheeks burn at my body's response, but I can't help it.

I tell myself it's just the aftereffects of nearly dying. That it's just biology, seeking heat and comfort. Celebrating that I am indeed alive. I am not—cannot—be reacting to him like this. He's a mythical creature, not a man.

And yet.

The steady flex of his muscles beneath me, the sheer power of him, the impossible contrast of brutal strength and the careful way he holds me—all of it coils together, winding tightly around something dark and unspoken inside me.

I shift, needing distance, but the movement only makes it worse. The friction of my thighs, the steady press of his body against mine, the way his breathing changes—deeper, heavier— as if he knows exactly what I'm feeling.

A new kind of panic grips me, one that has nothing to do with fear and everything to do with the fact that I might be enjoying this too much. And maybe he is, too.

I don't know how long we walk like this—minutes, hours— but eventually, the rhythm changes. His steps slow and his muscles shift with the change in incline. We're going up.

I frown, trying to make sense of it. Shouldn't we be descending toward Migdhari?

I take a breath to ask, to say something. But I don't know what to say or if he can even understand me. In the quiet of my uncertainty, my mother's voice drifts through my memory, *Sometimes, the only way left to go is up, honey.*

I bury my face deeper into the delicious warmth of his skin, and decide to give myself over to finally doing something I shouldn't. My eyes drift close again as the final thought curls my lips into a crooked smile. Yeti or not, up we go.

A chill creeping over my skin wakes me some time later, the heat from being held so closely by the Migoi dissipating into the cool air. I blink against the dim light, my surroundings swimming into focus.

Gone is the raging storm, the endless white, and the relentless wind. In its place is something both impossibly different and completely unexpected—a vast cavern.

I sit up, fascinated by the change in scenery. The air here is thick, rich with minerals. Stalagmites rise like frozen sandcastles from the ground, while stalactites hang like jagged chandeliers overhead. Light refracts off the embedded crystals, casting a soft, shifting glow through the misty air.

A sound pulls my attention away from the beautiful view. Is that water? I get to my feet and walk over to find steam curling upward from a massive pool in the center of the cavern. It seems alive, a bioluminescent glow dancing across its surface.

When I dip a finger in, heat and light shimmer in its wake. Enchanted, I swirl my hand through the warm water, surprised by the faint glowing trail it leaves behind.

Where am I?

A shift in the background pulls my gaze upward, away from the magic of the living water, and has every muscle freezing into place. Adrenaline courses through my body, panicked sweat blooming in its wake.

A shape detaches from the shadows and coalesces into myth made flesh. My pulse races, a fine tremor running through my locked muscles. I should be afraid. I should turn and run. But I already know who it is, and my damned innate curiosity is pulling me towards something that feels an awful lot like fate.

The Migoi.

Unsure what to do I give a little half-wave, then kick myself for making such a silly gesture at the legendary guardian of the mountains and forest. I flush as red as my hair, embarrassment heating my skin, the flush creeping up my neck erasing the chill from earlier.

He steps forward into the dim glow, and my breath leaves me entirely. Gone is the long, white fur that blanketed me against the cold. The great shaggy head that eclipsed my vision after the avalanche has been replaced, leaving in its place a figure that looks more man than beast.

My swallow is audible over the soft backdrop of the water. He is as ruggedly handsome as the harsh terrain he calls home. Still otherworldly, yes, but undeniably gorgeous. His white hair is tousled, thick waves tumbling over his forehead and fading into the short fur that courses over his shoulders.

The luminescent silver eyes that have been haunting me stare back, glowing in the dim cave like moonlight over the snow-covered mountains, studying me just as intently as I am doing to him. They are framed in a harsh yet beautiful face that is all angles—chiseled cheekbones, straight nose, and a sharp jawline.

The only softness is his full, lush lips. Pointed teeth peek past them, and gods help me, but all I can think about is running my tongue over each white tip, or better yet, having them run over me.

Tall, broad, and carved from shadow and ice, every inch of him is honed and hardened, power coiled into every line. My eyes trail over his broad shoulders that taper into a chiseled torso, down to the sharp ridges of his abdomen, the deep V of his hips, and...

My jaw falls open as I finish my survey. I don't know what I expected him to be wearing. Fur pants? A strategically placed snowflake? But the fact that he is absolutely, gloriously naked is not exactly disappointing. My face burns as I realize I'm staring, but how can I not? He is magnificent.

He takes another step closer, moving cautiously as if I'm a scared rabbit, muscles rippling with every movement. I watch, mesmerized as he dips his large hand into the steaming water, the faint blue-green swirling around it. He pulls his hand out and smooths back his thick shock of white hair.

He turns his intense gaze back to me, the silver eyes unreadable. The same piercing stare I've been dreaming of.

Unconsciously, I have drifted closer to the magnificent creature, only realizing my hand is outstretched towards him when my fingers brush against the hot, velvety plane of his abdomen, mere fuzz where before there was fur.

Grazing my fingertips over the dip and swell of each muscle, the words slip out before I can stop them. "The abdominal snowman."

A startled laugh bubbles out of me, half-delirious from exhaustion, half-horrified at what I just said. I snatch my hand back and drop my eyes, face once again burning, but before I can retreat, he swoops in and catches my chin between his calloused finger and thumb.

He tilts my face up, forcing me to meet his gaze. His skin is warmer than even my embarrassment flushed skin. Gently he turns my face from side to side, eyes tracing over every freckle as he regards me with inscrutable intensity, and maybe a faint touch of amusement, before gently brushing a thumb over my bottom lip.

His eyes darken as he follows the movement of his finger, reigniting the earlier desire that pooled in my belly. He is looking at me like I am his next meal after all, and despite my brain screaming at me to run, I can't help but wonder what it would be like to be devoured by him. I had hoped I wasn't going to be his snack, but now—

A sharp inhale escapes my lips at the thought, anticipation building as I wait to see my fate at the hands of this creature. At the soft sound, his eyes turn hungry. Feral. I should pull away. I *should*.

But I can't. And not just that, but I don't *fucking* want to. My lips fall gently open in instinctual invitation, and I'm barely breathing as my body aches for something I don't fully understand, something impossible. Because for being lost somewhere in the Himalayan mountains, I have never felt more found.

"Where are we?" I whisper, my voice barely audible. But I think I'm asking myself so much more. I'm asking, *Dahlia, what the hell are you doing? What are you thinking?*

I don't know if he'll answer. I don't know if he even *can*. But I do know one thing. This Migoi rescued me. He pulled me from death, shielded me from the cold, carried me into the safety of the depths of the earth itself. And for the first time in my life, I feel like I'm exactly where I'm supposed to be.

I am not chasing down the next thing, looking for love, searching for answers. I have arrived. I am *here*.

"What is this place?" I try again.

He drops his hand and looks around the cave as if seeing it for the first time through my eyes. I follow the path of his gaze, taking in the beautiful glowing pools, and, now that my eyes have adjusted to the dim lighting, the natural rock formations and what appear to be deeper caves judging by the way some areas fade to a deep, inky black.

The cave's warmth should comfort me, but the heavy air reminds me of my fall—the suffocating snow, the weight of death closing in. I would have died out there. I know that. Everything feels so unreal.

I need some type of connection to reassure me I'm not dead after all so I reach up, daring to lay my hand on his arm. My voice shaky with nerves, I say, "You saved me."

Not a question, but a statement of fact.

He shoots me a very human-like smile as we stand with the steam curling up from the pool and filling the air between us. I'm not sure which is more surreal—this hidden oasis in the midst of the mountain's snowstorm or this creature, smiling at me like I just hung the moon.

But I am sure that he saved me from an icy death, and now I owe him my life. A shiver that has nothing to do with the cold has me wrapping my arms around myself.

Concern flickers in his eyes as he reaches out and tugs me by the hand to follow him, engulfing my much smaller one in his grasp. His skin is thick and rough, calloused like leather in a sharp contrast to the other parts of him I've been privileged to touch.

We walk along a small path that leads up and around the pool, coming even with its surface. The trail narrows, but instead of dropping my hand, he switches his grip so that I'm trailing behind him.

I can't help but run my eyes down the thick columns of muscle that frame his spine, following them down to where they meet a perfectly sculpted ass over thighs like tree trunks. He is massive, maybe eight feet tall, judging against my height, but the large caverns may be making the proportions seem off.

Since he has yet to talk, I assume I can speak freely and say under my breath, "That ass though."

I'm so busy enjoying the view that has no business being on a mythical creature, that when he abruptly stops I crash into his back. With a startled yelp, I lose my balance and topple straight into the glowing water. It rushes over my head, and as my heavy clothes and coat soak through, I'm pulled down deeper.

Panic claws at me, the feeling of being deprived of oxygen yet again clawing at my throat and impairing my ability to think. I thrash blindly, lungs burning, eyes shut tight under the unfamiliar water. I am so overwhelmed with the sensations and fear I can't even try to surface. I've been saved, only to die.

Once again strong arms wrap around me and pull me against hard and unyielding muscles. I feel my face break the surface and start choking and sputtering in my haste to take in a greedy breath.

CHAPTER FIFTEEN

She is waking up. The change in her breath, the subtle shift of her weight in my arms. She does not know where she is or that she is the safest she has ever been. But she will.

Before she can fully wake, I carry her into the cavern, cradled in the warm embrace of the mountain. The storm could rage on forever, and we could hide away here, just the two of us. The thought sends a secret thrill through me, and I pull her closer, savoring the feel of her against me.

I take us deeper as she shivers in my arms, closer to the warmth of the water. At the edge of the spring, I kneel and for the first time since I pulled her from the snow, I release her.

My arms ache without her.

She shifts, murmuring in her sleep. Her body protests the absence of my warmth, instinct pulling her toward where I kneel beside her. My hands clench, resisting the urge to reach for her. I force myself to step back and wait.

At length, she stirs, eyes fluttering as she blinks them open. Her arms shake with the effort of pushing her exhausted body upright. She blinks, her gaze unfocused as she takes in her surroundings. Her breath catches as the cavern comes into view—the towering walls, the crystals, the steam curling lazily from the pool, the strange glow of the water reflecting against the stone.

Then, she sees me.

I feel the exact moment her eyes find me in the shadows, her gaze locking onto my form where I stand at the far edge of the pool.

She freezes.

I do not move but study every flicker that crosses her face, searching for a reaction. Her pulse kicks up, her breaths come faster. But it is not fear that stiffens her limbs—it is something else. Something hungrier.

She looks at me like she does not know what to make of me. Like she does not know whether to run.

Or come closer.

Her gaze drags over me, tracing the breadth of my shoulders, the lines of my chest, the heat of my skin where my fur thins. Her breath catches as she sees what was hidden before—what I am beneath the beast. Her scent changes—desire threading through the fading chill of fear.

Then—she moves. A step forward, as if it is unconscious yet inevitable.

I can't help but meet her as she crosses the space between us. Drawn forward not by logic, but by something deeper. A driving force older than even this mountain.

She stops just within arm's reach, so the heat of her breath fans against my skin. She does not flinch. She does not look away.

I do not break her trance. I let her look though I ache for her to not just touch me, but to see me. See who I am despite the differences between us. I need her to open herself to the possibilities of two souls meeting despite their physical forms. Of the forces that can transcend the flesh.

She moves slowly, hesitantly, eyes flicking to the steam curling from the water, the glow of the cave reflecting against my skin. Curiosity lights her eyes beyond the exhaustion rather than the fear I was worried about.

I should have known better. My fierce Winter Star is too brave to be afraid, even if, by all reasoning, she should be.

I cover my nervousness as I wait for her to pass judgment by dipping my hand in the water and smoothing back my hair. For the first time in centuries, I feel vulnerable. Even a little exposed.

As her eyes follow the reflections dancing over my body, down the muscles honed over so many years even I have lost count, her hand lifts—hesitant, drawn by something she doesn't yet understand. Her fingers hover, unsure and I count the beats of my heart, until finally, *finally*, her touch brands my skin.

Light as the brush of a moth's wing, yet searing as a lightning strike leaving electricity crackle in its wake. Her fingertips graze the ridges of my abdomen, heat meeting heat.

I tense, every muscle locking beneath her touch as she traces a slow, reverent path over my flesh. Centuries of resolve hold me in place by the merest thread. But only barely. I grit my teeth so hard I'm surprised they don't crack under the strain. Blessed mother moon, how I want to sweep her into my arms and lay claim to her right here, right now. But I vowed to wait until she made her choice, so I will abide.

"The abdominal snowman," she mutters, her voice barely a breath, a flicker of amusement cutting through her shock.

A strange sound rumbles in my chest—half growl, half laugh. I can't recall the last time I laughed. The noise sounds strange to my ears, but the feeling, the joy that bubbles up to my heart is a welcome stranger.

She startles, blushing a furious red to match her glorious

hair, and jerks her hand back as if burned, embarrassment tightening her features. She drops her gaze, her lips parting as if she might apologize.

I do not let her. Will not. With slow, deliberate intent, I reach out and catch her chin. She stiffens, but I do not force her. Just hold her there. Just enough to make her look. To keep her seeing beyond my skin, so different than hers. To keep her seeing—me.

Her eyes look up to meet mine, those iridescent pools of violet-blue, still heavy with exhaustion but alight with something else. The twin flame to my own.

I study each tiny dot on her face, like the smallest snowflakes left a tiny kiss across her nose and cheeks. I will count them all, commit them to memory like the stars of the night sky. I will trace constellations in them created from our story and add them to the walls of this cave.

My hungry eyes devour every inch of her face, down her tiny upturned nose to the soft, flushed lips above my fingers. She is so small, so different from me. I cannot hold back the desperate need to explore her, to feel the textures of her. It drives me to drag my thumb along her lower lip.

She gasps. Her pupils blow wide, but I know she is not afraid as the scent of her desire reaches for me until my restraint hangs by an ever fraying thread.

I let her see the vow reflected in my eyes. The hunger thrumming through my veins. The thing inside me that declares, *mine.*

"Where are we?" she whispers. But the words hang between us, a thousand more questions shimmering in the air.

I do not answer at first, because I do not know how. At least not in a way she would understand. Not in a way that would not change everything.

Home, I want to tell her. *You are home.* Instead, I drop my hand from her chin, but do not step back. I cannot leave her side now that I have tasted the sweet air that surrounds her like an aura.

She sways, caught between instinct and reason, between the safe boundaries of the known and the pull of something darker. Forbidden.

My vow binds me. Holds me back and stops my hands from taking. But I am still a beast. Still a thing made of hunger and instinct, and she stands before me half-wild herself. It would be easy, *so easy*, to take.

The thought is as intoxicating as it is dangerous.

I could pull her against me, answer her question with my mouth instead of mere words, feel her soft skin beneath my hands. I could sink my teeth into the delicate curve of her throat, claim her in the way my instincts demand.

And she would let me. But she nearly died, and that is heavy on the body and the soul. And I made a vow. I will not take what she does not freely give.

She is trembling, but it is not the cold. She shifts, wrapping her arms around herself. A shiver courses down her spine, and I know it is not only from exhaustion. She is looking at me like I am no longer just a myth, but like I am something else entirely.

Hers.

"What is this place?" she asks, still looking for answers.

I do not speak, but instead, as she shivers again, I reach for her hand. A silent invitation. A choice.

She hesitates. Then, slowly, she takes it.

I stare down at her tiny hand in mine, the contrast stark— her fingers delicate where mine are thick and scarred, roughened from centuries of survival. Her skin is still chilled, her fingers trembling. I do not think—only act. My thumb sweeps over her knuckles, slow and careful, chasing away the last of the cold that tried to steal her from me. If it had a form I would slaughter it in retribution.

Her breath shudders, sharp and unsteady. A small sound escapes her lips—not quite a gasp, not quite a sigh. As if she, too, feels something shifting beneath her skin, something too vast to name.

She does not pull away. Instead, her fingers curl slightly, gripping mine in return. The smallest movement. A whisper of a choice. But I feel it sink into my palm, through my skin, and settle deep into the marrow of my bones.

Not just warmth returning to her skin in response to my heat—but something more. Something *becoming*. A beginning.

I lead her along the edge of the pool, steam curling in the air between us. When the path narrows I cannot bear to drop her hand; I just move so that we are still touching, still connected. Behind me I hear her murmur under her breath, barely audible—

"That ass though."

I go rigid.

I do not know the phrase, but I know the words and, more importantly, the way she says them. I can feel the scorching heat of her eyes as they explore my body, sense the vibration of her throat bobbing as I hear her swallow hard. I can smell the way desire overpowers her sweet Spring scent.

A rumbling growl slips from my chest before I can stop it, and I freeze, locking every muscle in response to the over-whelming desire to spin around and take her in my arms, vow be damned.

She crashes into my back, lets out a startled yelp, stumbles and falls.

I whirl around to see the pool swallow her whole. For a fraction of a second, she vanishes beneath the surface. The water surges in around her, the glow rippling outward, distorting the outline of her flailing limbs.

Her panic echoes through me. The sharp intake of breath before she went under. The way her limbs fight against the pull of the water. The frantic, uneven quickening of her heart audible to my sharp ears.

She thrashes—wild and disoriented. The weight of her soaked clothing drags her down. She does not recognize that she is in water shallow enough to stand. This can't be panic from the fall.

This is something deeper. A fear that does not belong to the water but to the avalanche, the suffocating cold. The way the snow swallowed her whole. She is there, not here.

I move before thought. Before logic. Before restraint. I jump down into the pool, and my hands close around her waist. I lift her effortlessly, quickly pulling her face above the surface and holding her close.

She gasps, coughing, fingers clutching at my shoulders as I steady her against me. Her body is soft in my arms, warm breath ghosting over my skin. Her fingers tighten into my fur, and she is no longer drowning.

But I am.

CHAPTER SIXTEEN

DAHLIA

Heat rushes over my skin as I cough and sputter, greedily pulling in air. The warm water sluices down my face, but it does little to stop the violent shiver wracking my body.

The Migoi's hands are solid against me, holding me effortlessly above the surface, strong and steady. I am pressed tight against him and can't help but remember he is very, very naked.

I feel it before I see it—the heat of his skin seeping through the soaked fabric of my clothes, bleeding into me like a slow burn. My fingers release their death grip on the fur that dusts his shoulders and slide down to his chest. The wet material of my clothes separates us, but even through it, I can feel him. The firm press of muscle, the steady rise and fall of breath, the pounding of his heart—just a little too fast beneath my touch.

Oh.

The realization crashes over me like a second shock to my system. I don't know why I expected him to be covered in fur again, he wasn't when I touched those damned abs, but without the fur, it's like there is no barrier of reason. Just his body and mine, flush beneath the steaming water.

I know I should look away from those mystical eyes. I should put some distance between us, give myself space to process this —the whole near-drowning, the mythical creature holding me, the fact that I was absolutely staring at his abs earlier.

But I don't move.

Because the longer I stay pressed against him, the warmer I become. The chill of my soaked clothes, the fear that clawed at my throat when I slipped under the water—it's all fading. Replaced by something heavier, something thick and languid curling in my stomach, something I should not be feeling.

And there's that damn word again, *should*.

Marvelling at his quick reflexes, I mumble, "Sorry."

He raises an eyebrow. "Do *not* apologize for giving me a reason to hold you in my arms."

My jaw drops as his voice rumbles through me like distant thunder, gravelly and rich as if he is pulling the words from the very heart of the mountain, carrying the weight of something ancient. And his English is flawless.

I stiffen with the realization—he speaks. I had assumed, maybe stupidly, that he didn't. Or at least, that he wouldn't speak my language. But his words are clear if slightly rough, as if he's unearthing them from somewhere long buried.

Which means... The singing. The abdominal snowman nickname. Oh gods, the ass comment. He heard, and understood, *everything*.

As my face flames, yet again, he raises an eyebrow and quips, "How did you survive without me?"

"To be fair, I don't usually try to die more than once a day," I say.

I aim for light, but the words land too sharp, too close to the truth. I almost died today. Sure, not really twice, but the first time? I was close. Really. Fucking. Close.

His lips part slightly, his warm breath ghosting over my temple as he leans closer. "I would hold you for far less than a life debt, Dahlia."

His words settle in my chest, curling around something fragile and unspoken. My pulse stutters, the weight of his gaze pressing into me like a vow.

I should brush it off. Laugh, maybe. But I don't. Because something about the way he says it makes me think he's not just talking about this moment, but something far more permanent.

A dozen thoughts collide at once—How do you know my name? How long have you been watching me? Why did you save me?

My throat tightens. I swallow, then add, softer, "I wasn't asking for a life debt. Just—maybe a temporary loan?"

"I rather enjoy you alive," he replies.

The way his voice rumbles over the word *enjoy* reverberates deep in my core. I need to escape, put some distance between this muscular myth and my rapidly devolving thoughts. I wiggle my way free but only succeed in dragging my body down against his.

I glance down past the warm spring water gently lapping at my waist as I find my footing and realize three things.

One—all I had to do to save myself was stand up in the shallow water. Instead, I panicked.

Two—for the first time in my life, I am *very* small. I'm used to being shorter than other people, but I'm barely half his width and hardly reach his chest. The water that was deep enough to pull me under doesn't even make it past his thighs.

And that's how I end up staring directly at realization number three—giant mythical creatures have giant mythical cocks.

Oh. My. Gods.

And said cock is now close. Very close. I can't help but stare. In awe. In curiosity. In *need*.

I should win a freaking award for the restraint I exercise not to reach out and caress its velvety length, just to see if it feels the same as the rest of his skin. I lick my lips as I imagine what the texture would feel like gliding across them and over my tongue. Or over my body, between my legs, and into my aching core.

He begins to harden under my intense stare, the already impressive member rising up through the air towards me as the thick, prominent veins on the shaft begin to pulse, and I realize how rude I am being.

I make a strangled noise in the back of my throat and snap my head up, but he *knows*. He definitely knows, because a smirk flickers across his sharp features, something far too human for my peace of mind. Cheeks flaming, I look away, searching for something, anything else, to look at.

"Um, thanks again," I squeak, looking up as if I am suddenly fascinated by the shimmering stalactites above us.

He reaches for the front of my coat, fingers brushing the zipper, and I slap his hand away. "Excuse me! Just because I had a little looky-loo doesn't mean you can start undressing me."

He blinks at me. Then—he rolls his eyes. Actually rolls them in a very human expression as he points out the obvious and says, "You're soaked."

I glance down at myself. My coat is dripping with water, and my clothes lie heavy against my skin, weighing me down in the warmth of the pool. I shiver, and his frown deepens.

"You'll catch a chill," he says, as if I am the unreasonable one here. "Give me your things, and I'll dry them by the fire."

Now that he mentions it, I realize he's right. I'm freezing. The heat of the spring is helping, but my clothes are still clinging to me, leeching the heat from my body.

"Oh. Oh! Right," I say sheepishly, fumbling with the zipper and passing the sodden mass off to him.

As I struggle to clumsily peel off the layers, he gestures with his chin toward a ledge built into the side of the pool. I trudge toward it, kicking up glowing swirls of color in my wake, and plop down.

I attempt to wrestle off my boots, but the wet laces are a hopeless disaster. After a minute of struggling, the Migoi strides over and hands me my coat.

Confused, I take it—just in time to see him extend a claw and slice through the tangled knots with ease, then retract the claw again to no more than a mere fingernail.

My mouth falls open and I mutter, "Built in multi-tool."

He smirks again as if proud of my reaction to his abilities and pulls off my boots, then holds his hand out for my coat. I pass it back over and begin peeling off layers, hyper-aware of his gaze following my every movement.

The glowing water flickers between us, casting strange shadows over his sharp features. His eyes track each article of clothing I remove, his expression unreadable. That is until I wrestle my bra out from under my tank top. It's not much but I leave it on, wanting some layer of protection between us.

His eyes sharpen as my peaked nipples peer out from the thin soaked material of my white undershirt, the darkness of my areolas visible even in this dim light. With nothing on but this and my wet, translucent panties, I am mortified. I pile my clothes into his waiting arms, the thick wool socks on top of my pants, and my bra on top like a damn trophy.

Removing my wet clothes was like wrestling a pissed off octopus, leaving me huffing and dashing strands of wayward hair out of my face. I meet his eyes again to find them crinkled at the corners as a small smile plays about his face.

"I'm glad you find this amusing," I mutter under my breath.

He wisely takes the clothes without comment, easily vaulting out of the pool and moving toward what I can now see is an adjacent cave where firelight flickers against the stone walls.

I sink deeper into the water with a muffled groan, tension slipping from my body. For the first time in hours, I stop fighting—against the cold, against the fear, against the relentless weight of survival.

The heat seeps into my bones, melting through every ache. My limbs float, weightless in the mineral-rich water, the faint, earthy scent grounding me as warmth swallows me whole. My heart beat slows, and I just relax, letting my head lie back against the edge of the pool as my hair swirls around my shoulders like seaweed. Sweat blooms on my face, and gods, does it feel good to be wholly and completely warm.

I hear his footsteps return, and I sit up slightly, waiting for whatever comes next.

His gaze, slow and deliberate, roves over my relaxed body visible in the clear water. It traces over my bare shoulders, my collarbone, the way the thin fabric of my tank top clings obscenely to my body.

I can feel the weight of it pass over the swell of my breasts, pause for a heavy heartbeat at my barely concealed sex, then continue along each relaxed leg to the very tips of my toes.

When his silver eyes snap back to mine, his expression is dark. Feral. Something flickers in the depths of his mercury gaze. The pearl and frost swirls have been replaced by something ancient and hungry.

My nipples tighten painfully, and I curse the interplay of warm water and cool cave air as I sit up a little straighter. Or maybe I don't. Maybe I know damn well the temperature change isn't the reason.

He vaults back into the pool and moves closer, an apex predator stalking his prey, and heat pools deep in my belly, far hotter than even the spring. He looms larger above me, and it's too much.

Too much heat, too much feeling, tightening my throat as claustrophobia claws at me. I grab at my neckline as if the wet fabric is to blame for the tightness consuming my breath. I'm suddenly too raw, too vulnerable for all that his eyes promise.

His gaze flickers to the movement, and his face immediately transforms to something softer. His looming form diminishes, and before I can process the change that has me breathing far easier, he holds out his hands.

I hesitate, but the fear is gone, replaced by the solid reassurance of my protector. Slowly, I take them.

His fingers engulf mine, so warm and solid, grounding me even as the water makes my body weightless. He guides me deeper into the pool, where the heat envelops me completely and my body goes weightless.

I let out a breathy, satisfied moan. I am warm. I am safe.

His hands tighten, and I feel his body go rigid in response. As he tenses, the glowing water shifts between us, curling in luminous tendrils. Fascinated, I let go of one of his hands to swirl my fingers through the colors, laughing softly.

He stills.

"Do that again," he murmurs.

I tear my gaze away from the symphony of light in the water to meet his eyes. The silver reflects the bioluminescence, turning them a rich blue-green. I blink up at him. "Do what?"

"Laugh," he says simply.

There is something reverent in his voice. Something softer than hunger that has a smile tugging at my lips. An answering one lights up his face, transforming him from fierce to fiercely happy as he sweeps me up bridal style and twirls me in a circle. As I catch sight of the glittering crystals in the cave's ceiling reflecting the beautiful pool's light, I can't help but let out a delighted laugh.

I am in a secret paradise, playing with a legendary creature in a hot spring. But I don't laugh because it's silly, I laugh because it's beautiful and free and simple and easy. I laugh because I think this is how life is supposed to feel. I had been so busy trying to get ahead and please everyone and achieve some elusive version of happiness that it took nearly dying to show me what it really means to live.

The snow and suffocation, betrayal and degrees, the elusive flower, even Ben, all just fall away. The simple joy of warm water, the natural beauty of the earth, a kind soul wanting to hear my laugh—this is living. I surprise us both when I reach up and lay a steaming hand along his jaw, finding his skin hotter than the water.

The second my fingers brush against him, his gaze locks onto mine, unblinking, hungry in an entirely different way. His grip on my waist tightens, his breath hitching ever so slightly. A flicker of something dangerous, something barely restrained, flashes through his eyes.

This time, safe in his arms, our laughter echoing in the caves around us, it doesn't feel too big or too much. It feels just right. I know I should move my hand. I should not want this. I should be terrified, running, questioning my sanity. But instead, I tilt my chin up, caught in the blizzard of his gaze, and think— maybe I was meant to be lost, just so he could find me.

Because right now, I feel like I'm drowning all over again. I need to be saved for the third time today. And the only thing that can save me is his mouth on mine.

CHAPTER SEVENTEEN

DAHLIA

The already humid air thickens with the tension that blooms between us like a rare flower, beautiful and exotic. His eyes reflect my hunger back at me, but where mine is uncertain, his is knowing. Calculated. Patient.

Instead of giving in to my clear, desperate desire for a kiss, he tilts his head, studying me like I'm something fragile. Like I am already his. Then, with deliberate slowness, he runs his tongue over his lower lip, sharp teeth peeking out just enough to make my stomach flip.

Hypnotized, I follow the motion, my breath stuttering, because I swear I can feel it tracing over my skin already—his mouth dragging over my throat, my collarbone, lower—the strong tongue and wicked teeth laving my flesh.

He slides me down his body and sets me back on my feet. But as if he can't bear to be away from my touch, he takes my hands. His fingers engulf mine, warm and steady, grounding me even as the water makes my body weightless. The calluses on his palms are rough, but the way he holds my hands is gentle.

Too gentle.

Because I see the way he looks at me. Like he's holding back a force more powerful than an avalanche, with the unshaken resolve of the mountain itself. His eyes burn brighter than the bioluminescence curling around us, the swirling depths of silver and gray mystical. A storm barely held in check. A beast in a gilded cage of control.

And I am so damn tired of cages.

I want to feel something real. Something wild. Something I don't have to apologize for wanting. I step closer, and his breath hitches.

I should be careful. I should think this through. But the words should and can't and impossible have been ruining my life for years, and I don't care anymore.

Not when his thumb traces slow circles over the back of my hand, as if memorizing the shape of me. Not when his chest rises and falls just a little too fast, his jaw tight, like he's holding himself together by the thinnest of threads.

Not when my body is begging me to break it.

I look up at him, tilting my chin so my lips part just slightly, an invitation without words.

And he—he doesn't move, as still as the stone caverns around us. The storm in his gaze rages, but he doesn't falter. Doesn't take.

Not until I give.

I reach up, pressing my palms flat against his chest. His skin is hotter than the water, a heat that seeps through my hands and arrows straight down to curl low in my belly, pooling between my legs.

His lips part on a sharp inhale and a tremor wracks his thick frame. He wants.

And so do I. My fingers trail lower, down the ridges of his abs, past the deep cut of muscle leading lower.

A flicker of a smirk ghosts over his lips. Then, without a

word, he takes my hands and starts moving, leading me deeper into the water. Into the darkness.

I let him. I should not, but I do.

The glow of the cave shifts, the bioluminescence trailing lazily over our skin as he maneuvers us into the deeper pools. The water changes here—hotter, stronger, more alive. As if it's a manifestation of the hunger pulsing between us, it swirls in currents that pulse over my legs and thighs, a steady, rhythmic pressure that makes my breath hitch.

The Migoi lifts me as the water deepens, angles my body, tilting me slightly, and the hot stream of water cascades lower—gliding down over my back, the curve of my ass.

I gasp, arching under the sensual attack, the current startling in its intensity but nothing compared to the fiery contact of my breasts grazing against his heated flesh.

A deep, pleased rumble vibrates through his chest, through me, pushing out into the dark corners of my body.

Before I can react, he moves as fast as lighting, spinning me in the water until my back is pressed flush against his front. The contact has me inhaling sharply, the scent of snow and pine washing over me above the mineral of the water as I am surrounded by him.

His massive arms cage me in, one wrapping across my breasts, dwarfing them in his hold, while the other grips my hip, anchoring me against him. His mouth hovers just over my shoulder, his breath searing against my exposed throat.

The faintest scrape of those elongated canines I had a glimpse of earlier teases my flesh as if he wants to bite me. And gods help me, I melt.

Because I feel him. All of him. His cock is like fire, pressed against my ass and reaching up to the small of my back, velvety and impossibly thick, the veins on his shaft pulsing with the warmth of his barely-leashed restraint.

Heat spikes through me, need unfurling low and dangerous.

I squirm, testing the strength of his grip, not sure if I am trying to get closer or further away when his growl deepens, his fingers turning possessive on my hip.

"Dahlia." My name is more snarled than spoken, gritted between clenched teeth. A blessing or a curse, I'm not sure, but the warning is clear.

But so is the way his hips twitch, as if his restraint is breaking, as if he is one heartbeat away from losing control. There is a fine tremble to the arms bracketing me, a frisson of energy coursing through him and into me.

A wicked shiver dances down my spine at the thought of him unchained. Unfettered. Wild and free, like I wish to be.

I tip my head back, exposing more of my neck, and his sharp inhale is the only confirmation I need. I can't help but strum this live wire, knowing full well I'm standing in water. The current is already surging, and if it kills me—what a way to die.

"I like the way you say my name," I confess into the dark caverns, voice breathy. Not the nickname I loathe, Dolly. Not Dahlia in Ben's mocking tone but Dahlia—strong, fierce, true. The way only he could say it.

His grip tightens.

"Dahlia," he growls again, this time lower, rougher, his lips brushing my bare shoulder, the scrape of his teeth more insistent, teetering on the edge of piercing my flesh.

Gods help me, I want more. Emboldened by his response, I thrust my ass back against him, and his growl snaps into something harsher, hungrier.

He angles me so that, once again, the current reaches for my body. It's everywhere, warm and pulsing, like a lover's hand—seeking and insistent. His fingers blaze a fiery trail from my hip down between my legs, shoving the thin fabric of my panties aside and parting my flesh just enough for the heated water to rush against my sex.

I jerk against him, a ragged moan slipping from my lips at the relentless current pulsing against me.

A dark chuckle falls from his lips, whispering over the shell of my ear, and I know we are crossing over into unchartered territory. Perhaps even more dangerous than that damn avalanche.

His muscles ripple against me, every flex deliberate, every motion agonizingly precise as he directs the jet exactly where he wants it—where he wants me to feel it.

And oh, I do. The water pulses between my thighs, demanding surrender, rolling over my clit in steady waves. Too much yet not enough. Not nearly enough. My head lolls against his chest as my legs tremble, but his arms hold me firm, his large hand splaying across my stomach to keep me in place.

I try to twist, to escape the onslaught of sensation, but it only makes it worse. He shifts his hips and moves so his cock, now fully hard, slips up between my thighs. It's scorching heat hotter than even his body.

Desperate for a mooring in this storm of sensation, my hands reach behind me, gripping his thick thighs, feeling the raw strength beneath his skin.

He shifts again, angling me just so, positioning my body so the water torments me further, cascading over my sensitive flesh. Each tiny movement causes it to wax and wane, teasing me until I'm panting.

Grasping the panties he had been holding to the side he gives a sharp tug. The fabric is there one moment and gone the next, a seamless motion beneath the water. No sound. No warning. Just *need*.

With his new unfettered access, he explores every inch of my skin with his rough fingertips, an agonized moan falling from his lips.

I cry out at the interplay of sensation, the smooth warm

water and his rough heated skin playing a brutal tug of war with my flesh.

His lips brush against my jaw, tongue flicking out to taste the steam and sweat from my skin as his fingers slide through my sex, teasing, circling, exploring me thoroughly but never quite giving me what I need.

I whimper, frustration curling into my pleasure, and he rumbles another dark chuckle. I need something inside of me. I need *him* inside of me to fill this desperate ache.

"So hungry," he muses, dragging his sharp teeth over the shell of my ear and working his way down my neck, trailing kisses and nips. His tongue sweeps out, tasting the pulse pounding at my throat.

His fingers press deeper, apply exquisite pressure to my clit, and fuck—I'm writhing and moaning and grunting, feral for him.

His cock pulses between my thighs. It's not just big. It's hot like fever-warmed silk, slick, the veins along the length thrumming against my sensitive skin.

I feel ruined already, and he's barely done anything. The only coherent thought in my mind is trying to get his massive erection inside of me.

A whimper catches in my throat at the thought of being filled by him, and I can feel his smirk against my temple as he leans in, lips grazing the shell of my ear.

"What was that you were singing earlier?" he murmurs, his voice a slow, sinful drag over my skin.

Song? What song? I can't answer him when all I can think about is his hand is roving over my breasts. All I can feel is the heat of his impressive erection grinding against me. And that damn relentless water is driving me mad.

"Back that ass up?" he murmurs, every syllable drenched in wicked satisfaction.

I choke on a laugh, but it melts into a moan as he moves his hand back to my hip to pull my ass back further into him then rolls his hips, thrusting his cock between my thighs. The head drags against my clit, and my vision blurs.

I cross my ankles instinctively, tightening around him. Desperate for more contact with the heat pulsing between my legs.

His breath hitches, and a low, rumbling growl rolls through him, vibrating into my back, my spine, my core.

I barely register that I'm whimpering until I feel his fingers drag back down my stomach while his other hand continues to worship my breasts.

The heat of his skin burns, and when he spreads me open again, the sudden contrast of hot water and fevered flesh against my sex is devastating.

Oh, fuck, oh, fuck—

I jerk in his arms, but he's already holding me open, holding me still, his massive fingers bracketing my aching clit, trapping me against the pulsing current while I grind my entrance down against his shaft.

The heat builds too fast, too sharp, like every nerve in my body is learning his touch too quickly.

"Please," I whisper, begging before I even know what for.

His dark, low chuckle echoes in the cavern. "You beg so sweetly, Winter Star."

His cock slides wetly between my thighs, thick and smooth, teasing against my opening without entering. But oh, how I want him to. I grind down, shameless, seeking more—but he doesn't let me have it.

Instead, his fingers replace the current, rubbing slow, lazy circles over my clit, making my body convulse in desperate, helpless shudders. Every time he rolls his hips, I feel another pulse of liquid heat against my thighs. My arousal—hot, slick, dripping between my legs, makes it even easier for him to glide against me.

"You are divine. Blooming for me like the rarest flower. I cannot wait to taste your sweet nectar," he rasps over my neck.

I moan at the thought of him feasting on me.

"That's it," he growls. "Let me feel how much your body weeps for me."

The glow of the water flickers, pulling my gaze down to see it reflecting off where our bodies slide, meet, and retreat in a dance as old as time, and I can't stop watching.

Once I see what his fully erect cock looks like, I can't help but touch it, desperate to heft its weight in my hand, explore the texture of something so fantastic and unknown.

I reach down past his hand working magic over my clit and wrap my hand around the head. In place of a flared crown is a more tapered head that quickly flares into a wide, thick shaft that I can't get my fingers fully around.

Exploring the new shape and texture that I'm starving for more of has him growling until it feels like a vibrating purr is emanating behind my back. He pulses against my palm, and I stroke slowly, worshipfully, exploring every vein, every ridge that I can reach. Precum coats my fingertips like liquid fire.

I pick up my movements, stroking the head and exploring his slit with my fingertips, marveling at its size, swirling the slick fluid, more viscous than the surrounding water, around the tip.

His movements pick up to match his heavy breathing until he wraps one great arm around me, stilling my movements, leaving me no choice but to submit to him as it explores my flesh and ride the hard cock pistoning between my thighs.

A litany of whimpers, moans, and half-spoken curses fall from my lips. I should be humiliated by how much I'm trembling; how easy he makes me come undone. How I've given over complete control of my body in total trusting submission to a mythical creature made flesh.

But I'm too far gone to care.

His cock glides against my entrance, bumping my clit with every pass. Each time, I wonder—will this be it? The suspense is killing me. My pussy clenches, desperate for something—for him.

He blocks the current with his large hand and says, "Your pleasure belongs to me and me alone. The mountain will not take you from me."

He slowly works a large finger into me and presses a spot deep inside as stars explode behind my eyes. My climax slams into me at finally behind filled—fast, violent, rolling through my body like that damn avalanche. Just like it, he consumes me completely, robbing the air from my lungs, claiming me mercilessly.

I scream, writhing in his hold, the pleasure too much, too much, too much—clenching around his finger, grinding into his palm.

"Please," I cry, hardly able to force a coherent word past my lips. My orgasm continues to roll through me in waves. I want him to stop but damn do I also need more.

He releases my sex and yanks my tank top to expose my breasts to his questing hands. He massages them, easily supporting my weight in the water so I can grind against him. I feel every ridge, every contour, and every pulsing, ropelike vein along the iron shaft trapped between my thighs. My soaked tanktop clings to my curves, nipples taut against his palm. I am lust incarnate.

Ben always made me feel like I was too much. Too soft. Too needy. But this creature—he holds me like I'm perfect. Like I was made to be worshipped.

He whips me around to face him with a dark, satisfied smile as he wraps my legs around his waist. Notching his cock at my entrance, he must have noticed the panic in my eyes bleeding through the fading aftershocks of the orgasm that continue to roll through me. His fingers twist into my hair, tilting my head back until I meet his gaze to find those silver storms swirling with hunger.

"You *will* take me, Dahlia. But not tonight. Tonight, you will only take my seed," he grinds out between clenched teeth, as if the restraint he is exercising is riding a razor thin edge of control. He pauses, the moment heavy with dark promise. He's holding back. And I think it's killing him.

I can't help but look back down, fascinated with the view of his enormous cock poised to spear me.

His fingers curl around my jaw, tilting my face back toward his. "But soon," his voice drops lower, rougher, "you'll take all of me." His voice is a promise. A warning. His thumb sweeps out to brush over my swollen lips. "Very, very soon."

He takes full advantage of my mouth—fallen open in shock—claiming it in a hot, rough, all consuming kiss. His tongue plunges into my mouth, stroking mine, chasing every retreat, swallowing every sound I make. The sharp edge of his teeth just grazes my lips and has me sucking in a breath.

It turns to a breathy moan as I feel his cock pulse at my entrance, desperate to penetrate me. I can't stop myself from grinding down against it despite my fear. The exquisite, burning stretch from just the tip has me gasping into his open mouth.

He groans into the kiss, one hand tangled in my hair, the other running down my back, over my ass, and moving lower until he's pressing a slick finger against my tightest opening. The water makes everything so damn slippery, and it slides in the smallest fraction on a moan.

The fear of his size drifts away in the swirling water as unfulfilled desires, locked away for years, come flooding to the surface, and I push myself further down over both his erection and finger, wanting to be filled by him everywhere.

Instead of thrusting up into me though, he continues to ease his thick finger into my ass while the other hand slides between us to pump his shaft. Desire unfurls, dark and wild. I writhe against him, undone, desperately trying to get more of his monster cock inside of me, but even with my arousal and this mineral water, it just won't fit.

Our kiss turns frantic, tongues dancing, sharing the same harsh breaths. He continues to pump his thick shaft with punishing strokes while he uses his other hand to slowly explore the tight ring of muscle behind me.

"You want me to claim every inch of your body," he growls, not a question but a declaration.

I nod, helpless, too consumed by the sensations to even speak, and it is his undoing. I'm close, so close to cresting another wave, as epic as the great creature surrounding me.

And then—heat.

He breaks the kiss to throw his head back, a guttural snarl breaks from his chest as his hips stutter, and I feel the first scalding pulse of his release flood my entrance.

Oh, gods.

The sensation triggers a wave of pleasure, my body milking the feeling, aching for more, clenching around the head of his erection as I shatter around him.

My body sucks and clenches at him, desperate to pull him inside. My ass tightens around his finger, pulsing, ravenous for more. The heat, the pressure of his release, the razor-thin control—it snaps. A second orgasm shatters me, more devastating than the first.

I let out a litany of nonsense, moans and half-uttered words falling from my lips until I scream out, "Fuck!" so loud it echoes in the cave pulling an answering deep rumbling from his chest, half-way between a growl and a chuckle.

My head drops to his chest as my focus coalesces to the point where we are barely joined. The exotic sight of his shaft illuminated by the living waters, barely penetrating me but held back by his incredible restraint, has me moaning and scrabbling at his chest for purchase, trying anything I can to pull him further into me.

His mighty roar echoes through the caves, hot, thick ropes of his seed surging into my channel, his orgasm endless, filling me, the heat pulsing inside of me like a living thing, branding me from the inside in a way that feels irreversible.

My body absorbs the heat, the sensation lingering like a slow burn beneath my skin. Like it's sinking in, changing me. The realization makes my breath catch, my vision hazy with the aftermath. I should feel satisfied. But I don't.

Because I already want more.

With a deep growl, he stalks over and balances me on the slick stone edge of the pool. My legs tremble as he throws one ankle over his shoulder.

"Keep my seed inside of you," he rasps, the possessiveness in his voice gathering like a snowstorm in my soul. "Hold it in your tight heat."

Before I can answer, he slides the head of his cock free. Thick, white cum drips from my entrance, and he tsks, swiping it up and using two thick fingers to push it back into me. He presses his other palm against the fullness of my belly like he's trying to imprint himself into my womb.

A feral moan tears from my throat. The sight of his release being stroked back into me, the way he watches me like I'm already his—it's too much.

My core flutters again, tightening. My thighs shake at the increased fullness with two of his large fingers but he doesn't stop. Thank the gods he doesn't stop.

One hand continues to stroke and fill me, while the other slides up to caress my breast, teasing the nipple until it's hard and aching.

"I want you to feel me inside of you for days," he growls. "I want your body to crave me. Hunger for me. Weep for me."

My body jerks and locks around his fingers, a gush of liquid pleasure pulsing out to mix with his seed, the water, the heat. Weeping for him, just as he said.

He lowers his great shaggy head and sucks my breast into his mouth, laving my nipple with his tongue before switching to the other side. His fingers continue to pump into me, and the sound of my desire echoes off the water and into the cave around us.

It is so real and raw. I chase his fingers with my hips, my head falling back in ecstasy as I grip the ledge. I am pure need. He sinks his sharp teeth into my breast, and my screams echo in the cave, a primal cry of surrender as my pussy clenches tight, locking down on his large fingers. My limbs shake, and my vision blurs as waves of pleasure cascade over me.

He holds me through it, strong arms anchoring me to him.

When I collapse against him, wrecked and boneless, he eases my leg back down and murmurs something soft in a language I don't know.

His breathing is still rough, ragged, but when I finally find some small bit of energy to pull my head away from his chest and look up at him, his eyes are already on me.

I shiver, not from the cold, but from knowing that this was only the beginning. And I won't leave this cave untouched. I won't leave the same at all.

I called him a beast in a gilded cage of restraint. But maybe I was never meant to stand outside the bars. Maybe I was meant to break them. Because I keep telling myself I shouldn't want this, that I shouldn't want him. But I do. I want to claw and bite and take just as much as I want to be taken.

He may have held back from fully wrecking my body tonight, but something tells me he's already ruined something deeper. Because the way he looks at me? Like he's been waiting for me just as much as I've been waiting to be free?

My body was never the thing in danger.

My heart is what's doomed.

CHAPTER EIGHTEEN

ERYON

I carry her from the water, her body sated with pleasure and limp with exhaustion. She is warm, but I do not trust it. The cold already tried to steal her from me once and may even now be tunneling its icy claws deep into her.

Humans are fragile things, and I will not lose her to something as preventable as a chill. As her skin pebbles, my nervousness has me increasing my body temperature until her skin turns pink.

I tell myself that is why I do not set her down. Not because she smells like me now—winter and woods mixed with the first Spring sunrise that is her essence. Not because of the divine way her body feels pressed against my skin. And definitely not because the taste of her is still bursting on my tongue like a ripe berry, yet I am already hungry again.

She has ruined me.

She curls against me, boneless, trusting in a way that knots something deep in my chest. My hands flex against her soft thighs, gripping her with more care than I have shown another creature in a very long time.

She is so small. So fragile. Yet she has survived. She has *fought*.

And I cannot stop thinking about how easily I could have lost her. How, if I had not followed her in the storm, she would be nothing but frozen remains beneath the ice. If I had not pulled her from the avalanche—if I had not kept her warm, held her close, willed my life into hers—she would not be here, pressed against me, filled with my seed.

Mine.

I do not say it. I do not want to let it take root, but it does not matter. The word has already embedded itself into my bones. I can try to fight it, but she is mine. If only she will choose me as hers. That is the way of balance, that is the way of the Migoi.

I step into the sleeping cave, taking her deeper into my world. A fire burns low in the corner, its glow flickering over the stone. Her clothes and boots are arranged neatly around it, faint wisps of steams rising into the air as they dry. I set her down, keeping my hands on her waist when she sways, her legs weak.

She blinks up at me, dazed. Her eyes are heavy-lidded, lips parted, the flush from her pleasure still staining her cheeks.

I want to kiss her.

I want to ruin her.

Instead, I slide the flimsy scrap of torn fabric down her legs and crouch before her. The sight of her bare body so close nearly undoes me. A groan escapes as her scent fills my lungs, her arousal mingled with my own essence. My gaze lingers on the soft wisp of curls framing her glistening pink center, and I marvel at her smoothness. Good thing she has me to keep her warm.

With resolve borne of my centuries of existence, I force myself to stand. I grip the hem of her shirt, peeling it up and over her head, removing the last barrier between my gaze and the rest of her body. She exhales a slow breath as I drag my fingers over her shoulders, tracing down her arms before pulling away.

She is breathtaking. My eyes greedily drink in the sight of her smooth skin, her lush curves. Every dip and swell made for my hands, made for pleasure. She is perfection. More of the tiny orange dots cascade over her flesh, just like the littles ones across her nose and cheeks. I cannot wait to count them.

I am lovingly cataloguing the differences between us when she flinches. Just barely. A flicker of movement, a hesitation, her hands lifting as if to cover herself. As if she is something to hide instead of worship.

Rage rises so fast it strangles me. Before she can fold in on herself, before she can shrink from me, I growl and swat her hands away.

"*Mine.*"

The word is guttural, ripped from my chest without my permission. My heart speaking before my head can temper my declaration.

Her breath catches, her eyes widening, but I do not take it back.

Does she not see what I see?

Her softness is not a weakness. It is a gift; one I would kill to protect. She is the perfect counterpoint to the masculine, completing the duality of nature. She is the curve of the river cutting through rock. She is the warm circle of the sun breaking the line of the mountain range. Breathtakingly beautiful.

She does not answer, her throat working as she swallows. I see the uncertainty in her eyes, the ghost of a wound left by another. I can only assume it was some lowly male who did not cherish what he had been given.

The thought of another seeing her vulnerable like this, touching her has the beast inside of me shredding at my skin to be unleashed. Did he dare to speak harsh words to her? Did he criticize someone so beautiful and lovely? Did he touch her in anger?

He is dead. He does not know it yet, but he is dead.

The fire snaps, spitting embers, a mirror of my rage. She jumps, and I inhale sharply, forcing the beast back down. I cannot touch her now—not the way I want. Not the way I should.

She is exhausted, swaying on her feet. Her body has been wrung out, her mind slipping into the haze of sleep even as she struggles to remain standing.

I lift her again, marveling over the feel of our skin ghosting over each other and carry her across the cave to my bed. It is nothing more than a pile of furs atop a wooden frame strung with rope that I pieced together over the years. Its simplicity suits me fine, but I worry this life will not be enough for her. Or maybe my true fear is that I will not be enough for her.

She makes a soft noise as I lower her onto the furs facing the fire. A sound of contentment. A sound of trust.

My throat tightens. I don't know if I can trust myself right now to let her choose me when my beast rages at me to claim her, claim her *now*. I should leave her. I should step away, retreat to the other side of the cave, let her rest without my flesh pressing against hers.

But when she moves to pull a fur over her body, I react, wanting to prove that I can provide her with everything she needs. I will keep her warm. I scold myself for being jealous of a fur, but it doesn't stop my body from moving.

An ache blooms in my chest as I curl around her, my body the only shield she'll ever need. My fur lengthens, softening as it spreads over her skin, covering her the way it was always meant to.

She sighs, and the sound is so right, so perfect, that I almost close my eyes. Consider letting myself rest.

But I do not. I cannot.

Instead, I will keep watch as I did for the weeks I tracked her through the mountains followed by the long cold days we were separated. Though they were few, they were some of the greyest of my existence. I will protect her as I protect these mountains. I will fulfill my vow, sealed with my blood and sworn to the earth.

I listen to the steady beat of her heart, feel the slow rise and fall of her breath. I memorize the weight of her against me, the way she fits so easily, so naturally, in my arms. Every curve is a perfect counterpoint to my body, as if she were carved from my very flesh.

I think about how much I do not want her to leave, but I know she will. That she must. But just for tonight, I can pretend that there is a world in which she is mine. A life where she can be with me here in this cave, cut off from the world and all of its problems. Just two mates with one heart beating between them.

I let my eyes slip shut, just for a moment, imagining what forever would look like for a Migoi and a human.

Screams of terror have me leaping from the bed to land in a defensive crouch between my Winter Star and whatever danger has come for her. My body instinctively reverts to my inner predator, my muscles bunching and flexing as my thick fur extends to its full length, useful for both weather and protection from injury.

My claws extend, and I bare my teeth in a feral snarl ready to kill. I sniff the air, scanning the surroundings for the would-be attacker. But I don't see or smell anything outside of the cave and her scent, the promise of Spring.

A small giggle has me whipping my head around to catch a

trace of fear spring into her eyes at my imposing facade. I retract my fur and sheath my claws, thankful for her sheepish smile that quickly replaces it as she blinks up at me from the furs.

"I'm sorry, I was dreaming of the avalanche. I didn't mean to alarm you," she says in a small voice.

I gather her up in my arms, this small, soft, precious thing.

"Tell me what you were dreaming," I murmur into her riotous curls that glow like the sunset in the light of the fire. She needs to speak the thoughts out of her mind where I can shred them into oblivion.

Holding her close, I trace the tips of my retracted claws up and down her spine, as she haltingly tells me of her dream.

"I'm in the dark, trapped and running out of oxygen. Powerless to save myself, knowing I'm going to die. I feel my body going numb, my strength giving out, and I have to decide whether to surrender to the cold and the dark, or fight."

I let the silence breathe, honoring her words, her shared vulnerability. My heart breaks at the thought of the nightmare that drug her back beneath the crushing snow and ice, where she was suffocating, where she was dying.

"But you did fight, that's how I found you. I heard you singing something about, 'Back that ass up.' Badly, I might add," I say to soften my retort.

She gives a soft laugh, but then sobers as she says, "If you hadn't saved me, I would've died."

I pull back and take her shoulders in a gentle grip, forcing her to meet my eyes. Fear of a world without her in it sharpens my tone. With a slight shake, I declare, "No. You would never give up. You are a fighter."

She hangs her head, shoulders slumping in defeat as she admits, "I don't know. I was giving up. And honestly, I don't know what I have left to fight for. I have no one to go home to and without my research, not only do I have no purpose, but I also have no chance."

No purpose? Nothing to fight for? I cannot, will not tolerate this belief, these careless words. She is everything. The sun that gives warmth to the world, the moon of creation. I lift her chin with a firm grasp, infusing my voice with the depths of my devotion and say, "You. You have *you* to fight for."

She looks away as if she can't bear to hear my words. As if she doesn't believe in herself even half as much as I do, and says, "I don't know. Everything just feels so out of my control."

And then, in a voice so small I can barely hear it even with my acute senses, she says, "I'm lost."

My jaw clenches. No. She does not get to doubt herself. Not when she is still here, still breathing, still mine. I understand all too well what it means to have no control. And what it means to be lost. So lost, you don't recognize your own soul.

I need to help her piece herself back together. I need to show her what I know to be as true as the rise of the sun each morning and the moon each night. As true as the Spring that inevitably breaks the long cold grey of winter. This is not something I can convince her of with words but something that she must learn for herself. I can only guide her.

"Let me show you that you are still worth fighting for," I say.

She glances at me and away again, uncertainty flickering in her eyes, but my words have caught her attention. I give her time to decide; she must choose this for herself. I let the heavy beats of my heart pass the time. Trusting her in the silence.

"Okay," she whispers, hesitant and unsure.

I wait, mouth closed but heart on my sleeve. I let her see the emotions blazing behind my eyes. I want to force her to choose this path through my will alone. But choose she must.

She clears her throat and with a decisive nod, repeats louder, "Okay. Help me see what you see."

Relief crashes over me. I knew she was strong. A warrior. But for this to work, I need more than her strength. I meet her gaze, steady and unyielding. "I need you to trust me. Completely."

Her hands lift, small and steady, pressing against my face. She searches my eyes as if seeking something unspoken. Searching for an answer hidden in the swirling silver. A heavy beat passes. Then, soft but certain, she murmurs, "I trust you."

I lower my forehead to hers as we sit in the stillness of the moment, breathing in the other's trust. She is starving for kindness, for compassion, and for the love that she so clearly deserves but has been denied.

Now that she is mine, she will never feel that way again. But first, I will show her who she is. I will prove to her that she is worth fighting for. I will make her see that I have been waiting for her, too.

A decision takes root before I can stop it. Before I can question whether it is right or fair.

I stand, cradling her against me as I take off into the tunnels, intent on a destination. The light fades and I know that all she sees is darkness, but I know every rock, every pebble of this cave system and I can still easily see what her human eyes cannot.

She does not resist. She trusts me. And that alone will be her undoing.

I take her into the darkness. I tell myself this is for her. That she must remember her strength. That she must learn to fight against the darkness that took her before.

But deep inside, I know the truth. I need this, too. I need to see her fight. I need to know she will not break. Not from this, and not from me.

I carry her deep into the mountain, where the air is heavy and still, and the quiet is so loud you can hear it. After my losses, I meditated in this silence for years. I drowned in it. Sat in the dark, waiting for the mountain to answer me.

It never did.

The mountain does not explain itself. It does not justify. It does not ask for forgiveness. It takes and gives as it pleases, and those who cannot endure are simply—gone. And no whispered prayer, no amount of endless meditation, no desperate plea would ever bring them back.

So, I became like the mountain. Unmoving. Unyielding. I buried my grief beneath duty, beneath the dharma of my existence. Protect. Preserve. Maintain the balance. That was all. That was enough.

Until her. My Winter Star. She was buried, too—swallowed by ice and fate. The mountain took her, just as it took everything else.

And yet—she did not disappear. She survived. Against all odds, she is in my arms because she fought.

I tighten my grip around her, feeling the warmth of her skin press into mine, and something inside me cracks open. This is not chance. It is proof.

Proof of what, I do not know yet. That she is different? That the balance has shifted? That the gods are cruel enough to put her in my path when I swore never to love again?

Or maybe—maybe it is proof that she is already mine. The universe has taken. And taken. And for the first time—it gives.

My Winter Star, defying fate itself.

Mine.

I ease her down, settling her gently against the smooth cavern floor. Hovering over her, I say into the dark, "I am going to show you that you are a warrior. Make you remember your worth. Show you what I see."

A soft murmur of agreement slips from her lips.

I stand guardian as her mind calms, watch as every muscle in her body slowly relaxes, her body attuning itself to the heartbeat of the mountain. There is no rushing this moment. I slow my breathing to match that of the caves. I attune every sense solely to her and let the dark pulse around us until I can hear her heartbeat quicken. Then, I know her mind has taken her back to the snowy prison, just as I thought it would.

Her breathing turns shallow, and I can imagine how she must have fought her fear, rationing every breath while she was entombed. I clench my fists until my claws pierce my own flesh, holding back the instinct to rescue her. Sweat beads across her skin despite the constant cool temperature of the deep caverns.

Yet still I wait for the exact moment to pull her mind back from the brink. To let her truly fight this battle she must believe. Her body must be flooded with fear and endorphins, returned to the moment of fighting or surrender. And damn it, she will fight!

A fine tremor wracks across her body and a whimper escapes her clenched lips. The desperate sound threatens to unravel the tightly held control that I cling to but still I wait.

I hear her heart stutter, and know she has reached the pinnacle. *Now*. Now is the time to bring her back to me, but more importantly, bring her back to herself. Show her just how fierce I know she can be. Show her that she is *everything* worth fighting for.

CHAPTER NINETEEN

DAHLIA

Despite my efforts to regulate it, my breathing turns erratic. The pitch black of the caves robs my vision, the weight of being deep in the heart of the mountain bears down on me, and the silence is so loud it's deafening. Just like that damn avalanche.

I'm back, trapped in the snow, wondering just how I am going to die. Debating the merits of suffocation versus hypothermia. Praying to anyone that will listen to save me. Wondering if I should bother to fight or just give in after all.

Just as panic threatens to consume me, the soft caress of velvet fingertips run lightly over my body. Long, smooth, unhurried strokes which pull my attention to the motion. The feeling of someone tracing my outline, drawing me here in this world bit by bit, grounds me.

I turn my mind away from my frantic thoughts and lose myself in sensation. The crushing weight of the mountain gives way to the featherlight touch of his hands skating over my flesh.

Painting me until I can visualize myself as an oil on canvas, a study in curves and shadows.

I am real, and I am here. I'm alive, not dying. The long, steady strokes come up and over my face, and I remember how I like the way the sunlight reflects off my hair. My eyes twinkle with mischief, my face is so expressive that no, I can't hide my annoyance behind a poker face but also, I can't hide my joy either and that's a gift to share with the world.

Tears prick my eyes as his gentle touch reflects my face back to me once again and I see, I am beautiful—flawed and imperfect but stunning in my true self. His hand runs over my mouth, and I smile.

The pleasant sensation is replaced by shock when he clamps his hand over my mouth and nose. Panic once squeezes my heart in its icy grip while my body rides the high of his other hand trailing down my breasts and the slope of my belly to trace over my sex.

Fear constricts my chest as the thought of suffocating to death rises back to the forefront of my mind. Any second now and he'll lift his hand; I just know it. But instead, its heavy weight remains while the other works its way between my folds. Instinctively I spread my thighs, eyes searching for his face to read his motivation.

But I can see nothing in the consuming darkness, hear nothing above my own frantic movements as I begin to struggle, the pounding of my heart as fear kicks in vibrating my entire body. I buck instinctively, heart racing, my lungs screaming for air. I need air!

He plunges two large fingers inside of me, and I try to suck in a breath at the invasion, at the glorious stretch of being filled by him, but I can't. Reaching up with both hands I futilely claw at his massive one covering my face, but his only reaction is to thrust his fingers in and out of me faster, deeper.

Despite my frantic struggle, a new sound greets my ears.

The obscene noise of my shameless, slick arousal flooding over his fingers. Each thrust curls deeper, stroking me like he's sculpting me from the inside out. Like he's claiming me from within.

I try to twist my hips, to wrench free, but the darkness makes it impossible to tell which way is up, which way is out. All I know is him. Surrounded by snow and pine, darkness and delight consuming me.

His breath is steady, controlled, as if my body's rebellion doesn't matter. As if he already knows how this ends.

As if I do, too.

My pussy clenches as he spreads me wider, rough fingertips dragging over my sensitive flesh, forcing me to feel every stroke, every invasion. Heat pools deep in my belly like a gathering storm.

He thrusts in again, deeper this time, harder, hitting something devastating. My back bows, my vision erupts into stars and I gasp—but no air comes.

The oxygen deprivation turns every sensation, every feeling, razor-sharp. My skin tingles, my thighs quake, my blood pounds against my skull. My mind screams that I need air, I need escape—

But my body? My traitorous, starving, desperate body?

It needs *this*.

A whimper breaks free, and he makes a sound—a low, pleased growl, reverberating into the earth and against my spine like an earthquake.

I claw at his hand and arm, my nails raking over his skin, but he only tightens his grip, as if to remind me—there is no running from this. From him. From what I am becoming in his hands.

His thumb presses down, circling my clit, a slow, agonizing drag that makes my toes curl. My body jerks—instinct, panic, pleasure too sharp to bear.

I writhe in his hold, trapped between torment and release, between fear and something far more dangerous.

His fingers stroke deeper, curving just right—so right—so devastatingly, impossibly right. The tension coils tight, razor-thin and fraying, every nerve crackling like a live wire.

The lack of air sends my body into freefall. Everything spins, shatters, reforms. A million stars burst into my vision, and I just know I am going to pass out. I am going to die. I am going to—

I come.

The violent orgasm overwhelms me, splintering my fear into oblivion. It slams through me like an avalanche, tearing the last mote of breath from my lungs, wringing me out until I have nothing left. A silent scream rips through my throat, raw and soundless, swallowed by the darkness, by his hand, by the universe itself. It's too much—too much—

I jerk in his hold, my body spasming, muscles locking tight before going completely, utterly boneless.

The moment my body breaks, he finally releases me. Air floods my lungs. My vision explodes with light, white-hot and flickering, my entire world drenched in sensation.

The first breath I take is not relief. It's possession. Because I know, in the marrow of my bones, in the echo of my own shattered scream, that I will never escape him now.

That I will never want to.

He didn't just make me come—he unmade me. Tore me apart and put me back together. And now? Now I don't think I can go back to who I was before. I don't think that I want to. Dahlia Wilde really did die in that avalanche. She is gone, lost to the cold, to the dark.

I am reborn of shadows and darkness. Of the heart of the mountain. This new version sees everything with freshly opened eyes.

The darkness isn't truly black at all—it's a thousand shifting shades of grey. Every contour of the stone floor beneath me presses against my skin, sharp and unyielding. The air flows over my body, brushing against every fine hair, carrying with it the rich scent of the cave, and the snow and pine scent of the Yeti's primal musk mingled with my own heated arousal.

What I first mistook for sensory deprivation is, in fact, an overwhelming cascade of sensation. With a sudden burst of understanding, I sit up and gulp down a deep, sweet lungful of air. My chest heaving, I feel a grin stretch across my face, wild and unrestrained.

I *am* worth fighting for.

But in the back of my mind, something new takes root, something undeniable. I came here searching for a plant. But in this cave, with this creature, I think I've found something else entirely. And I don't know how I'm supposed to leave it behind.

I turn my head and set my sights unerringly on the Yeti's face and can see an answering smile blooming. Meeting his beautiful silver gaze, I launch myself at him.

He catches me in his arms and rolls to his back, allowing me to straddle him. My thighs tremble as I settle over the expanse of his chest, the hard ridges of his muscles teasing against my slick flesh. His hands grip my hips, guiding me, sliding me over him, every inch a deliberate torment. Each ridge, each dip, teasing at my sensitive flesh.

Heat pools low in my belly as he moves me higher. I realize, too late, what he's doing. A sharp inhale breaks the silence as he buries his face between my thighs and breathes me in. I try to hover, to hold myself above him, but I can't fight the iron grip pulling me closer.

Silver eyes flare up at me as he growls out, "You couldn't drown me if you tried. I was made to breathe you in."

My breath stutters, anticipation crackling over my skin like lightning before a storm. I bite my lip, wanting, waiting, until his mouth finally claims me.

I gasp as he drags his tongue through my folds, deliberate

and slow, tasting me like something sacred. His groan vibrates against my clit, sending a sharp pulse of pleasure through me. I choke on a moan as his lips close around me, as he feasts on me with a hunger that borders on reverence.

He doesn't just devour me—I feel him savoring me, like he's memorizing every shudder, every breathless sound I make as he laps at my arousal and explores every inch of me with his teeth and tongue and lips.

I reach down, threading my fingers into his thick white hair, marveling at the silk-soft strands tangling around my fingers. I fist the locks, gripping tight for leverage as pleasure pools in my belly, but all it does is spur him on.

A growl rumbles against my core, a primal sound of satisfaction that makes my stomach clench. He delves deeper, his tongue spearing into me with devastating precision, stretching me open, wrecking me. My thighs shake as heat radiates from my belly and out through my limbs.

I ride his face, rocking into him, chasing the crest of something unstoppable. His sharp teeth just graze against me, a wicked contrast to the heat of his tongue, and I cry out, my body tightening, chasing the pleasure his skillful mouth promises. When I dare to look down, his silver eyes are open, locked onto mine.

Dark. Starving. *Possessive.*

I lift and drop my hips, fucking his tongue, gasping as it snakes ever deeper, until the tip is caressing some undiscovered spot inside of me. He helps guide me with his hands, taking over my weight completely as I lose myself to chasing pleasure. My arms shake as I use my grip on his hair to support my weight. I don't want this feeling to end, I want to live in this moment of bliss for all time but when my hardened clit brushes against his sharp teeth—I explode like a supernova.

Pleasure detonates through me, so raw it strips me bare, leaves every muscle trembling in the aftermath. My movements are jerky and uncoordinated as I writhe above him, barely conscious of the hands steadying me, of the mouth that refuses to stop, drawing out every last pulse of my release until I am nothing but breathless, spent, undone.

I gasp as he lazily laps at my oversensitive flesh, as if he just can't stop himself from continuing to feast on me. His large mouth practically engulfs my entire sex as he licks every inch of me clean.

As my orgasm fades away, I'm flooded with the desire to touch him. The curiosity to explore the body of a mythical but very real creature takes hold of my brain. I want to trace every hard line of his body with my fingers, taste every texture with my tongue.

I try to tell myself it's the scientific part of me wanting to research the unknown. But the truth is ever since he notched his enormous cock at my entrance and filled me with his release, I've been thinking about how to fit him inside of me. I need to get a better idea of what I am working with. More data for my hypothesis. The latter being, make it fit.

Breathless, I whisper, "Please, let me touch you."

The Migoi lifts me effortlessly from his face, setting me down beside him. My legs are weak, trembling, my skin still flushed from the way he just unraveled me.

For a moment, I think he will let me—think he will allow my hands to roam over the body that just drove me to madness. My fingers twitch with the need to explore, to return the pleasure he gave me.

But instead, he stands, towering over me, and shakes his head.

"There is nothing I would love more," he murmurs, voice dark and rough, thick with restraint. His thumb drags over my bottom lip, teasing, yet reverent. A promise. A warning. "This was just for you."

With a smile he pulls me by the hand after him. I try to keep up but even with my improved perception, my smaller steps over the unfamiliar and uneven cavern floors are no match for his sure and steady stride.

Noticing this, he scoops me back up against his hot, velvety skin. I can't help but let out a small noise of contentment at how good he feels pressed against me. In no time, we are passing the pool with its glowing waters and making our way back to the bed next to the fire.

He sets me down gently and passes me a water jug. I had no idea how thirsty I was, and after I chug the sweet cool liquid, I find him holding out a small basket full of fruits, seeds, and nuts.

As I sit and eat, I watch him walk around the cave, straightening some things and folding my now dry clothes. He spins my boots around next to the fire, getting them to dry thoroughly.

I watch him and realize soon my gear will be dry and I'll be able to go, head back to the guesthouse and continue my search for the elusive plant I had returned for. I should be thrilled; this is my whole purpose after all. But I can't deny the thought of leaving this magnificent Migoi has my dedication to my purpose wavering.

He was supposed to be a distraction. A stolen moment. But now, I can't ignore the dangerous ache blooming in my chest. The kind that says *stay*. Make this your forever home.

Despite just meeting, he sees me more clearly than Ben ever did in all our years together. With him, I feel safer and more cherished than I have since my mother was alive. I want to hide away from time, and genetics, hell hide away from the whole world here in these caves. After everything that has happened, don't I deserve a break?

I decide I'll give myself one more day in this suspended reality. Just one more day of this delicious pleasure we've been discovering and the chance to explore the fantasies that have been unfulfilled until now.

With a full belly, I lie down in the mountain of furs, full and warm and content in a way I didn't know I needed. The Migoi hums low under his breath as he tidies, something ancient and rhythmic in the sound. The softly crackling fire mixes with it to make the perfect, relaxing background soundtrack.

He returns to my side, lowering himself behind me where he curls his massive body around mine like a living shield. His heat seeps into my skin as his breath ghosts over the back of my neck.

I let myself sink into his arms, into this strange little world we've carved out of stone and ice. It feels so comfortable, so warm and safe. *Home,* pulses again in my heart, more sensation than thought.

Gods help me—I don't want to go. Tomorrow, I'll start thinking again. Tomorrow, I'll figure out what I have to do. How to not just leave, but tell him that I must.

But tonight, I belong to him.

CHAPTER TWENTY

DAHLIA

I wake to find the fire banked low, cold seeping through me in the chill of the cave. The furs have slipped off, leaving my flesh rippled with goosebumps. I grope around, seeking my warm, fuzzy companion, but the bed is empty.

I stand and stretch, crossing to where my clothes are neatly stacked. I slip them on, minus the ruined panties, and grab my boots. Sitting down I cobble the laces back together from where he cut them with his claw, a delicious shudder ghosting over me at the memory of what came next.

Looking for my missing Yeti, I venture out to the large pool, but not finding him, spin in a slow circle and take in the expanse of the caves. I know better than to go wandering in the dark alone, risking getting hurt or lost. One end of the cave appears lighter though, so I head towards it.

As I walk and more light filters in, shapes begin to emerge along the walls—paintings. Not crude or primitive, but ancient. Older than the famous cave paintings of France or Argentina, untouched by time yet holding the weight of centuries.

I reach out, fingers skimming just shy of the surface, afraid to disturb something sacred. The paintings tell the story of the Migoi's world—a world that once held more of his kind. They show glimpses of their lives, their purpose. Guardians, protectors of the forest, just as Sita had said.

The beginning starts with a Yeti and a woman with the moon. Then, towering figures move through the mountains, their massive forms blending with the snow, nearly indistinguishable from the landscape itself. In another, two groups appear to come together, perhaps for a joining of families? My stomach twists as I follow the progression, tracing the changes with my eyes.

Further along, the figures dwindle. What was once a thriving presence slowly fades, replaced by emptier landscapes—mountains bare of their massive shapes, forests that feel hollow. A chill crawls up my spine.

And then, as the light grows brighter, I come across one final image. Larger than the others. A massive Yeti, standing tall. Beside it, another, slightly smaller. And between them, a small, rounded figure covered in thick fur. A baby.

My heart tightens. I step closer, breath shallow.

I don't know why this painting affects me more than the others. Maybe it's the way they stand, their bodies angled inward, protective. Maybe it's the simple, aching familiarity of it —two parents, their child between them, their world reduced to this tiny, precious thing. A family. Gone, just like mine.

A lump rises in my throat as I wonder—what became of them? What became of all the Migoi on these walls? And why— why does my chest ache as if I already know the answer?

A breeze pulls my attention, and I turn from the somber story etched into stone and follow the whisper of fresh air. The tunnel widens, opening to the world beyond, and I step out into the fading light of sunset.

The sky is painted in deep violets and fiery reds, the last

breath of the sun slipping below the jagged peaks. A few stars blink into existence, pinpricks against the twilight. The air is still, the hush of approaching night settling over the mountains like a blanket.

I exhale, tension bleeding from my limbs as I tilt my face toward the sky. The vastness stretches above me, boundless, a stark contrast to the enclosed cavern walls I have spent so much time within. For the first time in days, I feel small in a way that is not suffocating but freeing.

Wrapping my arms around myself as the temperature plummets with the setting sun, I decide to say put, not wanting to chance wandering away and getting lost in the dense forests surrounding me. As I sit on the ground, the sounds of the forest start to surround me, and I feel at peace.

In fact, this is the happiest I've been since I can remember. No frantic research, no Ben, no spiraling thoughts. Just the unique stillness that comes from being enveloped by nature rather than the noise of humanity.

It's short lived as I feel a subtle shift in the air around me and sit up straighter, my senses sharpening. Fear ghosts over my skin as I realize how defenseless I am sitting out here alone in the darkening night. Plus the Migoi might worry if I'm gone too long. I stand and stretch my arms up to the sky and take a deep breath of the cold, crisp mountain air, then turn back.

But the entrance is gone. A frisson of fear skitters down my spine. I haven't moved more than a few feet away, yet the opening that I just walked through is nowhere to be seen.

Frowning, I step forward, scanning the rock face, my fingers brushing against the rough stone. Hadn't it been right here? I pace back and forth from where I swear I came out, my heart rate spiking as the wind shifts, curling around me like unseen hands. The mountains seem to stretch taller, the trees standing just a little closer than before.

The cave entrance has vanished. And I am alone.

Every second that passes, I hope that the Migoi will come to find me. But as the time ticks by, suddenly I'm not so sure. At least physically, I had felt a connection with him. And I thought there was something beyond even that, but perhaps he did this with all the women he rescued from avalanches?

Frowning, it dawns on me that I don't even know his name to call out for him. Well, shit. I walk a little further, determined to find the entrance, when a noise breaks the stillness of the night. I freeze, hoping I can somehow escape whatever is out there.

I turn towards the noise and see the beautiful twilight has exchanged its dusty purple hue for a shadowy grey and black landscape as the light fades behind the mountains. The forest noises which were soothing just minutes take on a sinister quality.

My heartbeat quickens as my primitive brain urges me to run. But where? A low growl has me sprinting into action, racing towards where I started and where I think the cave's entrance must lie. I can't help but look back over my shoulder, wondering how much time I have to escape whatever is after me.

While my head is turned, I slam into a solid wall of heat and dense fur. The snow and pine scent of my Yeti surrounds me as a large arm sweeps me behind him to safety. He turns and lunges at the creature chasing me. I lean to the side, brave enough in his presence to see just what he is protecting me from.

A large wolf with raised hackles, gnashing teeth, and dripping saliva strains and snaps on a leash. I frown at such a ferocious thing being owned. Following the long leather lead, I trace it back to its owner standing at the tree line, heavily cloaked and hooded.

The Yeti lets out a fierce roar, echoing through the forest. The wolf tucks its tail and runs back to its owner, clearly knowing it is not the alpha here. Despite the distance and the dim lighting, the man's face transforms, sheer terror overtaking him as he falls to his knees in supplication at seeing the mythical guardian of the mountains.

At the low growling that continues to emanate from my savior, the man gets his feet under him, backing away while still bowed. He unties a sack at his waist and tosses it towards us. Within seconds the woods swallow him, and I can hear the frantic crashing sounds of his running away.

The Yeti spins around to face me, and I'm confronted with the sight of just how fearsome he is. He appears larger than I've ever seen him, muscles rippling with each heaving breath. His normally luminescent eyes are almost completely black in the darkness of the night, and his pointed teeth also appear larger.

I should probably be stumbling backwards, away from this creature that is more beast than man in this moment. But I've had enough of doing what I should. Of shrinking myself down, listening to others, being practical, sensical. I want some damn *nonsense*. I want to be hedonistic and chase down my desires. It's time for me to be Dahlia fucking *Wilde*.

So instead of running away, I race forward and launch myself into the air, trusting his strong arms will catch me. And they do, a split second before our mouths crash into each other. I swallow his snarl with a moan as the sharp edge of his teeth drags over my lips and tongue, the tang of copper blooming on my tastebuds.

Burying my hands in his thick white hair, I angle my head to kiss him deeper. I'm so lost in the claim of his mouth that I barely notice the impact of the stone wall behind my back as he slams me back against the mountain.

A groan escapes me as he trails kisses down my neck, nipping at my pulse point. Rough hands rip open my flannel shirt, sending the buttons flying. His claw-tipped fingers grazing my flesh have me tipping my head back, a loud cry echoing into the night air.

Above us, the full moon stares down from a velvet sky, a million stars scattered like distant embers. Now that I have stepped beyond the world I once knew, embraced something wilder, freer, how will I ever return to living in captivity?

The thought unravels as his mouth finds my breast—hot, demanding, insistent. A gasp slips from my lips, my fingers tangling in his hair as reason melts away.

Despite having shrunk back to his merely large size, looking more man than beast once again, I still marvel at the differences between us. His thick white hair, coarser than a human's yet soft as silk, slides through my fingers. The smooth velvet of his skin is pure indulgence beneath my touch, a stark contrast to the sharp teeth that graze my nipple—a reminder that he is still, in part, the beast.

A curse slips from my lips as his tongue follows, swirling soothing heat over the sting. My hands fist in his hair, my body arching into his mouth, torn between craving his bite and the way he soothes it after.

One shove, and my pants are down. He drops to his knees, and his mouth finds my dripping core, dragging a strangled curse from my lips between panting breaths. The rapidly fading, rational part of my brain catalogs one last, glorious difference between us—that fucking tongue.

Even with my legs tangled in my pants, he manages one impossibly long lick, tracing from the seam of my ass to my aching clit, sending a full-body shudder through me. My thighs tremble as he presses the firm base of his tongue against my sensitive flesh while the wicked, flexible tip works its way inside, curling and teasing. Filling me with pulsing heat.

A choked moan rips from me, my need spilling down my thighs as the realization slams into me—this is something no human man could ever do. This is something Ben never even wanted to do.

Not that I'm thinking about him now. Not when my body is wound so impossibly tight, my pleasure shimmering just out of reach. I try to shift, to throw my legs over his shoulders and ride his face properly, but my trapped ankles keep me from moving the way I need.

I let out a groan of frustration.

His response? A sharp nip to the soft flesh of my inner thigh. A warning. A promise.

I yelp in response, but he looks up at me, face shining with my arousal, and says, "What do you need, *Sruhnar?*"

I repeat the name back to him, tasting it on my tongue. "Sruhnar?"

The word hums between us, carrying something I don't yet understand but somehow it feels—right.

He chuckles against me as he gently corrects my pronunciation, rolling the R softly. He translates, "Sruhnar—my Winter Star."

I hold his face in my hands, staring down into his eyes, which reflect the night sky above us. I marvel at their beauty and feel pride overflowing my heart that he would compare me to the heavens above.

I say, "And what do I call you?"

He looks away for a poignant beat, hesitation flickering across his face. Then, as if making a decision, he meets my eyes again, almost shyly, and whispers, "Eryon."

This time, I take care to pronounce his words the same way. "Air-ee-on."

I let the name settle on my tongue, the syllables feeling ancient, powerful—fitting for the creature before me, the one who saved me. The one who is becoming mine. His name settles into my soul like a shadow of my own.

At the sound of his name on my lips he takes my mouth in

what starts as a soft, sweet kiss. Gentle. Warm. As his hands sweep over my body I can't help but wonder how long it's been since he has heard his own name.

The loneliness and longing for a kindred spirit resonates within my soul and pours out through my kiss. The simmering intensity shifts until it boils over, raw and unchecked. Until I'm kicking frantically at my pants, twisting, and squirming to free myself. But the fabric stays stubbornly tangled over my boots.

Eryon huffs a quiet laugh at my struggle, his eyes gleaming with amusement and something darker. Before I can protest, he grips me with ease, hoisting me up as if I weigh nothing.

The flannel slips down, and I gasp as my shoulders scrape against the cold stone, a sharp contrast to the feverish heat of my skin. But the gasp melts into a moan as he loops my legs behind his head, settling my weight over his broad shoulders.

I barely have time to process the sheer strength in him, the effortless way he holds me, before his mouth is on me. And then I stop thinking altogether.

His lips, his tongue, his teeth—he devours me like he's making up for lost time, like he's been starving for this. For *me*. I arch against him, crying out as he drinks me down, tracing every fold, every trembling inch, as if it was always his.

I bury my fingers in his hair, clutching tight as he wrings moans from my lips like confessions—raw, unfiltered, undeniable. But as the pleasure builds, cresting like a wave too powerful to fight, my grip loosens. I fling my arms wide—part surrender, part exhilaration—offering myself to the moment, to him.

The precarious height beneath me adds a delicious edge of fear, a razor-sharp contrast to the pleasure overwhelming me—a heady, intoxicating thrill, like gasoline meeting fire. Besides, I know he won't drop me. I trust him.

When his tongue spears into my entrance, thick and impossibly deep, I cry out, the sound echoing off the stone around us, multiplying, surrounding me. The wildness of it, the raw hunger, makes me feel untamed, unbound.

I am here, beneath the open sky, surrounded by the pulse of the earth itself—while the guardian of the forest feasts on me like I am the only offering that matters. The realization crashes into me, surging through my body as my climax rolls deep and unrelenting, pulled from the very core of me.

My thighs shake and toes curl as I ride wave after wave. When I feel too sensitive, unable to take anymore, I bury my hands deep into his hair and try to wrench his face away from me. I'm met with a fearsome growl and may as well have tried to push away the stone behind me, as unyielding as Eryon is.

With wide eyes I look down to where he continues to lap at my pussy. The sight of his tongue disappearing inside of me is so erotic and wickedly taboo I can't help but stare down at him. I thought I was done but already pleasure is building again, a swirling vortex pulling me in.

Another gush of arousal has his mouth falling open on a groan and the sight of his sharp teeth grazing my skin as he devours me has me arching closer, lost to his hunger, grinding my hips harder into his face as he returns to consuming me like a starved creature.

With his large, calloused hands he shifts his hold to my thighs and spreads me open even further. Meeting my eyes he uses his long tongue to snake back to my ass, the probing lighting up erotic nerves I didn't know existed.

When his tongue breaches me, I can't help the squeal that escapes my lips. I know it should be in shock, in reproach, but instead it turns into a deep moan as pleasure blooms within me. My pussy clenches at the emptiness, aching to be filled.

He buries his nose into my entrance, face flush with my body so my clit can grind into his forehead. The motion allows his tongue to slip further into my ass. I am so consumed with pure animalistic lust, I would have ground my flesh into the mountain itself at this point and not given a damn.

The sensations pulse and swirl, an unfamiliar molten pressure building deep inside me until it feels as though the very mountain he holds me against might erupt.

I pant out raggedly, "Eryon, please."

At the sound of his name, he thrusts his tongue deeper and groans against me, the vibrations echoing into my center and reverberating through my core. The mountain does not break, but I do. The pressure peaks and releases in a blinding rush, and I scream at the intensity, shocked at the eruption that completely drenches his face.

"I—I'm so sorry," I stammer out, mortified that not only did I just squirt for the first time ever, but I did it directly into his face. His. Face.

Eryon pulls back to look at me. But instead of the disgust I expect to see written there, he tips his head back and groans a deep guttural sound. He lets my body slide down the rock face, so I am pinned between him and the mountain, legs still tangled in my pants looped around his body.

Meeting my eyes, he flashes me a wicked smile, more teeth than lips, and says slowly, "You marked me."

Chapter Twenty-One

Eryon

In the face of my declaration, she apologizes profusely, turning her head away as redness creeps up her neck and over her face. I love when she turns as pink as the sunrise, but for some reason I cannot comprehend why she seems to be embarrassed. As if she has done something shameful. As if she has not just rewritten the entire fabric of my existence.

My chest rises and falls with a deep, heaving breath as I fight the urge to snarl. She doesn't understand. She doesn't know that in a single, fated, instinctive moment—she has *claimed* me.

My body reacts before my mind can catch up. I rip her hands away from her face. I need to see her. Need her to look at me. To know.

Her scent—her essence—clings to my skin, so rich, so thick I can still taste it on my tongue. It sinks into my fur, seeps into my flesh. I drag a hand over my face, down my jaw, gathering every drop of her release into my palm like the precious gift that it is.

She watches wide-eyed, lips parted, unaware of what she's done.

Of what I am about to do.

Still holding her gaze, I drag my soaked hand down my throat—pressing her nectar into my skin, letting it seep into me. Across my chest, over my heart, branding me. I coat myself in her, tracing it over every ridge of muscle, drowning myself in her scent.

Her breath hitches, but she does not look away. Something deep inside me shatters at the hungry way she watches me. I drag my hand down slowly, loving the way her tongue peeks out to trace over her lips as I reach lower, down my stomach, and fist my aching cock.

Hand slick with her release, I stroke myself in slow, punishing pulls, spreading her over my length, marking myself with her until there is no part of me she hasn't touched. Until I don't just smell like her, but until she is imprinted on my body just as much as she is in my soul.

She watches, and I see it. The flicker of understanding. The realization of what this is. Her cheeks burn hotter as her thighs clench together. She knows. And she wants.

The hunger in me is unbearable. I waited with barely contained restraint for her to choose me. It was an agonizing wait, but now that she has made her choice, it is done.

The thin thread of control that I have been clinging to since the first time I saw her in the mountains snaps, reverberating straight down my spine and into my cock. It bobs and strains toward her, flushing a deep purple as my desire pounds with my heartbeat. The beast within roaring that I finish this. That I lay my claim.

"My turn," I growl.

She barely has time to gasp before I tear her pants apart and sweep her up into my arms. She is weightless in my grasp. Her lips are on mine before she can even exhale, my tongue stroking deep, learning every inch of her mouth. She tastes like me now. Like *us*.

Just as winter melts the snow from the pines, she melts against me. My harbinger of Spring, my Sruhnar.

She kisses me back just as fiercely, her small, clever tongue daring to explore my teeth, my lips, my jaw. She is not timid. She is curious. Bold. Unafraid. All of our kisses before this moment seem chaste by comparison.

Something violent pulses through me. I should not love her like this. So fiercely. So recklessly. So utterly, devastatingly mine.

I do not even realize I have placed her back on her feet until I am forcing her down to her knees, pushing her where I need her the most. I have dreamed of this moment from the first time I saw her beautiful face and those lush lips. I have ached to have them wrapped around me.

The look she gives me is devastating. Head tilted back, eyes glinting in the moonlight, cheeks flushed, and lips swollen from my kiss. A goddess of ruin, kneeling before me. Her breath ghosts over my length, her lips parting as I guide her face against me.

I drag myself over her skin, rubbing my scent into her, coating her. My musk will linger in her hair, her cheeks, her throat—so that if she dares to leave this mountain, if she dares to leave me—she will forever smell like mine.

She moans, and the sound is sacrilege. I have waited, but I can wait no more. My hands tighten on her head as her tongue darts out, tasting me. I hiss as her lips part wider, as she pulls me into her mouth, hot and wet and so impossibly small. It feels better than I dreamed.

I will not fit. And yet—she tries. She worships me with her hands, her tongue, her lips. Takes as much of me as she can. Sucks and licks and strokes, her little moans vibrating up my spine, rattling my very bones.

She does not just take me into her little pink mouth. She consumes me.

I cannot breathe. I cannot think. When she chokes on just the tip, some distant part of my mind tells me I should stop her. But my beast is mindless, clawing for more, panting and snarling as I hold her still and fuck her mouth with slow, brutal thrusts.

She lets me, relaxing and breathing through her nose, taking every inch I give her. I know I cannot fit, but she tries anyway. I feel her gag again, swallow, fight for air—but her hands tighten around my thighs, pulling me deeper, as if she wants to choke on me.

The sight of it—her watering eyes, my cock stretching her lips wide, her throat working as she takes me deeper—is too much. I have dreamed of this moment for so long. The very mountain could come down and take us and still I would not, could not, stop this claiming. It is written in the very stars above us.

She moans around me, and the air thickens with the scent of her desire, like the first rain of Spring, and I lose control.

I yank myself from her mouth just as the heat explodes up my spine, her hair wound tight in one hand while the other fists my cock, painting her with my seed. I roar my release—a guttural, primal, possessive sound echoing back from the rocky mountain walls around us.

My body convulses, every muscle locking as wave after wave of pleasure spills onto her. Thick steaming ropes coat her lips, her chin, and drip down her throat to her breasts.

She gasps, blinking up at me, wide-eyed and wrecked.

I do not hesitate. I take the last of it into my palm and smooth it over her. I mark her the way she marked me. I drag a heavy hand down her chin, over the rapid pulse fluttering in her throat like a butterfly's wings. Once my hand is coated, I caress the swell of each breast, making sure to circle each rose colored nipple. Then, I rub my seed down the soft round slope of her belly and across each thick, creamy thigh.

The moonlight highlights my glistening touch, gilding her in perfection. She has never looked more beautiful. Finally, I reach up and swipe a finger across her lips, swiping up one last drop, and reach down to slip my fingers into her tight, welcoming heat one last time.

She whimpers as I press my seed deep inside her. Her body shakes and mine does, too. Because there is no going back now. She has marked me. And now I have marked her. She is not just mine. She is mine forever.

And she does not even know it yet.

CHAPTER TWENTY-TWO

DAHLIA

I eye the hot springs longingly as Eryon carries me back to his bed. My skin is sticky, and in some places, we're glued together, dried fluids tightening with every step. He doesn't seem to mind. Unlike me, he doesn't seem to be in any hurry to bathe after our mutual marking.

I insisted I could walk. He insisted harder. And truthfully—being carried in his arms, wrapped in his scent of pine and snow, his velvety skin brushing mine—is no hardship.

Eryon chuckles before tossing me onto the bed like I weigh nothing. I let out a breathless laugh, landing in a tangle of limbs and contentment in the furs. My cheeks are starting to ache from the nonstop smile he has plastered on my face.

As he stokes the fire, I watch the embers drift up with the woodsmoke and out the small hole in the very top of this particular cavern that seems to be his bedroom. I'm amazed at how comfortably he lives in such a primitive set up.

There are large hot springs for bathing and drinking. A smaller one leads out and under the wall of the cave that he explained to me was for the bathroom. A series of niches in the wall serve as storage for what few belongings he has, and there is even a pantry with baskets of food. The bed, furs piled on top of a rough wooden frame twice as large as my king bed back home, rivals the comfort of my pillowtop back home.

Once the fire crackles to life, he dumps out the bag retrieved from the man in the woods, revealing several fat silver fish. My stomach growls at the sight—I hadn't realized how much I missed eating something besides plants.

It reminds me to ask him, "Do you eat meat?"

"Rarely," he replies, arranging the fish over the flames. "I will tonight—wasting them would dishonor their lives. But I am a guardian of the forest. I take only what is necessary. And I can survive without killing those I protect."

I run my fingers through the soft furs on the bed and ask, "What about these?"

"I take the pelts of animals that have already fallen, so they may still serve a purpose. Some things are given to me as offerings."

"Like when you help people?" I ask, remembering Sita's story—how her family had been saved from freezing when the Migoi brought them firewood. Though I hadn't believed it when she told me, now I know it was true.

He throws me a half smile and admits, "When they deserve it. But my first responsibility is the earth and its creatures. Humans are pretty good at putting themselves first."

His words cause a slight twinge in my gut, and I push away the thoughts of leaving that they stir up. Instead, I get up to go sit beside him as he roasts the fish over the fire, the rich, savory scent filling the cavern. As I wait, I nibble on dried fruit and nuts, the sweetness a poor substitute for the protein my body craves.

When he hands me the steaming fish, I don't wait for it to

cool and burn my fingertips and the roof of my mouth. But it's worth it.

He chuckles, eyes warm with amusement, and passes me a waterskin. I take a grateful sip, the cool water soothing the burn.

The simple meal is delicious, but it's the company that makes it better. We talk about our lives, laughing at the stark differences. When I confess my surprise at how much he knows about the modern world, he gives me a flat look.

"I have ears," he says dryly, rolling his eyes. "I have listened to people for years, and have even seen television through people's windows. Which is the greatest waste of time I have ever witnessed. There is much I have learned over the years. Languages, stories, songs. Maybe not your ass backing up song, but others."

I laugh and try to explain the plots of some of my favorite shows and movies to him but even I have to admit, they seem inconsequential when I try to put them into words. I don't bother with trying to sing since we've both heard enough of that.

My life seems like another world entirely sitting here in the cave next to him. One that I'm not sure I want to go back to. But we can't always get what we want.

"I'll show you something worth watching," he says, tugging me away from the fire by the hand as we finish eating.

He leads me through another maze of twisting tunnels, the air growing lighter and warmer with every step. I get the sense that we are climbing both higher and deeper, ascending into the very heart of the mountain itself.

I let out an audible gasp as we emerge into an ethnobotanist's paradise. Lush greenery sprawls before me, a hidden oasis cradled within the stone. Broad-leafed plants ripple in the breeze, their silvery-green leaves catching the starlight. Thick vines drape from the cliff walls, their delicate flowers nodding like a thousand whispered secrets. The air is rich and warm, tinged with minerals and blooming life.

I tip my head back, following the sheer walls of the basin up as they stretch toward the heavens, forming a great domed ceiling. At the very top, a jagged skylight yawns open, spilling moonlight into the sanctuary below.

Stars wink and shimmer through the gap, distant and infinite, like silent watchers peering into this sacred place. I throw my arms wide and spin in a slow circle, taking in the beauty around me. A slow, wondrous smile spreads across my lips as Eryon sweeps me up and spins me, with a delighted answering smile.

Shyly he asks, "Do you like it?"

"Like it? I love it! Truly, Eryon, it's magical. What is this place?" I ask, breathless as he sets me back down on my feet.

"A sacred place," he murmurs reverently. "*I've* never brought a human here before."

His silver eyes flicker in the moonlight, searching mine as if to impress upon me the gravity of this moment. "This is the heart of the mountain."

He leads me toward the center of the alcove, where steam rises in soft, ghostly tendrils from a deep, mineral-rich pool. The water bubbles up from beneath the earth, its gentle currents lapping against carefully stacked stones.

Even in the dim glow of the stars, I can see it—the way the rocks have been fitted together by careful, deliberate hands. Not by chance but intention. A sanctuary, shaped by time and devotion.

I realize now the heat in this secret garden isn't just rising from the water; it's held captive by the towering cliff walls, caught within the embrace of stone and sky. A world preserved in warmth, untouched by the ice beyond.

The botanist in me aches to return in daylight, to study the plants that must flourish in this hidden cradle of life. The ethnobotanist in me wonders how the people of the region might have used them. Were they ever known? Gathered? Revered? Or has this place remained a secret—untouched, unseen, waiting?

I desperately want to ask if perhaps the Migoi have used them. But those questions belong to another time. Right now, the world is awash in silver and shadow, bathed in moonlight so soft it feels otherworldly and magical.

I turn back toward Eryon, my breath hitching as I find the night sky reflected in his eyes. A galaxy of light and longing.

Something takes root in my chest. A shift that has me realizing a quiet, inexorable truth. And as I watch him—watch the same feeling take shape in his gaze—I know I am no longer lost.

I try to push it down—to starve it of air, to keep it from taking root like the lush foliage around me. But love, like life, is relentless. It grows where it will, thriving in the harshest climates, in the smallest cracks of a rocky mountain. It is a force of nature beyond our control.

Yet no matter how beautiful this place is, how peaceful, how welcoming—I know I can't stay, no matter how much I want to. I cannot fall in love with a Yeti. And even if I could, if I let myself, I would still die here.

If I don't find my way back to town, if I don't finish this expedition to find this damn plant, then love, like me, will wither before it has the chance to bloom. The genetic flaw that took my mother's life in her fifties will take mine too—unless I stop it.

The *Silene vitalis* carries the precise enzyme my body lacks, the key to breaking down the proteins slowly poisoning me. I need time, maybe even years, to extract it, to perfect the delivery mechanism.

And I won't find my cure hiding away in a cave with a Yeti. Tomorrow, I'll ask him to take me back to Migdhari—before these feelings can blossom. Although I think it might already be too late.

I school my face, bury the thought deep, and let him guide me into the steaming water, my body surrendering to the inviting heat—even as my heart refuses to do the same.

The stones are smooth beneath my feet as I cautiously make my way to the built-in stone bench. He sits on it and then settles me between his legs and pulls me against his chest. Together we recline in the gentle current, watching the stars cross the sky above us.

He points out a shooting star, and I say, "You're right. I've never seen a better show than this."

His soft laugh rumbles beneath my ear. Reaching over, he plucks something from a nearby plant and lathers it between his hands.

"Oh, a soapberry!" I exclaim.

I watch, captivated. I've spent my life studying how humans use plants—for medicine, food, ceremony. But this—this is something else. An entirely different sentient species, with knowledge all its own. And I'm witnessing it firsthand.

He smiles at me as he works the lather into my hair. I groan as he massages my scalp with his strong fingers, grateful to finally be washing away the remnants of his marking. It had been intoxicating in the moment, but I was ready to be rid of the sticky, dried patches. He seemed to suffer no such qualms, happily sporting spiky clumps of fur where I had marked him.

I reach for the soapberry and step onto the bench behind him, returning the favor. As I lather the suds and work them through his thick hair and fur covered shoulders, I marvel at how his body shifts—not just with threat, but with the world around him. The heat of the spring coaxes him into something softer, his form relaxing, his edges blurring.

As I knead the tension from his neck and shoulders, I admire just how much his form can change. His skin is slick beneath my fingers where most of the fur has receded. A dusting of white remains, framing his chest, trailing down his abdomen, before thickening into a short crop at his groin.

In the dim glow of the cavern, with his body softened by warmth, I can almost imagine—almost pretend—that he could be human. That we could leave this cave, step into the world beyond these mountains, together.

But even if his size alone didn't set him apart, one look at his luminous eyes, at the sharp cut of his teeth, and the truth would be undeniable. He is not human. He never could be.

And yet, I still want him.

He melts into my touch as I massage the soap down his back until he lets out a groan and snags me with one massive hand, bringing me to stand in front of him again. Taking the soapberry back from me, he lathers it between his hands, staring into my eyes as he runs them up and down my body.

My skin flushes under his attention, the slippery glide of his fingertips lighting up my nerves as they slide up and over my breasts, then back down along the curve of my belly. With each pass he brings his hands lower until I'm spreading my legs in anticipation, desperate for him to touch my aching center.

I arch into his hands, breath catching every time he almost gives me what I need—only for him to retreat, teasing, pulling at my pebbled nipples again instead. A huff of frustration escapes me as I shift forward, trying to guide him lower, to where I really want him.

When I reach for his hands, determined to take what I need, he only chuckles and pulls me into him. His breath is warm against my ear, his voice a deep, wicked promise.

"My greedy Winter Star," he murmurs. "Let me show you again. Let me show you how much you are worth saving."

I nod, desperate to agree to anything if it means he'll touch me again.

He tugs me deeper into the pool, pulling me into the

unknown. The moon has drifted past the natural skylight, plunging us into shadow. The water, once silvered with light, now swirls black around us.

"It's dark here," I whisper shakily, the memory of the avalanche's crushing blackness pressing in.

Warm hands find my waist, grounding me. His voice is a fierce vow, a lifeline in the dark.

"It is never dark where you are," he breathes, his grip tightening. "You are the light."

The earlier feeling in my chest blooms despite my best effort to keep it from flowering. I can't stop the tendrils of love from growing, even knowing that I have to end this. Tomorrow, I'll leave. I have to. If I stay, I will lose sight of why I came. Of what I need to do to survive. But gods help me, I don't want to go. Not yet.

Just one night. One night to pretend.

"Show me. I trust you," I say with my lips. But in my heart, I whisper, *You are my light, too.*

He tows me through the deep water where my feet no longer touch the smooth stones, guiding me toward the far side, beneath a thick canopy of foliage. Lifting me effortlessly, he sets me on a broad, flat rock just below the water surface, and presses me back until I'm lying down.

Heat cradles me, the water lapping at my ribs as my head tilts back, ears dipping below the water. Sound muffles, leaving only the steady drum of my heartbeat and the hush of my breath. I float in the warmth, cut off from everything but sensation.

I tilt my head back to keep my nose and mouth just above the surface, letting the hot water cascade over my eyes and ears. The current surrounds me, caressing my arms and legs, while my breasts peek out into the air.

For a flickering second, a shadow of the avalanche presses in —the weight of the cold, the suffocating dark. I keep reminding myself I am warm, I am safe, and Eryon will protect me, yet again. The hot water erases the memory of the cold, and then Eryon's hands erase the fear.

He trickles warmth over my peaked nipples, dragging a gasp from my lips. I reposition slightly, keeping my airway just above the surface. Again and again, the water trails over my flesh, alternating with the teasing pinching and rolling of his fingers. I can't see him, can't hear him, can't anticipate his next touch—only surrender to feeling.

Then, his mouth is on me, the heat of his tongue sealing around my breast, sucking, nipping, drawing sharp moans from my throat. My thighs part instinctively, my body aching and restless at the unbearable teasing. My hands scrabble at the smooth rock, desperate for more.

Then nothing but silence. Stillness.

A ripple brushes my skin. The slightest shift of water. But before I can react—a hot, wet tongue flicks over my clit, stealing the breath from my lungs.

I jolt, my gasp echoing in my head with my ears still submerged. There's no warning, no build-up—just the shock of pleasure, white-hot and all-consuming.

Eryon doesn't give me time to recover. He licks deeper, his tongue gliding down, circling my entrance, teasing before retreating. I writhe, chasing his mouth, but strong hands grip my hips, pinning me in place. Over and over, he alternates, lashing my clit with his tongue and teasing my pussy.

Just as I think I'll go mad, one large finger thrusts into me, and my breaths turn to pants as he expertly licks me, tongue circling while he drives his finger in and out of my core. But it's still not enough.

"More," I plead, barely able to form the word.

He laughs against me, the deep vibration rolling through my belly. A second finger joins the first, stretching me, filling me, pressing against that devastating spot inside. I cry out, my body tightening around him, pulling him deeper. When another finger probes my ass, I know I am going to drown, albeit a very happy woman.

I cry out, my hips jerking against him, but the pleasure stays just on the right side of overwhelming. I'm too wet, too slick, my body yielding to him, taking everything he gives.

The pressure builds higher, sharper. My breath shudders. I can barely keep my mouth and nose above the water as I thrash against the pleasure swallowing me whole. My hips remain pinned, and I can only take the assault of pleasure.

And then—his tongue pushes inside. I choke on a moan. My back arches. The stretch is exquisite, his tongue working alongside his fingers, stroking, tasting, consuming me. The thick muscle is a delicious counterpoint to his questing fingers.

His thumb finds my clit and rubs slow, firm circles that send sparks shooting up my spine. The whole world disappears to coalesce in this one singular focus.

He pushes hard against my clit, and pleasure detonates through me, violent and endless. I convulse, writhing against him as I shatter, the orgasm slamming into me like a tidal wave, pulling me under.

The water surges over my head, muffling everything but the relentless storm of sensation between my legs. Sight, sound, hell even breathing—none of it matters. Nothing exists beyond the liquid heat of his mouth, the deep, aching pull of his fingers, the consuming pleasure crackling through every nerve.

It builds, higher, tighter, curling in on itself like a supernova ready to detonate. My body is no longer my own—it belongs to this feeling, to him, to the unstoppable force unraveling me from the inside out.

My lungs are bursting, stars dance in my vision, and I don't want to come up for air because this is the best damn orgasm, the best damn *anything*, I've ever had in my life. My limbs are getting heavy, and at any second, I am going to drown. To surrender. But this will have been worth it. I drift in relaxed bliss and open my eyes, noting from somewhere far away how the stars ripple and shimmer from below the water's surface.

Eryon yanks me up out of the water just as I inhale, saving me from choking. Sweet air fills my lungs and, with it, frantic need. I don't just want him. I fucking need him. If I am his light, he is my very breath.

Still trembling, still drunk on the aftershocks, I launch myself at him, surprising us both. But he catches me, he *always* catches me, his heat searing against my water-slicked skin.

I don't want to think. I don't want to fight this. I only want him. The warmth of his hands, the fire of his mouth, the promise of his body sealing me to the earth. I press against him, breathless, desperate.

"Eryon, I need you," I pant out between frantic kisses.

CHAPTER TWENTY-THREE

ERYON

Her words wreck me. Not because she is begging—but because she says my name. In hunger. In worship. It falls from her beautiful lips in her soft, reverent voice. She does not call me a monster. She does not call me Migoi.

She calls me Eryon.

I did not know how much I needed to hear it. Not until now. Not until it leaves her lips, soft and desperate and pleading—curling into my chest like a living thing.

I snap.

She barely has time to gasp before I crush my mouth to hers, dragging her on top of me, shielding her from the stone. Her lips are swollen and delicious, and I drink the remnants of her moans like I'm drowning.

She has no idea what she does to me.

I take her mouth the way I will take her body—without hesitation, without mercy, without regret. I chase every retreat of her tongue, swallow every tiny sound, scrape the sharp edge of my teeth along her soft, bruised lip just to taste the copper bloom of her life force to bring us that much closer.

She wants this. She needs this. She *chooses* me.

And I will give her everything.

I break the kiss to snag a leaf from the shoreline, crushing it in my hand, reaching between us to coat my cock with its slick gel until I glisten under the night stars. I hold my hand out to her in invitation, giving her one last chance.

She places her small hand in mine, and I draw her closer, guiding her hips to straddle me, notching my head at her entrance. She should not want this. She should not want me. And yet—here she is. Here she stays.

The knowledge sends a sharp pulse of heat through my veins.

She braces her small hands on my shoulders, and I steady my cock at her entrance. Her eyes meet mine, and I marvel at her bravery as she takes just the tip. Guarded yet determined. As I slowly slip into her body with the plant paving the way, her eyes widen in surprise.

Her mouth drops open as she guides herself down slowly, inch by inch—glorious, excruciating—as I smooth more of the gel that will ease her way between us. Even with its help, the tight vise of her channel can barely contain me.

I hold myself back, every muscle shaking with the effort of letting her take her time, shifting her hips to accommodate my size takes effort even with the help of the plant.

"Eryon," she breathes, "I'm not sure I can."

I swallow her fear with a kiss, reassure her with my lips while my hands come up to tease her beautiful breasts. I want to thrust up and sheathe myself within my mate, but I let her slowly take me. Retreating and then claiming ground by fractions.

I marvel at the way our flesh blends together, until it feels like we are no longer two separate beings but one. The sight alone threatens to tear me apart. And then the way she looks at me—wild and unashamed, a woman claiming her own desire—has my restraint ready to shatter.

I grip her hips, my fingers spanning her waist, holding her steady. She is so small, so impossibly soft, and yet she takes me with a ferocity that threatens my razor-thin control.

"Look at you, opening for me like the beautiful flower you are," I murmur, voice thick with awe, dragging my lips over her jaw as she circles her hips, desperately trying to take me.

I feel a gush of her arousal with my words so continue. "I knew your body would yield to mine, Sruhnar. You are radiant. A gift from the divine. You are meant for me."

She gasps, her lashes fluttering, and I feel her clench around me like a vice as I push ever deeper into her. A low growl rumbles from my chest as I sink deeper into her heat.

"You pull me in like you were made for me, like we were made for each other," I snarl against her throat, nipping just enough to mark. "The way you take me—so eager, so fierce—gods, you'll wring every drop from me."

Her nails sink into my shoulders as I roll my hips, grinding into her, burying myself ever deeper. The small breathy moans that fall from her lips are the sweetest music to my ears. I want to hear every note.

I do not withdraw, do not retreat, my only salvation lies in moving forward, claiming her more fully until I am completely seated. I cannot stop now. There is no force on this earth that could make me. I thrust into her, steady and merciless, letting her feel every inch, every stretch, every claim.

"You want this," I rasp, biting down where her pulse hammers in her throat. "To be filled, to be claimed, to be taken so deep I ruin you. You can run, but your body knows the truth. Your soul knows the truth—you are meant to take me, to hold me. I will fill you, again and again, until you cannot think of anything but the way I mark you from the inside out, branding my claim on you."

I thrust up, gaining precious ground. Another pulse of her pleasure leaks down over me as I grunt out, "Inside you."

She trembles in my arms, her breathless moans only spurring me on. Every word that falls from my lips, every declaration of my claim driving her higher.

I pull her closer, feeling her heat, her wetness, the way her body clenches around me. My voice is low, guttural, barely human as I lose myself to her. "Or shall I paint you in my seed again, let you wear me, let you feel what it is to be mine?"

She moans my name, her hips rolling against me, desperate, pleading as she rides the waves of pleasure.

Her head drops back between her shoulders, putting the round globes of her divine breasts on display. I fasten my mouth to one, devouring it, sucking the whole delicious mound into my mouth. I release it with a pop and tease the other side and feel her sink down another inch.

I slide one hand from her hip, back over the perfect swell of her ass and run my finger down the cleft, finding the spot that makes her skin redden.

"Do you want me to claim all of you?" I tease with my words and my finger.

"Yes," she whimpers. "Eryon, please. Fill me up. I need it. I want it."

Her words are my undoing. Her desire for me, my name falling from those lips. I lose all restraint, all finesse. Instinct takes over. I am not thinking anymore—only feeling, consuming, penetrating. A surge of precum fills her tight channel, and I must have more of her.

I flip her onto her back, hauling her to the water's edge, caging her beneath me, locking her to the earth itself. She is so small, so perfect, and so completely mine.

I brace myself over her, watching as she unravels beneath

me. I sink into her—deep, unyielding—until there is nothing left between us, until I am buried in her heat. Then, I begin to move. A punishing rhythm. A relentless claiming.

Every thrust *carves* me into her, binding her to me. I *watch* it happen—the way her body clenches around me, taking me deeper, accepting all of me.

"Sruhnar," I growl, feeling the heat coil tight in my core, the unstoppable pull of release. The feel of her, the vision of our joining spiraling my pleasure out of control. "You are wringing me dry. Take what you need—let me feel it, let me drown in you. Now."

My command is a desperate plea. She obeys and finally, *finally*, I am fully inside of her. I can't help but look down, marveling at where we are joined. I note in rapt fascination how each time I pull out to the very tip and then drive myself home, the rounded curve of her belly swells.

Her entire body tenses beneath me, her legs locking around my waist, her fingers clawing at my back as she comes undone. Her core clenches at me, milking me, stripping away all restraint, all control. Freeing the beast that scrabbles at my skin just to be nearer to her.

Her heartbeat thunders in my ears, echoes through the chambers of my own heart until it reverberates through my marrow.

Mine, it whispers into every shadowy corner of my soul. *Mine*.

The moment she breaks, I lose myself. A snarl rips from my throat as I thrust deep, burying myself to the hilt, filling her, marking her, binding her to me.

Pleasure detonates, raw and relentless, splitting me open like a fault line in the earth. Heat and pressure coil tight, then release in a rush, flooding her, claiming her. She clenches around me, her body milking every pulse, wringing me dry, dragging me under until there is nothing but sensation— nothing but her.

She shudders, whispering my name like it belongs to her.

And perhaps—it does.

As I hold her, panting, trembling, filled with me, I know this was no ordinary joining. This was not just pleasure, not just need. This was devotion.

I tip her chin up, forcing her to meet my gaze. I need her to see what I already know—that she is mine. That she has always been mine. That she will always be mine.

But in her eyes, I see something else—something dangerous. It *guts* me.

She is already leaving me—if not now, then soon. The sadness of goodbye dances behind her eyes even as her heart pounds and she labors to catch her breath.

And for the first time since I pulled her from the snow, I feel something I cannot fight, cannot conquer.

Fear.

Because if she walks away from me, I do not know if I will have the strength to let her go.

Chapter Twenty-Four

Dahlia

Eryon pulls me close and sinks us back into the hot spring. The warmth of the pool washes over us as the sky above begins to blush with the first hues of dawn, dappled light filtering down to paint the scene in soft golds and pinks. His heartbeat thumps beneath my ear as I rest against his chest, and for a moment, I wonder if this is what paradise feels like.

My jaw-cracking yawn breaks the peaceful silence, pulling a laugh from both of us as he mirrors mine with one of his own. I promised myself today would be the day I leave, but the pull of this place—and the weight of my exhaustion—make it impossible to go just yet. First, I need sleep or I can't possibly hike away from here and continue my search.

And I don't know how I'm going to explain to Eryon that I need to go. Especially after this time together. My heart is trying to dig in its heels and keep me here, but my mind, and my will to survive, insist that I go. There is no choice.

As he scoops me up bridal-style, ignoring my usual insistence that I can walk, I can't help but take in the local flora, now painted with the soft hues of the breaking dawn. The early light slowly reveals the amazing colors around me, erasing the muted greys of night.

Yellows and peaches and corals compete with reds and oranges and a thousand shades of greens. Even blues and whites emerge in the morning sun, speckled with dew. All the colors of the rainbow are here in this amazing flora.

My gaze catches on the plants clustered near the head of the spring, their delicate leaves and flowers struck by an errant ray of dawn light filtering down through the trees above. Something about them tugs at my memory, and a frown creases my brow as my sex-addled brain tries to figure out why this plant seems so familiar.

The heart-shaped leaves, the compact growth, the star-shaped flowers nodding gently on their delicate stems—petals the exact violet-blue of my unusual eye color passed down to me by my mother.

My breath catches as my heart beats out a staccato rhythm. The realization strikes with the force of an avalanche. My lips part, but no sound follows. There are no words when my thoughts are spiraling, frantically clawing at something impossible—something that can't be.

Silene vitalis.

The name blooms in my mind, unbidden and impossible. I want to scream at him to stop so I can share this amazing discovery, but in my state of shock, it's all I can do to weakly pat his arm in protest. He walks on, up and out of the water, passing by the plant without a second glance—while I am left grappling with the impossible truth it holds.

I have spent months searching for this. Weeks trekking through these mountains. I nearly died in a fucking avalanche. And it's here. It's been right *here* the whole time. I twist in Eryon's grip, struggling to free myself, desperate to touch it—to prove it's not a dream.

"Eryon, stop," I force out through the lump in my throat, wriggling free and sliding to the ground.

Racing over to the plant, I collapse to my knees. My hands move without thought, reverently tracing the heart-shaped leaves, the velvet-soft petals with shaking fingers. The key to everything I've searched for lies right here, within my reach. I never would have found it tucked away in this specialized micro-climate. Never.

"Sruhnar," he calls sharply.

As if calling to me from a great distance, Eryon's voice breaks through my excitement, its sharp tone a strange juxtaposition to the elation coursing through my body.

My heart stutters as his shadow falls over me, stretching long in the morning light, and suddenly, the weight of his presence feels immense. Something is wrong. I can sense it.

I snap my head around, and my stomach clenches.

He isn't moving. He isn't blinking. He simply stands there—still, silent, as unreadable as the mountain we stand on.

The air thickens, so charged it crackles like a coming storm. But I'm too caught up in my discovery to understand what's wrong. What could possibly be wrong in a moment like this when all hope has been restored?

I'm already explaining, the words pouring out in a rush. Already assuming he'll understand.

"Eryon, this is the plant I was looking for." My voice cracks, a mixture of disbelief and relief flooding me. "This is the entire reason I came to the mountains."

He still doesn't move. Doesn't smile, doesn't acknowledge the biggest discovery of my lifetime. The discovery of my life itself. My excitement falters but doesn't die. The cognitive dissonance is too much to process.

"I was going to have to leave to find it, but it's been right here the whole time." I swallow hard, still shaking, still breathless. "I'll need to take it with me."

The words feel huge, as if speaking them aloud makes it real. Frustration gnaws at me as I think over the supplies I lack. Without my pack, I don't have what I need to preserve and transport the plant properly.

I launch into a rush of problem-solving, speaking more to myself than him.

"I'll have to extract it here. I need something sterile—a way to store it without breaking down the enzymes. It might be heat-sensitive, so I'll have to find a way to cool it—maybe wrap it in damp moss. Then I'll need to leave quickly, get back to Migdhari and my supplies."

I spin toward Eryon, reaching blindly, my hands brushing his chest, seeking his help and understanding.

"Eryon, do you know if there's more of it? If the population is stable? If there's enough, I might be able to—"

"No," he says flatly, his tone leaving no room for argument.

The word is devoid of all feeling like his eyes, the swirling silver mystical luminesce gone and replaced by the flat leaded grey of threatening storm clouds. Unyielding like the tense muscles under my hands.

I blink up at him, unable to process his words. "No? What do you mean, no?"

He still doesn't move. He doesn't even blink. He repeats, his voice as cold as the North winds blowing down the mountain, "No."

A tight knot forms in my stomach, frustration spiking. I know he will support me, be happy for me, he just doesn't understand yet, that's all. I need to explain it better.

"Eryon, I don't think you understand. This plant—it's everything. It's not just another discovery, not just some academic pursuit. This could save lives." My voice pitches higher, more frantic. "It could save my life."

Nothing.

The silence feels like a wall, thick and unmoving. As suffocating as being trapped under that damn snow and just as hopeless. Just as lethal.

"I have a genetic disorder," I rush on, my words tumbling over each other. Overexplaining in an effort to get him to understand. "A change, a defect in how I'm made. My body is missing an enzyme, a special chemical. My mother died from it in her fifties. I—" My throat tightens. As soon as he hears this part, he'll understand. He has to. "I won't make it past that unless I find a cure. And this plant—Eryon, this plant is the key. Please."

I grab his hands. He doesn't shake me off. And for a single agonizing moment, I think that maybe I've gotten through to him. I wait the span of a heartbeat. Then two. Three.

But he doesn't soften. He just stares down at me. Unmoving. Unflinching. Unyielding.

Raw, visceral pain flares in my chest as hope withers like the last bloom of summer.

"Eryon." I whisper his name, pleading. "Please, just let me take a few. I swear I won't take them all. I'll only take what I need. You don't have to help me—I'll do it myself. I just—I need it."

I squeeze his large fingers, and for the first time, his skin doesn't blaze with its usual heat. It's ice-cold just like the light in his eyes.

His hands flex beneath my grip, so tight they shake with the effort. His throat bobs, a slow, deliberate swallow audible in the heavy silence between us. His fingers twitch—as if, for the briefest second, he wants to reach for me.

He closes his eyes as if he can't bear to see my face as he gives his final answer, "No."

I flinch as if he'd struck me, my hands slipping off of his. The sound isn't loud. It isn't cruel. It's just final. A cold and quiet whisper of death. A fatal blow, in the most literal sense of the word.

Chapter Twenty-Five

Eryon

She pleads with me, but I cannot hear her over the slow, splintering crack of my frozen heart. The weight of her words settles like fresh snowfall—soft, quiet, deceptive. She does not know it, but she is now the avalanche. A tremor in the ice, a whisper of movement before the mountain gives way. And I can feel it coming—the collapse, the ruin, the moment there will be nothing left of me but the wreckage.

Her voice cracks, breathless and desperate. Her hands clutch at mine. I look down at them against my own as if seeing them for the first time. They are too small, too fragile. They are human. Her warmth presses against me, but I do not let it in. I cannot. I was foolish to allow her past my defenses, to allow hope and love to thaw my icy solitude.

She is the one who does not understand.

"This plant has already cost lives." My voice is steady, but the ground beneath me is not. The whole word feels unstable, the eternal foundation of these mountains beneath my feet reduced to quicksand. "Nothing can leave this basin. I am its protector, and I will not allow humans to destroy my family, my home, or the balance of this sacred place again."

She stumbles under the weight of my confession. "Eryon, I thought you said you'd never brought a human here. What do you mean, 'destroy your family again'?"

Despair and anger flavor the air, turning the usually sweet scent of her and this sacred place bitter on my palate. The morning sun hides its face behind a cloud, casting my world back into a grey shadowy landscape to match my heart.

I do not wish to speak of it. I've never told the tale, never shared this grief. I thought I was honoring my family by locking them in my heart. I thought—I thought she was the next chapter in my story.

But she was always going to leave. She never meant to claim me. She never felt anything for me. Just used me to get to this plant. Another human, leaving a trail of devastation in their wake.

I exhale, slow and deep, willing my rage to still. But it does not. Cannot. It grows and builds, pushing against my skin, clawing at my throat, shredding my heart.

She flinches as my form grows, as I let my presence swell, towering over her, forcing her to feel the weight of what she is asking. The weight of what she is undoing.

She does not know that I am already hers. That I have already chosen her. That I have already been claimed by a small human who is fierce and brave. Who has eyes the color of the cursed plant that has both blessed and plagued my existence.

I tear my gaze from hers and begin to pace, letting the fury escape through me, letting it spill out into my powerful movements.

"Humans," I snarl, low and menacing, "take and destroy, leaving nothing but devastation in their wake." My blood hums, restless, my muscles tight with the urge to move, to rage, to stop this before it is too late.

"Everywhere I walk in the forest, I see it. Plastic water bottles choking the rivers. The sky, suffocating with pollution. The ancients of the forest, sentinels of time, razed for roads and houses that will never be enough. And the creatures who once roamed freely? Slaughtered for a few bites of meat, the rest of their bodies discarded as if their sacrifice meant nothing."

As if I meant nothing. My sacrifice meant nothing, my heart cries.

I do not look at her. If I do, I will see her eyes, wide and searching, trying to understand. I do not wish to be understood. I wish to be heard. Obeyed. Feared even. Anything would be better than this emotion that scrabbles at the inside of my chest like a caged beast.

"Humans believe they have dominion over the earth and exercise their right to take and take without giving anything back, no matter the cost. I've witnessed their greed and devastation right here in this very spot. No, *I* didn't bring a human here to this sacred place."

She does not speak, but I hear the breath she holds, waiting for my next words.

"But my mate did. She brought a human here for that same flower. She was kind, always trying to help. Too trusting. He befriended her, gained her trust over time. The human told her he just needed one. *Just one.* Pleaded for it, like you do now. Do you know how he repaid her trust? Do you know?"

A roar shreds its way out of my throat, echoing in the oasis I've shared with my Winter Star. The mountains shudder beneath my anger, and she trembles like the plants around us, but holds her ground, waiting for my words to strike.

"He took it. Not just one, but every single one he could find. She begged him not to, tried to explain that we needed it for our little Snowling, who had fallen ill after his first visit. We didn't realize, until it was too late, that a simple human sneeze would cost us his life."

I draw in a ragged breath, wanting to stop the torrent of words but unable to now that the floodgates have been opened on my pain. "Yes, the winter star can save lives—ours and maybe yours. But it's also taken them, and I'm not willing to sacrifice any more for this plant."

I grant her no mercy. I gut her like I am gutted. Hurt her like I am hurting. "Or for a human."

She inhales sharply. *Good.* Let her feel it. Let her *see* the past as I do, etched into the marrow of my bones. Carved from my heart itself.

I do not tell her that I can still see my mate's hands, frantically searching the earth for a single flower to save our child, her wails of despair echoing in the valley, the caves, the basin, my mind.

I do not tell her that I still feel the small weight of a snowling in my arms, light as snowfall, heavy as grief. I do not tell her how small he was. How fragile. How he had fit perfectly against my chest, tucked beneath my chin, his fur the color of the first snowfall. Or the way his tiny fist would wrap in my hair.

I do not tell her how my mate had withered. How she had stopped eating, stopped speaking, stopped living. She could not survive the loss of the snowling. And so, the mountain took her, too.

For a long time, I wished it had taken me, too. But I was not granted the mercy of death. Instead, I found one last winter star buried in the soil. A shriveled, dying thing. A single, withered root of the damned plant. We were kindred spirits. It should not have survived and neither should I.

But I made it live just as I did. For decades, I tended to it. Fed it, coaxed it, willed it into bloom. Hand pollinating it with loving care. It became my only purpose. My only reason for existing.

Until Dahlia blew into my life like the first breath of spring. I knew her eye color, the exact shade of its petals, was no coincidence. I knew it had given me her. Just as I had known it was too good to be true that after all of this time I would have a mate again. Maybe I had recognized all along that this was the plant she had been searching for.

And now, this damned plant that brought her to me is taking her away, too.

Her voice breaks through the storm raging in my skull.

"Eryon, I'm so sorry for your family. I'm sorry about what humans have done and still do. For all the destruction we cause. I can see now how much damage we've done, and it breaks my heart. But you don't understand—" She breaks off to clear her throat, dashing the tears from her eyes.

"I *need* this plant. I'm not just here for myself, for research. This isn't about taking or destroying—it's about survival. My life is at stake. Without the *Silene vitalis*, I won't make it. I know it's hard to trust humans, and I understand why you'd want to protect this place, this plant. But please, don't let my desperation make you think I'm like the ones who've hurt you."

Need.

Need.

She speaks of need as if she knows what it is to lose everything. She does not understand that I am already hers. I would give her my breath, my blood, my very soul. I would die before I let her slip away.

And yet she is asking me to give her the one thing I cannot.

"It took me decades to save this plant. The only thing that kept me going—the only thing that gave me hope—was the possibility of someday having another snowling. I did this for them. For my family. For my future. And now—" The words bring me to my knees, staggered by the weight of my grief. All I have lost; all I am losing. The plant is taking its toll again. But I cannot betray the ghosts that haunt me.

"Maybe you can still have a family, a snowling. I hope that for you, Eryon, I do. Not to replace the one you lost, but because I can see how important it is to you. I would never take all the plants. I would never try to hurt you."

But she already has. She is choosing the plant over *me*. She said it was the only thing that had brought her to my mountain. I am not enough to keep her. I am not enough. I was not then, and I am not now.

"I haven't seen another of my kind in centuries. I don't deserve another family. And I was foolish to think I would ever have another mate. But I am the sworn protector of this place, of the forest. And I will not allow you to destroy all I have left," I say, my voice sounding as old as my years.

The sun dares to show its face. Mocking. I make the mistake of meeting her eyes again. The violet-blue pulses more vividly through the tears clinging to her lashes, reflecting the sunlight back to me as if to remind me that she is my light.

Her chin quivers. What a small frail thing. What a beautiful thing. And now, I must make her go. Attempt to save my shattered heart, attempt to survive heartbreak again.

"Leave," I growl.

She stiffens. "Leave?"

I bare my teeth in the need to make this easier for me because I am one second away from complete annihilation. "*This plant* is the only reason you came here," I spit her own words back at her. "You are no different than those that came before you. You want to take it for yourself, and damn the consequences."

Another lie, my mind says. But my heart, it knows. My soul *knows*. She is different. She is mine. But the biting words come anyway. A torrent of pain once unleashed, unable to be damned.

"Leave me here with my ghosts. The world is vast, but this corner is mine. Go find something else. I won't be used, not again." I rip my eyes away and stare into the bright morning light, marvelling that the sun has not fallen from the sky and that the world still spins.

And when she goes—I let her.

Even as I shatter.

CHAPTER TWENTY-SIX

DAHLIA

The weight of his words crushes me, pressing down with the same force that buried me beneath the avalanche. Only this time, no one is coming to save me.

I always thought that finding the *Silene vitalis* would mean salvation, that I would leave these mountains victorious, my hands full of something precious, something powerful enough to change my future. Dreamed that, at the end of this journey, my heart would be bursting with triumph, with possibility. Instead, I am leaving with nothing. No plant. No cure. No Eryon.

Nothing. Again.

A black vortex of grief opens inside me, swallowing every-thing—hope, purpose, even reason. I thought this place, these stolen moments, was paradise, but now I see it for what it truly was. Just another dead-end, another dream slipping through my fingers.

Had I ever really had a chance? Or had I been clinging to a fantasy that was never meant to come true?

The thought chills me deeper than the cave air. I have spent my entire life searching for knowledge, chasing meaning, convinced that I was building something greater than myself.

Do the research. Find the plant. Ensure my survival.

I thought it would be simple. I thought all I had to do was follow the thread of science, of truth, of the one thing I had always believed in. The one thing that, no matter what else had failed me, was my true north.

But standing here, gutted and empty, I wonder—what is the value of a life, human or otherwise? Would it have been right to take what I needed, even if it cost him everything? Would I have done it anyway if given the chance? Am I any better than the man who betrayed him before?

After all, I had been planning to leave him despite knowing that we had forged some type of bond. But would I have left if he hadn't forced me? Or had some part of me already belonged to him from the moment he saved me?

The weight of the questions has me staggering, trailing a hand against the stone wall to guide my exit through the dark tunnel. My fingers drag over the rough, damp rock as I force my feet forward. The cold leeches into my skin, but I barely feel it. My mind is too tangled with everything I wish I could take back.

My fingertips catch on an uneven ridge of stone, and something about the texture stops me. Not the slick dampness of the cave walls, but something smoother.

Paint.

Although I can't make them out in the dim lighting, there are more cave drawings here. I remember when I discovered the others—tracing the ochre shapes with my fingers, marveling at the figures—how they faded and dwindled until only two remained. The last of their kind, drawn together, standing over something small, nestled between them.

A child. A family.

I looked at those paintings with the fascination of a scientist, an observer, a researcher standing at the edge of someone else's story. I thought them beautiful, thought them historical—proof of something that once was.

But now, I see them for what they truly are.

Not history, but his life. Eryon's life. It was the weight he carried in his bones, the story of everything he lost. And I stood before it like it was an exhibit in a museum, admiring it with detached curiosity, unable to understand that I was staring at his grief carved into stone.

I press my forehead against the cool rock, my breath shallow, wondering if I had ever understood him at all. When had I ever understood anyone?

Certainly not Ben, until it was too late. I can hear his voice echoing in my mind, the way he called me *Dolly* even though I hated that nickname. The way he doubted my abilities, my hopes, my dreams. He told me more than once that I put too much value on the *ethno-* aspect of ethnobotany. Encouraged me to ground myself in the science of just the plants and drop the humanity.

Maybe he was right.

Because everything that came with this plant—the loss, the lies, the culture surrounding it—had ruined lives. It was better when it was nothing but a specimen, a chemical, run through the mass spectrometer. It was better as a dream.

I had let myself believe in something that was never mine to have. I let myself believe in Eryon. And for what? To be thrown away like I never meant anything?

I swallow hard, pushing past the painful lump in my throat. Maybe I don't know how to separate passion from purpose. Maybe I don't know how to tell the difference between reality and dreams. After all, I thought I was falling in love with a Yeti. But maybe I was just falling for a fantasy.

Maybe *I* am the one who is broken.

By the time I stumble into the sleeping cave, lost in my own grief, my body is numb, mental exhaustion weighing me down like lead. Heartache blooms in my throat like a noxious weed, choking, suffocating.

I don't know what to do. I don't know where to go.

I sink down next to the fire, staring into the embers as if the answer lies in their dying light. But there is no answer. Just the quiet, steady glow of something already lost.

Like me.

The faint rustle behind me should pull my attention, but I can't find the strength to turn my head until heavy footsteps announce his arrival. I drag my gaze to find him, standing there. Hope flickers in my chest for a single, aching second. He's back. He understands. He—

He doesn't look at me. Doesn't say a word. Just disappears into the cave's shadows, returning a few minutes later with my pack. I had no idea he rescued it along with me. He drops it at my feet.

In a clipped, emotionless voice, he says, "Get dressed."

I blink, my brain still struggling to catch up to the change in our relationship, uncomprehending. But then my fingers move, automatic, reaching for the clothes I abandoned days ago as my nakedness no longer seems natural, but a vulnerability.

They feel strange in my hands. The fabric is stiff and unfamiliar, too civilized after days wrapped in nothing but Eryon's heat, his scent, his touch.

I pull on my pants. Tie my boots. And with every motion, I feel it happening—my wildness bleeding away until I am human again. And I hate it.

I *fucking* hate it.

Eryon doesn't wait for me to shoulder my pack. He grabs it from the ground, slinging it over his shoulder as if it weighs nothing, then turns and walks away, leaving me no choice but to follow.

I zip up my jacket and stumble after him woodenly, each booted step echoing through the tunnels. Too loud. Too unnatural. My toes feel strange at the lost contact of the earth. Just another layer of constraint creeping back in.

By the time we emerge from the tunnels, daylight sears my vision, the brightness a cruel contrast to the darkness I carry inside me. The sunlight stabs at my eyes, making them water, or maybe that's just another wave of tears.

I blink them away and follow Eryon's broad back through the deep snow, my steps clumsy compared to his. I try to walk in his footsteps, but his stride is too long for me to match. The cold presses against my skin, sinking into my bones. I feel so much smaller without him, as if his affection had me bigger than, somehow more than, Dahlia. He made me Sruhnar.

He doesn't speak. Doesn't turn back. But he waits when I stumble and lag behind, standing still as the mountains themselves until I catch up. And then he moves again.

It is not kindness or affection, but his duty to protect. As if I were no more than a rabbit under his watch. That realization breaks something deep inside me. My knees buckle, exhaustion both physical and mental, finally dragging me under. I make no effort to stand again on my shaking legs. My breath saws in and out of my lungs, and I simply sit there, slumped, curling in on myself like a frozen shell of who I was just hours ago.

Eryon does not leave me, of course. A strange, fallen knight cloaked in white fur instead of armor, comes to gather what's left of me from where I kneel in the snow. He takes me into his arms, strong and unyielding, lifting me as if I weigh nothing at all.

But this time, I do not sink into him. This time, I keep my hands to myself, my body stiff against his. I ignore the crisp scent of snow and pine that threatens to envelop me, and I force away the memory of the first time he carried me. Refuse to remember how safe I felt in his arms.

Because this time, he is not saving me.

This time, he is carrying me to my death.

Chapter Twenty-Seven

At some point I must have dozed off, because suddenly the air is warmer, and the forest is changing. I can feel it thinning around us, and the daylight is fading again. In the place between awake and asleep, I nuzzle into Eryon's arms until I remember why we are here and jerk my face away from him, stiffening. He must have carried me for hours while I hid from sorrow in sleep.

I hear the rushing of the river as he sets me down on my feet and steps back, giving me the space I wanted so desperately just a moment ago. Instead of relief, the desperate urge to reach for him floods me, my fists clenching with the effort of keeping my arms at my sides.

He stands in the shadows of the trees, all but an invisible part of the landscape, as if he really is made of stone and ice. But I know that he is scorching heat. He is safety in the storm, comfort in the dark. He is my light, too. And damn me, but I should have told him. I should have told him everything.

I tear my gaze from him and look towards the water to see if

I can figure out where we are, and when I turn back to Eryon—he's gone. Disappeared back into the woods he protects with only my backpack sitting on the ground to mark where he had been.

No goodbye. Not even a fuck off.

I swallow against the raw ache clawing at my throat. Was he even real? Or did I simply conjure him from frost and fever, a snow dream woven from ice and longing? But the pain gripping my heart and soreness between my legs are visceral reminders of just how real he is.

I follow the sound of the river, blinking back more tears. I'm not sure how I have any left. The wind whips through the valley, sharp against my skin, and I drag my pack more securely over my shoulders before gripping the rope railing of the precarious bridge to cross the river.

The old Dahlia would have hesitated. Would have feared the height, the raging water below. But I have nothing left to fear. Death is already hunting me, and it's not the river that will take me.

The bridge sways beneath my feet, but I press forward, climbing the hill on the other side until I reach the edge of town. The tiny mountain village is half-buried in snow, eerily quiet in the dead of winter. There are no pilgrims here now, no bustling voices or temple bells. Just the muffled stillness of the cold and the pale wash of twilight, softening the hard edges of the world.

My breath puffs out in little clouds as I push onward, my boots crunching through the icy slush. A cold gust pushes me back towards Eryon, but it would take more than the North winds to bring us back together. I lean into it and head towards the familiar guest house that I spot just ahead. As if Eryon knew exactly where to bring me back to.

I almost collapse with relief at the sight of home. Or at least, as close to one as I have right now.

I trudge up the stone path, my body aching, my hands numb as I fumble for the key tucked in the side pocket of my pack. I half-expect the door to be locked with someone else inside, my room long given away in the time I've been gone. How many days did I hide away from the world?

When the key slides in and turns easily, something in me uncoils. Inside, everything is just as I left it. The bed. The thick quilt thrown back in a hurry. The small desk covered in my notes.

I long to crawl beneath the blankets and disappear into sleep. Just let oblivion take me. But I owe it to Sita and Tenzig to check in, let them know I made it back safely, and ensure Sita did the same. With a final reluctant glance at the bed, I close the door behind me and head to the lobby to find my friends.

The fire is burning strong when I step inside, the scent of incense thick in the air. I rush toward the warmth, holding my hands out, the tingling sensation returning to my frozen fingers as the heat seeps into my skin.

The sounds of a door creaking has me turning just in time to brace myself before Sita barrels into me, nearly knocking me over. She wraps her arms around me, crushing me in a warm hug. My throat tightens and tears sting my eyes as the urge to unburden my soul overwhelms me.

I step back and shove my feelings down deep because if I start crying again, I'll never stop. And Eryon's secrets are not mine to tell. My lips clamp down hard in an effort to hold the words that threaten to overflow at bay.

Sita grips my shoulders, eyes wide as she studies me like I might disappear again. "*Hai Migaia*, I can't believe you're alive! We looked for days, but we had given up hope of finding you!"

Guilt crashes over me in a sickening wave. They searched for me. They thought I was dead. And while they were combing the mountains, fearing the worst, I was—with him. Heat floods my cheeks, but I welcome the warmth when my whole existence feels frozen.

"I'm so sorry, Sita. I can't imagine what that must have been like. But I'm so happy you made it back okay," I say.

Tenzig appears, carrying a steaming mug of chai. He hands it to me with a smile before settling into a chair beside the fire.

I cup the mug, letting the heat seep into my palms, and take a careful sip. The sweet, spiced tea should be delicious, but it tastes like ash. I've come full circle over this drink, from first sighting to final goodbye. I set it down, suddenly unable to take another sip.

Sita sits across from me, still watching me like she's afraid I might disappear again. "How did you survive?"

I swallow hard, carefully crafting my answer. "I was able to dig myself out of the avalanche and find shelter in a cave."

Technically not a lie. Just an omission of everything that came after.

Sita shakes her head in disbelief. "I know you'll find your plant now. The gods have surely smiled upon you."

Her words twist like a knife in my chest. I did find the plant, only to lose it again. But instead of voicing my heartbreak aloud, I force a tight smile and say, "I don't know that the price is worth it anymore."

She leans forward, her brows knitting together. "What do you mean? You must find it! You'll die without it, Dahlia. Your life is worth any price. And not just yours—this could help others, too."

I place a hand on her arm, my voice soft but firm as I say, "It's okay. I'll have to find another way."

Sita opens her mouth to protest, but Tenzig interrupts her. "Even the worst storm must pass. When the snow settles, you will see the path forward."

The words blanket me, heavier than the dread that's curdled

in my belly. I nod, grateful for his wisdom, even if I don't believe it yet.

They don't press me for details, don't ask how I made it back. Instead, they fuss over me, refilling the tea I've hardly touched and bringing me food. I eat mechanically, more out of politeness than hunger.

Numbness creeps in, settling deep in my bones. I tell myself that I'm just exhausted, that as Tenzig said, I'll find that path forward. But the truth is, I don't know if this storm will pass. I don't know if this snow will ever settle. And even if it does, I don't know that my heart will ever thaw again.

After my third yawn, Tenzig bids me goodnight, and Sita insists on walking me back to my room. She sets up a small space heater before leaving with a lingering look of concern.

Once the door is locked behind her, I cross to the window and stare out over the river, my breath fogging against the glass. I drag my finger through the condensation, drawing the chemical formula for Silenol, the compound I was hoping to extract from the flower.

But it no longer looks like salvation. It no longer looks like hope. It's nothing but a barrier between me and Eryon. I dash it away with my sleeve so my eyes can search the darkness for him even though I know he's not there, no matter how much I wish he was.

If Eryon hadn't even bothered to say goodbye, he sure as hell wouldn't be standing across the river in the trees, watching over me now. But I ache to see him. To know he hasn't disappeared from my life completely.

The memory of his silver eyes flashes in my mind. How they burned into me that first night I saw them. The way they softened when he whispered my name, *his* name for me—Sruhnar. The sound echoes in my ears, curling around me like a prayer. Or a curse.

My fingers clench the windowsill, knuckles white. If I just stare long enough, maybe—

But the night remains empty. The dark woods hold no silver glow. Instead, the shadows swirl with secrets, and I am nothing but an outsider. I drop my forehead to the cold glass and close my eyes.

I didn't just lose him. I lost everything. I'm left with nothing but the icy wind and the weight of my failure. But I have to move forward, because there is no other choice. I hear my mother's voice in my mind again.

Onwards and upwards honey.

If only rock bottom wasn't so much deeper than I thought. Exhaling, I force myself to sit at my desk and open my laptop. The scientist in me won't let me waste time—not while I still have the memory of the plant fresh in my mind. I begin typing notes, logging every detail I remember. Although, now that I know how the specimen was originally obtained, I see its promise through a different lens.

The glow of the screen blurs as exhaustion presses down on me. Eventually, I shut the laptop, my brain unable to form one more coherent thought.

With a heavy heart, I crawl into bed, curling into a ball beneath the thick quilt. Sleep takes me fast, pulling me into restless dreams of endless caverns, iridescent violet-blue flowers, and silver eyes that I will never see again.

Chapter Twenty-Eight

Eryon

I do not look back. I *cannot*. If I do, I will go to her. And if I go to her, I will never let her go.

I take the punishing route home—the path that demands blood. Snowdrifts claw at my legs and sharp rocks pierce even the thickness of my skin. The wind howls through the valley like a living thing, but I do not feel any of it. I only feel the absence of her.

It is an emptiness I have known before. One carved into the foundation of my soul long ago, a chasm of grief that time never completely filled. I thought I had made peace with it. Thought I had accepted my fate.

And then she came—my Winter Star.

The one I should not have touched, should not have wanted. Yet fate had thrust her into my arms, again and again. And I am not as strong as I thought I was for all of these centuries. Not strong enough to keep her from slipping through my fingers like melting snow, even as I tried to hold on.

As I climb, a squall kicks up. Ice crusts the edges of my fur, driven against my skin in sharp, stinging waves. I could increase my temperature or lengthen my fur to protect myself, but I don't bother. I welcome the pain. It keeps me from thinking. From feeling.

The wind screams in my ears like my bleeding heart as I make the steep ascent. I push myself until my muscles ache, my breath a ragged thing torn from my chest. Perhaps I will die after all. Perhaps the mountain will finally take me.

But it does not.

I pass between the sentinel stones, their jagged peaks towering above me like ancient guardians. I trail my fingers along their rough surface, as I have for centuries, but this time —this time, they feel like grave markers.

I press forward through the whispering gorge, where the wind wails so loud it drowns the sound of my own thoughts. Yet beneath the mountain's agony, I hear something else. The phantom echo of her voice.

"You don't understand—I need this plant. I'm not just here for myself, for research. This isn't about taking or destroying— it's about survival."

I clench my jaw, my breath coming in ragged bursts. She was not the first to say such things to me. The man that came before also spoke of healing, of discovery, of a future where knowledge could change lives. He, too, swore that he would only take what was needed.

And then he took everything. The plants. The chance to save my snowling. The last light in my mate's eyes.

I stagger. Just for a breath, just for a single misstep, but it is enough. Rocks cascade over the edge of the narrow path where my foot is poised. I am unraveling, and I welcome it. It's what I deserve for failing everyone I have ever loved. One strong gust, a fraction of a shift in my balance, and I will fall.

The squall vanishes as suddenly as it started, and I sigh in acknowledgement. The mountain is not done with me yet. I force my leaden feet to continue on until I reach the frozen waterfall that marks the threshold of my solitude. It looms before me, caught in eternal stillness, its surface so smooth and clear that my own reflection stares back at me.

A beast looks out from the ice.

Snow clings to the thick white of my fur. My silver eyes are hollow, empty pools in the face of a creature who no longer knows himself. I have never looked more like a monster. I bare my teeth as if to snarl at my own reflection. But there is no one to witness my rage. No one to hear my grief.

I am alone.

A single tear falls from the eye of the beast who stares back at me. I wrench my gaze away from the pathetic creature and continue toward the cave, its darkness yawning open to swallow me whole. Inside, silence presses in, thick and suffocating. My home, once a sanctuary, now feels like a grave.

The fire is still warm from the night before. The furs on the bed still hold the ghost of her body, her shape pressed into the soft pelts. Her scent remains, winding through the air like a spirit refusing to leave.

I sink onto the edge of the bed, curling my hands into fists against my thighs to keep from gathering the pelts into my arms, desperate to be closer to where she had been, where the traces of her still linger.

I can still feel her here—the way she fit against me, the way her fingers traced over my skin as though I were something sacred. The way she looked at me—not with the fear of a monster, nor the reverence of a guardian, but with recognition. Of something more. Someone more.

She saw *me*.

A shuddering breath rips from my lungs, and I press my hands to my face. For an ancient and wise guardian, I have been a fool. I should not have let her touch me. I should not have let her in. She was never meant to stay.

I knew this, even as I let myself believe otherwise. Even as I let my hands roam her skin, as I whispered her name into the hollow of her throat, as I claimed her like she was mine.

But she was never mine.

I lurch to my feet, shoving the thought away. I move through the caverns and tunnels, the places that once felt like shelter. Now, they are only prison walls.

The darkness presses in, but my hands know the way. My fingers skim the rough stone, seeking something I should not reach for, but I do. The place where I traced the ochre lines of my past. My grief, carved into stone.

I let my forehead rest against the wall, the cool rock grounding me even as my thoughts spiral. I have carried this loss for decades. It should not feel new. It should not hurt.

And yet, it does. Because for a moment, I let myself believe I could have it again. I let myself believe in her. In us.

I turn from the paintings, my claws pressing into my palms as I clench my fists, grounding myself in the pain. The past does not matter. My duty has not changed. I am the guardian of these mountains. The keeper of the balance. I exist to protect, not to want.

I tell myself this, over and over, as I have for centuries. But as I step outside once more, the wind biting at my skin, I find myself looking toward the village. Toward her.

The sky has cleared, the storm has passed. And yet, the path before me is no clearer than the day I lost everything. Because no matter how much I try to convince myself otherwise—

I am not sure I can survive losing her, too.

Chapter Twenty-Nine

Dahlia

A few days later, I wake to the pale grey light of winter leaking through the window and the muffled sounds of voices outside.

For a moment, I burrow deeper under the covers, chasing the last fragile wisps of dreams where I am not hopeless, not alone. Where silver eyes still watch over me and strong arms still wrap around me like I belong. Like I am his.

But then—a voice.

Every muscle locks into place, my breath turns to ice in my lungs. My body is already processing the danger that my mind is slowly coming to realize. I know that voice. And it has no place here.

"Ben," I hiss. I bolt upright, my heart scrabbling against my ribs like a caged, frantic thing bent on escape. No. It's impossible. But even as I think it, I already know the truth.

I throw off the blankets and stumble to the dresser, yanking out clothes with shaking hands. The room is freezing, but the chill barely registers. Adrenaline has wiped away the last traces of sleep, leaving me hyper-aware, my mind a frantic mess of questions.

How is he here? Why is he here? And how the *hell* did he find me?

I pull on thick socks, gloves, my parka—layering up as if armor could protect me from whatever is about to happen. But no amount of fabric can guard against the sickening, crawling dread twisting in my stomach.

By the time I lace up my boots, my fingers are numb—not from the cold, but from how tight I've been clenching them. I shove my scarf up over my face, drag my hood low over my forehead, and force myself to breathe.

I wrack my brain, trying to recall if I had told Ben the name of the guesthouse I was staying in. But I must have, because how else could he have found me?

I need to find Sita and warn her not to tell him I'm here. She was wrong. The gods haven't smiled down on me. I'm fucking cursed.

Moving with slow, deliberate care, I crack my door open and peer outside. The bright glare of snow makes me squint, but the path to the lobby is clear. I slip out, keeping my footsteps light.

But the second I step inside, the air whooshes from my lungs on a startled gasp. Ben is casually sitting in front of the fire, a cup of tea in his hand like he belongs here. Like he's been waiting for me.

My stomach drops as the world tilts sickeningly sideways. He looks exactly the same. *Exactly the fucking same.* As if he isn't the shadow of a life I tore myself free from. But it's the expression on his face that turns my blood to ice.

A smirk sits on his lips. Smug. Satisfied. Expectant. As if he knew I would come.

I rip my hood back and yank down my scarf, my voice like steel when I spit out his name. "Ben."

His evil smile widens, slow and condescending. "Hello, Dolly."

Rage flashes through me, hot and violent. "Don't call me that."

He chuckles, shaking his head. "Still so sensitive." He tsks, then lifts his tea as if in a mock toast. "It's good to see you, Dahlia. I was starting to think you wouldn't show."

I cross my arms over my chest, holding myself back to keep from lunging at him. "What the hell are you doing here?"

He takes a slow sip, as if he has all the time in the world. Then, like he's enjoying this, he says, "I've come to obtain the *Silene vitalis*."

A sharp, dizzying rush of panic slams into me. No. No, no, no—

I school my expression, stalling for time. "Too bad you came all this way then, because I don't need your help."

He lets out a humorless chuckle. "I didn't say I was going to help you. I said I was going to *obtain* it."

This is so much worse than I could have ever imagined. I school my voice, remove all traces of emotion, and say, "You don't even know where it is."

His smirk doesn't falter. "Lucky for me, you already found it." He stands, zipping up his new, top of the line parka, and points to a logo emblazoned on the chest. "And unlike your feeble attempt at a one-woman research expedition, I have the backing of not only the university, but a pharmaceutical company funding mine."

His eyes gleam with triumph. "Unlimited money. Unlimited *manpower*. You were right about one thing. Turns out that enzyme you stumbled on? Pharma is very interested in it. The drug they'll develop will be worth millions. Maybe billions."

It feels like ground has opened beneath me and is swallowing me whole, down into a deep, bottomless pit. He's taking it. He's taking everything.

Not just my research. Not just my discovery. But, more importantly, Eryon's home. His last link to his family, his past, and his grief. His future. An unholy trifecta of exploitation.

"No," I cry, horrified by the thought of pharma sweeping through Eryon's caves, destroying his home, his paintings, the heart of the mountain where the *Silene vitalis* grows. I bite back my fear for my Yeti, but I can't help but say, "This area will be ruined. The people, the environment—"

He cuts me off and says, "You still don't get it, do you? You could have been something with my backing. Instead you're nothing but a stupid fucking girl chasing stories instead of science. You should have stuck to plain botany, no one cares about people or culture when there's money involved."

Ben turns, brushing past me like I'm nothing. As if he's already won. He knocks into my shoulder as he passes, spinning me around to look after him. But then he pauses at the door, glancing back with a wicked glint in his eyes.

"I've told you before, you really should secure your files better," he says as if he just can't help but gloat, and walks out, the door swinging closed behind him.

I can't breathe. The walls press in, the fire flickering wildly in my peripheral vision as the realization crashes over. My files. He was in my *fucking* files. This whole time, after being so dismissive of everything I had ever worked on, he had been keeping tabs on my work.

Oh, Dahlia, of course he had, I lecture myself. He had always fallen back on me "helping" him with his, both when he was getting his degrees and as a professor. When in actuality, everything had been my ideas, my research, my hard work and long nights.

All those years, making me feel small. Doubting my research. Calling my passion for ethnobotany a distraction from the true science of botany. He never respected my work, much less me.

But even if he hadn't respected it, he still used it. Just like he used me. I was always the brains. The talent. The one who did the damn work. And now he's trying to take everything I have left.

I'm not a "stupid fucking girl." I was always the woman with the brains in this relationship. And I need to be the brains now.

"Think, Dahlia. Think!" I coach myself out loud. I wrack my brain, trying to remember what I had typed into my notes when I had returned.

Sure, Ben has money. Resources. A team. But he doesn't know where the special cave is since the exact location isn't in my notes. But I do. I know I can find it again.

The faint flicker of hope flares in my chest as a plan forms. If I can get to Eryon first—if I can *warn* him—maybe, just maybe, I can fix this. I just need to find my way back to the main cave system and then make my way back through the tunnels.

The hope quickly dwindles, chased by fear and doubt. I can only hope Eryon will listen to me after I'm the one responsible for bringing this threat to his doorstep. My heart breaks for him as the price of this plant just keeps getting steeper.

I have no choice but to try. I sprint back to my room, hands shaking as I power up my laptop. I need my files. Coordinates, notes—anything that can give me an edge. But when I try to log in, a message pops up.

Access Denied.

Frowning, I check my internet connection and then carefully retype my password and try again. Frustration at wasting precious time courses through me. I know this is the password, I just logged in the other day.

Access Denied.

Frantically I try to reset my password, but when I enter my university email, the same one I've used for years, I get another error.

Unknown user.

"Un*fucking*believable," I complain to the empty room.

He had the university lock me out. The realization slams into me like a physical blow. Ben didn't just take my research. He took my identity, my work, everything.

The sound of voices has me pressing my face to the window, trying to see what is going on without running into Ben and risking another confrontation. As I see his large, well-outfitted group heading out, I hold my breath, waiting to see what direction they head in.

To my relief, they don't head towards the river, rather they turn south where the more populated end of town lies. A slow, burning rage rises in me, steady and all-consuming.

He thinks he's won. He thinks I'll just roll over and let him take what's mine. What's Eryon's. He thinks I'm the same girl he used to manipulate. The same girl who let him take credit for her work.

But I'm not a girl, not anymore. I grab my pack and shove some extra supplies on top since I don't have the time to repack it. I stand tall and throw it over my shoulders, yanking the straps tight. I am a woman on a mission.

Ben may have unlimited money and *manpower*. I can't help but sneer as I remember the condescending elitist tone he used. But I have something he will never understand.

I have *Eryon.*

And I'll be damned if I let him take away the one thing in this world worth saving. The sudden threat has made me realize I love him, and I'm going to protect him. No matter the cost. He's paid enough. It's time for someone to show Eryon that he is worth saving, too.

CHAPTER THIRTY

ERYON

Awareness pulls me from the solace of my meditation. The thick fur along my neck and spine bristles, every muscle coiling with instinct before I've even opened my eyes. My claws unsheathe, curling into the rock beneath me, my body already poised for a fight it has yet to see but knows is inevitable.

The wind shifts.

A small thing, imperceptible to most, but I feel it ripple through my bones like an omen. The storm is coming. Not just the snow, not just the bitter wind. Something else. Something worse.

The air changes, and I taste it first, sharp and acrid on my tongue. Something not of this world of stone and ice. The scent of men drifts toward me, foreign and wrong, wrinkling my nose. Synthetic fibers. Gun oil. The stale, metallic tang of greed. A pestilence seeping into the mountain's sacred space.

I rise, unfolding to my full height, scanning the vast white expanse below. The mountains breathe, whispering their secrets through the drifting snow, passing messages through the roots of the trees, calling to me through the aching bones of the earth itself.

The balance has shifted.

Intruders.

A deep growl rumbles low in my chest, rolling through the empty caverns behind me. They are here, in my domain. I move, silent and unseen. Nothing more than a ghost in the coming storm. I am a flicker in the long shadows of winter, the movement of a breeze in the trees. Invisible.

Before long, I come alongside the hunting party. For that is what they are. They do not move like men on a simple expedition. There is too much tension in their movements, too much nervous shifting of weight, hands adjusting gear, eyes flicking to the sides of the trail as if they expect the shadows to swallow them whole.

They are not just searching for something. They are hunting me. A wicked smile curves my lips, exposing my sharp teeth. My favorite kind of humans to realign the balance with. And one among them knows just how very real the danger is.

Their guide is the same man who had stumbled upon my Sruhnar with his vicious wolf yet ran away when confronted by me. I should have ended him when I had the chance. Instead, I showed him mercy. Let him leave unharmed. And now he walks among those who would desecrate this land, this balance. Who would take what belongs to me.

The animal is restless. It whines under its breath, ears twitching toward the trees, sensing what its master cannot.

Unseen, I bare my teeth at them anyway and slink further into the shadows. Let them believe they are alone. Let them believe they are safe. For now.

Their guide may know these mountains well, may have walked these paths since birth. But I have lived in and protected these mountains for centuries. They are carved into the long lines of my bones, etched into the tapestry of my soul.

I *am* the mountain.

I press forward, keeping to the higher ridges, watching and listening. The mountain hides my every move, covers my tracks, blows away any sound I make. The voices of the men carry through the stillness. They are loud. Careless. Their tracks evident all over the pristine landscape they desecrate, their trail so visible even a snowling could track them. They do not know how to respect a world that is not of their making.

And then, the scent of the promise of Spring reaches me like a phantom. Her scent. Faint and distant but real. Is it really here or do I desire her, long for her so deeply, that my poor mind is manifesting her here with me? I stumble as I search for her, a single misstep resulting in the sharp crack of a branch underfoot.

The guide's head snaps up, scanning the trees. I freeze, scarcely daring to breathe until his attention shifts back to the man prattling on beside him.

Something about the foreigner is wrong. His voice creeps under my skin, sets my rage simmering. He reeks of arrogance, of control. A man who does not fear what he cannot understand.

I circle them, moving closer. Silent despite my rage. Finally, I am close enough to discover he is the one who carries her faint scent. Why does it cling to him? The sacred essence of spring, of my Winter Star, polluted by his presence.

Had she turned to him after I cast her out? Reached for him in loneliness, let him hold her the way I did? Let him touch what was mine as if not only I had meant nothing, but all that we shared meant even less?

The thought is a blade, twisting deep, shredding through my ribs, carving something jagged and unholy into the wreckage of my heart.

She desperately needs the plant. Perhaps she is desperate enough to trade me for it.

The rage surges, dark and blinding, slicing through my

reason until the world narrows to bloodlust and betrayal—until another, more horrifying thought buries the blade to the hilt and collapses me to my knees.

Had she sent them? Had she led them to my home, knowing what they would do? Had my grief, my pain, my life meant so little to her? Had I ever meant anything to her at all?

And then I hear her name—Dahlia.

The word from his mouth is a desecration. They way the sound falls from his lips not in worship but in mocking is wrong. She is not their flower, but mine. Not Dahlia, but Sruhnar, my Winter Star.

"She really thought she was going to find this plant," he says, shaking his head with a smirk. "Like she was some kind of genius. Please, she is nothing without me. She never had the guts when things got tough. Always clinging to her ethics, her precious research integrity."

His face twists as he scoffs. "She would've wasted years studying it, learning its history, figuring out how the locals wave it under the moon or some bullshit. Me? I have the brains. And the balls."

Laughter ripples through their group as he lewdly grabs the front of his pants.

Another of the men claps him on the shoulder, saying, "Good one, Ben. Good one."

The one called Ben chuckles, shaking his head. "I'll take the plant. No hesitation. No second-guessing. I could give a shit about the environment. I'll rape and pillage this whole fucking mountain to get it. And the best part? She handed it to me without even realizing it. Bitch served up a fortune on a silver platter."

Ice floods my veins. My claws unsheathe, slicing through the frozen ground as I dig my fingers into the earth to keep myself from tearing into him now.

He pauses, then adds with a sneer, "Not surprising, though.

She was always desperate. Desperate for a win. Desperate for purpose. But most of all, desperate for love. She clung to me like a lost little puppy because she had no one else."

More laughter.

I am going to kill him. This is the man who haunted her eyes. Who made her feel less than her divine self. This is the man who did not treasure the gift bestowed by the gods themselves. He has no place here.

He has no place anywhere.

Every muscle in my body tightens, my teeth grind together as bloodlust surges through me, and a battle drum pounds in my chest, demanding violence. I can picture it too clearly—the snap of his bones, the wet crunch of his throat collapsing under my grip.

But I do not kill him.

Not yet.

Not here, not now, not where others could witness his death and escape to bring more in his place. The entire expedition must be disposed of. Order must be upheld.

I force myself to breathe, pushing air in and out of my constricted chest. To listen past the rushing of rage pulsing in my veins.

"The plant can only be in the Migoi's cave system, Mr. Ben," the guide says.

If I hadn't already fallen to my knees, this would have felled me. They know. But how?

He continues, "I've lived my entire life in these mountains, and that's the only place it could be. Never saw anything like what you describe anywhere else."

Fool.

"And I saw her there—the woman. With the Migoi. He protected her. I retreated to the woods but then I saw them, together." He pauses, as if considering what to say next. His face contorts as he continues. "They were doing unnatural *things*."

The guide is a dead man walking. He has sealed his fate, too.

Ben scoffs. "My god she really is desperate for love. So desperate she'll turn to a monster?"

One of the hunting party shakes his head. "Wait. You're saying the girl was with it? Like, fucking some kind of animal?"

The guide's face is grim. "Not an animal. The protector of these mountains. I saw them together with my own eyes."

The group mutters, shaking their heads, making snide remarks to one another. Oh, I cannot wait to kill them all. How easy it is for them to judge what they do not know. What they cannot possibly comprehend. They call me a beast, a monster. I cannot wait to show them the true meaning of the word.

"And if that beast shows up?" another of the men asks, hesitant.

Ben laughs, sharp and triumphant. "It better."

And then—confirmation.

"The plant is just the beginning," Ben says, smirking. "But let's be honest—the real prize is the thing guarding it. You don't just leave a discovery like that in the mountains. We take the beast, too. Can you even imagine?"

He raises his hands, as if showing off a marquees, *"Professor Ben Thorne Captures Legendary Beast.* I can see the headlines now, fellas. The kind of fame that lasts forever."

He lets out a low chuckle, adjusting the straps on his pack. "But even better than fame is the money. Pharma will pay anything for the enzyme—the drug alone will be worth billions. But the creature?"

He shakes his head, eyes gleaming. "That's a once-in-a-life-time discovery. The kind of thing that changes everything. If this best is real—and from what you're telling me it is," he says, pointing at the guide, "then we're talking about exclusive research grants, government funding, museum exhibitions—hell, maybe even movie deals."

He spreads his hands as if this is some grand revelation.

"Think about it. A species that's survived here, undetected, thriving in conditions that should've killed it. The kind of adaptation that rewrites biology books. If we can capture it, study it? We're looking at the greatest scientific breakthrough of our generation. Hell, maybe of all time."

His grin widens, and he gestures around at the men. "This is history in the making, gentlemen. And I intend to be the one who makes it. I'll get a fucking Nobel Prize for this."

A low, rumbling growl I cannot contain escapes my throat, barely audible but reverberating into the night air. The dog whimpers, tail tucking tight against its belly. The guide's eyes flick to the tree line, his breath hitching.

Fear bleeds into his voice as he murmurs a prayer and then says, "Maybe we shouldn't be here."

Ben smirks and claps him on the back. "Oh, we should definitely be here. Lead on."

The others chuckle. They have no idea what they are walking into. They want to take me. They think they can cage me. Little do they know, they have already lost. Their fates are sealed in this mountain.

But now I know what I needed to. Ben is the enemy, not my Sruhnar. Never her.

I turn away, the plan forming like a snowdrift in the wind—shifting, building, waiting to bury them whole. Let him believe he is the hunter. Let him believe he will take what is mine.

By the time he reaches my cave, he will know *he* is the hunted.

I move quickly, away from the East trail the guide is directing the crew along. Let him think he is closing in. I will loop around the base of the mountain and come up the North side.

The sun breaks through the gathering clouds, a gold beam of light caressing my face with its warmth. Despite the depths of winter, Spring floats to me on the beam of light.

My heart cries out for my Winter Star, and her essence washes over me as if the universe itself is giving me one more taste of her, one more chance at the warmth of her before I cleanse this world of Ben and the men like him.

Perhaps I will finally die after all. It will be a worthy death. I close my eyes and picture her face in my mind, all the little sun kissed dots, "freckles" she called them.

I imagine the flush of her skin beneath me, the little cries she makes when her pleasure blooms. The vision is so real, I can not just sense her, but I can smell her. Not just a drift on the wind but something tangible.

My eyes snap open as her presence becomes stronger. I'm not just imagining her here. She is near.

The realization that she has chosen to return has my heart pounding and a strange ache twisting in my chest. She has chosen me. Not the plant. Not the world beyond these mountains.

Me.

She was desperate for the flower before. Desperate to save herself. And I let that desperation convince me she would never choose me. That I was only an obstacle, a means to an end. And maybe, in the dark and lonely place deep in my soul, I thought I wasn't worth choosing.

But now—now, she stands on my land again. The mountain and the trees whisper to me excitedly, the land itself rejoicing in her presence. She is facing the storm, the cold, the danger. She walks this path knowing what waits in the shadows. Knowing *I* wait in the shadows.

And still, she comes.

I should not want this. I should not care.

But I do.

She has made her choice. And in doing so, she has undone the doubt I tried to carve into my own bones. She has sealed the bond I tried to reject.

She is mine. And I am hers.

I repeat my vow, just as I did when I first watched her. No one will harm her again. No one will take her from me. Not now. Not ever.

I swear it to the river that carves the stone, to the wind that howls through the peaks, to the mountain that will bury the bones of these men. I swear it to my Sruhnar, my Winter Star.

I drag my claw across my palm, let my blood spill onto the frozen earth. She has chosen. And so have I.

She must make this journey. This is her path to walk. I will watch, and I will protect, but I will not, cannot, interfere. She does not need to be saved—she needs only to see the strength that has always been hers.

I mark the path, knowing she will see and she will understand. I carve her name into the sentinel stones, dragging my claws through the frozen rock with slow, deliberate strokes. I rub the fresh cut of my palm over the etching. A guide. A claim.

I move quickly now, leaving more signs—breadcrumbs in the snow. Markers only she will recognize, meant for her eyes alone.

She will follow them. I know she will come. And when she does, I will be waiting.

I lift my gaze to the sky as the first howling gusts of a storm begin to pick up, swirling around me. Ben and his men have sealed their fate. They have shattered the balance. The mountain will take its due.

A deep, rumbling growl builds in my chest as I step back into the shadows.

Let them come.

CHAPTER THIRTY-ONE

I glance around to make sure no one is in sight before heading north, back toward the bridge I crossed just yesterday. The river is swollen from the fresh snowfall, its roar filling the air as I grip the rope railings.

"Dahlia!"

I spin around, my heart leaping into my throat at the sudden sound of my name. Relief floods me when I recognize Sita instead of Ben or someone from his group.

"Sita! You scared me half to death!" I press a gloved hand to my chest, my heart pounding beneath my parka.

"I'm sorry! I didn't mean to," she says, breathless. "I heard you and Ben. I had no idea you weren't together anymore when he checked in. If I'd known, I would've come straight to you! Then I saw you leaving the guesthouse and knew something must be wrong for you to head back out so soon."

I sigh, guilt and exhaustion pressing down on me. "I didn't tell you when I first got back. I was heartbroken—and obsessed with finding that damn plant."

I step closer and place my hands on her shoulders, steadying both of us. "Sita, there's so much I haven't told you. But I don't have time to explain everything now. I need to find that cave I was in before Ben does."

She frowns, worry etched into her face. "Dahlia, it's dangerous to cross into these woods. The—"

I cut her off. "I know. The Migoi." I hesitate, knowing how absurd it will sound. "Sita, the Migoi—he's the one who saved me."

Her eyes widen, but I press on before she can speak. "And now, I need to save him. I already found the plant—it's in his cave. Ben is here for it, too, and we both know what people will do for money and fame. Especially Ben. Sita, I can't let him get there first."

Sita flips up her hood and pulls the zipper up to her chin. With a sharp nod, she says, "Let's go. You can fill me in on the way. My family owes him a debt, too. I'll help you protect him as he has always protected us."

"I don't know where I'm going. He might be angry that I've brought danger to him, just as I'm bringing you into it. You don't have to come with me. Really."

The hope she'll back down and stay safe wars with the desire not to fight this battle by myself. Her presence isn't just help— it's risking someone else's life for my choices. And if something happens to her? That's on me. I'm left once again grappling with the question of the worth of my life.

Would I trade her life for mine? If this goes wrong—if she dies because of me—what then? I've fought so hard to believe I deserve saving, but what if the cost is too high?

Sita shakes her head firmly. "I think I know where to go. I've heard enough stories from travelers and passed down within my family about landmarks to reach his territory."

She steps closer, her voice softer now. "And of course I have to go with you. What kind of friend would I be to let you face this alone? Besides," she glances toward the mountains, as if seeking their silent blessing, "surely the gods will smile upon us for honoring a dharma as sacred as protecting the protector."

"Right now, I need all the help we can get. I'd be foolish to refuse you. Thank you, Sita." My voice catches as my eyes sting with unshed tears, moved by her loyalty and unwavering commitment. I was wrong—I don't have nothing. I have everything. Friendship, integrity, intelligence—and I'm in love with a Yeti.

I echo her phrasing, a small smile tugging at my lips despite the gravity of the situation. "Let's go protect the protector."

Taking a deep breath, I step onto the bridge, the ropes creaking under my hands as the icy wind whips around us and the river rages below. Sita follows close behind, her presence a quiet reassurance.

We retrace my earlier steps as far as I can remember, the path narrowing as we push deeper into the forest. The dense trees cut the wind but also the light, lending an eerie gloom. We quickly exhaust the extent of my knowledge, so Sita moves ahead.

As we move forward as fast as the trail and weather allow, she begins to recount the stories passed down through generations in her family and overheard snippets from the many travelers who have stayed at her family's guest house.

"My grandmother always said the Migoi are guardians of more than just the forests and mountains. They keep the balance between the human world and the wild, between man's greed and nature's abundance. Let's follow the landmarks from the stories, and if they're right, we should end up at the caves."

Her voice carries conviction, each word pushing back against the cold and hopelessness threatening to set in. It's enough to spark hope. Even with the wind biting at my face and the trail ahead uncertain, I can't help but think we might just make it.

Hours later, doubt begins to creep in. The trail has become a monotonous cycle of cold and up. Our conversations have dwindled, replaced by the sound of heavy breathing, and our stops to rest are more frequent. Both the trees and the air have thinned with our ascent, which means we're hit harder by the cold and icy wind.

We're both struggling to keep up the pace and look for the first landmark, something about watching stones. Darkness is falling fast, but we push forward, determined.

When we both stumble again, I call out, "Sita! We can't keep going like this. We need to find somewhere to stop for a bit. We won't be able to find these eyes in the dark, anyway."

She nods, gesturing to a rock face ahead. I return the nod, following her, though every step is longer than the last. My toes are numb, and despite all my gear, my face is like ice. When we stop, the rocks help to block some of the wind making me realize just how brutal it is. I drop my pack and stretch, feeling the tension in my muscles.

Sita pulls off hers and, with practiced ease, sets up a compact four-season tent. Designed for extreme conditions, its heavy-duty poles and tightly sealed seams are a stark reminder of the mountain's unforgiving nature. She works quickly, the low-profile design minimizing the wind's bite, offering us a small but essential refuge from the elements.

My spirits lift at the thought of even a little time out of the weather. I'm beyond grateful for her presence and grab her bag to help. "I couldn't have done this without you."

She flashes a quick smile. "I grabbed the emergency pack when I left. When you grow up in these mountains, you learn to keep one ready at all times. Let's rest. We'll leave at first light."

We crawl into the tent, and while I'm still chilled, the warmth inside is such a relief. Sita pulls out a small stove and starts heating water. She hands me a sleeping bag, then unrolls her own. I can't believe how poorly prepared I was for this journey. I really wouldn't have made it without her.

By the time our beds are set up, the water is hot. While she makes tea, I dig out the protein bars I had hurriedly thrown in the top of my pack. My fingers and toes tingle as they warm up, and my face feels like it's finally thawing. Our simple dinner tastes like a feast, and the hot tea fills me with warmth, rekindling my energy and hope.

Despite the physical exhaustion, I struggle to fall asleep. My mind keeps rehearsing what I'll say to Eryon if we find him. When we find him, I correct myself.

Still, a part of me can't shake the worry that he won't listen—or worse, that he'll blame me for Ben's pursuit. And, honestly, I wouldn't blame him. After all, if he hadn't rescued me from that avalanche, none of this would have happened.

I regret the danger heading his way, but I can't regret the time we spent together. It was cathartic, and I've come out of it stronger. Fiercer. Unlike Ben, who I sure as shit regret my time with, but all these experiences, however painful, have shaped me into who I am today.

The old Dahlia never would've rushed off into the Himalayan mountains to save a Yeti. But the new Dahlia does. Because I'm Dahilia fucking Wilde.

But what if this new Dahlia is still not enough? What if I can't find the cave? What if Eryon won't forgive me? What if I've led Sita to her death? The questions swirl in a chaotic vortex in my mind. A tornado of fear and worry until the anxiety is coiled deep in my center.

I stare at the roof of the tent, my breath curling in the cold air, doubts settling over me with the weight of that damned avalanche. I've come so far, changed so much—but is it enough? Will it ever be?

A gust of wind rattles the fabric, and for a second, I swear I hear something outside. The snap of a branch. The whisper of something moving just beyond the edge of camp.

My pulse jumps. Could it be Ben, lurking in the shadows? Has he found us already? Or could it be Eryon? Hope flares in my chest, that he's out there, watching, waiting. That he sees I am coming for him.

The wind stills. The night holds its breath, and I hold mine, too. But nothing happens. Ben doesn't break through the tent walls, and Eryon doesn't scoop me up in his arms. Sita shifts beside me, her breathing deep and steady, and as I count the thudding beats of my heart, they slowly calm. I take myself back to the quiet and dark of the caves and the stillness there. With one last slow deep breath, I close my eyes, and let exhaustion finally win.

CHAPTER THIRTY-TWO

DAHLIA

Sita wakes me in the early dawn when the sun is just a whisper on the horizon. We roll up our sleeping bags, our movements stiff from the cold, hands fumbling over frozen fabric. The air is thinner at this altitude, biting at every exposed inch of skin. My breath curls in the breaking light, ghostly wisps vanishing into a paling sky.

Sita hands me a steaming cup of tea, and I cradle it between my palms, letting the warmth seep into my frozen fingers. The first sip scalds my tongue, but I don't care. I need the heat, the illusion of comfort before we begin another grueling day.

The morning is silent but for the rustling of fabric and the distant groan of shifting ice. The mountains are waking, stretching beneath the weight of the cold.

I pull on my gloves and move to break down the tent. That's when I see them. Just outside the perimeter of our small encampment are impressions in the snow. I blink, the breath stilling in my lungs.

Bigger than any human boot print. Too deep to be from the wind.

I crouch, pressing my fingers to the edge of the indent. The snow is packed firm, the print deep—whatever made this was big. Heavy. A flicker of warmth blooms in my chest before I can stop it. A pull, sharp and aching.

I swallow hard and shove it down. It could be anything. A trick of the snow, a settling drift, or even an animal. Probably the latter.

But still, my fingers linger over the edges of the print, tracing the symmetry of it. A gust of wind kicks up loose powder around me, and I shiver, but it has nothing to do with the cold. Something in my bones hums with awareness, and I know Eryon has been here.

Sita zips up her pack and glances over. "Dahlia?"

I startle, snatching my hand away from the print as if I've been caught touching something sacred. The hope is too fragile to voice it out loud, but my heart knows it was him despite my rational mind denying it.

"Yeah," I say quickly, standing and brushing off my gloves. "Just zoned out for a second."

She eyes me, then the ground where I was crouching, but doesn't push.

"We should get moving as soon as you finish your tea," she says, and I nod, forcing my feet to move. Forcing myself to leave the proof behind, but not the hope. I hang on to it like a lifeline.

As we shoulder our packs and begin our trek upward, I feel it —the weight of unseen eyes. The feeling is burned into my memory, returning ripples along my skin with delicious awareness, and gives me the strength I need to keep going.

The air thins further as we ascend, each step a battle against the mountain's relentless pull. My thighs burn, my lungs ache, and yet I push forward, refusing to slow. The trail grows more treacherous with every passing hour, and as I dig my boots into the frozen ground, a thought strikes me.

Eryon carried me down this. What had taken him less than a day is taking us, two determined women, a damned eternity. It's humbling.

I picture his massive form moving through the snow, effortless and swift, his white fur blending with the storm. Twice he had held me, shielding me from the worst of the cold, never once faltering in his steps. My fingers tingle with the ghost of his velvety skin deep under the fur.

I press a hand against my chest, as if I can still feel the lingering warmth where our bodies had pressed together. Instead, a gust of wind cuts through my layers, and I grit my teeth, pulling my scarf higher over my nose. The world around us is nothing but white and gray, a never-ending blur of snow, stone, and sky. The silence is vast, broken only by the crunch of our boots and the occasional howl of the wind.

Just when I thought it couldn't get any harder, the squall hits. It comes without warning, a violent roar swallowing the world in a matter of seconds. Snow whips through the air, turning the trail into a blind, white abyss.

"Down!" Sita yells over the wind.

We press ourselves into the mountainside, huddling close for warmth. My heart pounds as the wind shrieks, tearing at us like unseen claws. My fingers go numb almost instantly, my thick gloves no match for the ferocity of the terrain. The cold is merciless, insidious, creeping into my bones.

Sita fumbles with her pack, managing to rip open a pouch of heat packs. We shove them into our gloves, into our boots, and drop them down our clothes. The warmth is fleeting, fragile, but it keeps us from freezing solid.

The wind roars and roars, and we have no choice but to wait it out. What I wouldn't give to be in a hot spring again with Eryon. Minutes stretch into eternity. My body stiffens from stillness, my muscles locking against the cold. I press my forehead against my knees, breathing through the panic rising in my chest. What if this storm doesn't pass? What if we're trapped here? What if I can't save him?

The questions are suffocating, but I force myself to stay calm. The mountain may be testing us, but we won't fail. We can't. There simply is no other option.

Finally, after what feels like forever, the wind dies down. The storm retreats as quickly as it arrived, leaving the world eerily still.

Sita is the first to move. She brushes the snow off and turns to me, breathless. "Dahlia, are you okay?"

I nod, though my joints are stiff as I push myself upright.

We stand and survey the damage. The bright sun staring down from an azure blue sky turns the landscape into a sparkling winter scene from a travel brochure. Despite the beauty, my stomach drops as I realize the trail is gone. The snow has shifted so much that the path ahead is unrecognizable. Panic gnaws at the edges of my resolve, and if the tears wouldn't freeze to my face, I would cry.

Why is doing the right thing so damn hard? I'm trying to save Eryon, save the land, and the mountain is testing me. Hell this whole damn life has been testing me. Where is Ben's test? Where is the fucking universal balance that Eryon is supposed to keep? When will I finally get what I deserve? Because Ben sure as shit isn't.

I look to Sita, hoping she can figure out where to go from here. She's already scanning the landscape, her sharp eyes darting from ridge to ridge, cataloging landmarks. I see a plan forming behind her sharp eyes.

"Didi, look!" she exclaims, pointing ahead.

I follow her gaze, my breath catching. There, partially uncovered by the shifting snow, are two massive boulders standing side by side. They form a narrow passage between them, like a gateway. Excitement hums through my veins like electricity, erasing the creeping despair.

The sentinel stones.

We had been looking for the landmark, but without this storm I doubted we'd have found them. We would have just stuck to the trail. But here they are, standing before us, as if they had been waiting here all this time. Maybe the mountain wasn't testing us, but helping us.

I can't take the time to overthink it. We shift our course, cutting a new path to the boulders. The way down is steep, treacherous. Snow slips beneath our boots, and we slide more than we walk, half-running, half-falling through the drifts. My heart pounds, exhilarated despite the danger.

It feels right. As if the mountain itself is leading me forward, not just toward fate, but to him. My Eryon.

When we reach the landmark, we pause, both of us staring up in silent awe. They're enormous, towering high above our heads. Their placement is too precise, too deliberate. My fingers brush over the weathered sacred stones.

As we step between them, I feel it. A shift, like crossing an invisible threshold. The air changes, thickening with something old and waiting. It feels like coming home.

As we walk through, I turn to glance back at the stones one last time and that's when I see it. My breath catches as I see writing scratched into the rock.

At first, the markings are faint, almost lost in the stone's natural grooves. But as the sun dips lower, its golden light strikes the surface at just the right angle, highlighting not just the carving themselves but a dark shadow pressed into the cuts —and the word reveals itself.

My pulse stutters. I know these letters. They are not fully familiar, but I recognize their shape, their weight.

"Sita," I gasp, pointing. "Can you read that?"

She steps closer to me, squinting at the carving above our

heads too high for a human to reach. Her lips move soundlessly as she pieces it together, mouthing different possibilities before settling on one.

"I don't know this language," she says slowly. "But it looks close to some words I do recognize. If I'm reading it correctly, I think it starts with Sru—?"

A shockwave ripples through me and my lips curve into a smile as my heart leaps. "Sruhnar."

She looks at me with wide eyes and then back to the carving, "Yes, that fits. But what is it?"

He carved my name into a rock. It's a gesture so simple, yet so profound. His way of marking our connection, like two lovers carving their initials into a tree. My spirits surge, and I'm suddenly re-energized. Without thinking, I break into a run, laughing, with Sita hot on my heels.

"My name," I call back over my shoulder.

She shouts after me, but I barely hear her over the bounding of my own pulse and my laughter. The air burns in my lungs, but I don't stop. Every step is one more step closer to him.

Gradually my pace slows with the fading light as the sun sinks lower. The excitement lingers, but reality creeps back in. We still don't know how far we've come. Or how much further we have to go.

The wind whispers through the stones, brushing over my skin with a chill that has nothing to do with the cold. I hate to stop when every instinct screams at me to keep going. But the darkness is relentless.

The wild does not wait. And the dark does not forgive. For every mark left on stone, the wild carves its own in flesh and bone.

Chapter Thirty-Three

Eryon

The mountain breathes, and I breathe with it.

We are bound by dharma—each of us playing our part in the great turning of the world. The wind carries my purpose forward, and I follow.

Snow drifts in slow, silent waves, curling through the air before settling into the folds of the earth. The storm is growing, gathering in the hollows of the ridges, sharpening like a blade. The sky is clear, but the mountain has begun its work, shifting beneath the weight of what does not belong. The trees whisper, branches shuddering beneath layers of ice, warning of what is to come.

But it is not the coming storm that commands my attention.

It is them. The intruders and the women both move steadily toward my home. One party is blind in their arrogance. The other is determined in their desperation. And between them, I wait.

I crouch along the high ledges, my form pressed into the rock, watching the first group below.

Ben and his men move in a tight, nervous cluster. Their scent is thick with sweat and nerves, their bodies sluggish under the weight of their gear. They move like prey, yet they believe themselves the hunters.

I have seen men like this before. The ones who come thinking they can conquer the mountain. That it is simply another obstacle to be subdued.

They do not listen. They do not respect. And they do not belong.

But the mountain will not be conquered. It devours. The wind cuts through them like teeth, stealing warmth from their bodies, gnawing at their resolve. They struggle over the uneven terrain, cursing each misstep and each other. Weakness spreads through them like rot.

Even the guide they have paid to lead them glances over his shoulder too often. His steps are halting where they should be sure and steady. He knows the mountain watches, and he knows *I* watch. He was right earlier. They should not be here.

But Ben? Ben is oblivious. He presses forward, driven by greed, too arrogant to understand that he is already lost.

I shift and climb, moving higher along the cliffs. The ice beneath my feet is familiar, the sharp ridges and deep crevices carved into my memory. This is my land.

But I am not only watching them. She is here, too. Dahlia moves differently. She is smaller, lighter. Though exhaustion weighs on her, she does not falter. She listens to the mountain. She reads its signs. She is learning.

My fingers press into the ice, gripping the cold even as fire races through my veins at the mere thought of her—her fierceness, her tenacity, her defiance.

She is not alone. Her friend and guide walks beside her, leading her toward me. Another human. Another risk. But the woman does not move with the greed of the others. She moves with reverence. She walks with the quiet knowledge of one who has heard the stories. She has seen my mercy.

I watch as they stop at the sentinel stones where I left a sign for her there. Not merely her name scratched into rock, but my claim. A guide for her on her journey. Will she find my mark and know my heart?

The wind shifts, carrying the sharp, bright sound of her laughter up the cliffs to me. It is a small thing, fragile in the storm. But it reaches me all the same.

She understands. She is coming. She is choosing *me*.

Yet still, a part of me hesitates. I have spent centuries alone. I have seen greed, betrayal, and destruction. I have known what it is to be feared, hunted, worshiped, and abandoned. I have seen what men do to the sacred things of this world.

Dahlia is not like them. I know this. I feel this. But she is still human. And humans are fragile. Their hearts. Their bones. Their trust.

And I—I am not made for fragile things.

What if I am wrong about her? What if she breaks under the weight of this land? Under the weight of me? What if I ruin her before she even has the chance to regret her choice?

A shift in the snow—small, barely a whisper—and suddenly, I am not here. I am elsewhere. I am *then*.

The snowling had been so small. No larger than my own hands. Yet it held the entirety of the universe in its eyes, reflecting the silver light of stardust and mystery and infinite possibility back at me.

The wonder. The exquisite love that sank into my heart with the weight of a thousand mountains when I held him close, tucked under my chin. I spent so much time marveling at how such a small thing could bring such great joy.

The first sneeze, I had ignored. It was a silly sound from a little snowling. The second, I had not. And then the coughing started, and when his strength gave out, when his tiny body slumped against my chest, too weak to even hold his head up—I knew.

The sickness had come from the man my mate had trusted. She had tried to help him by giving him shelter, offering him kindness. And in return, he had left us with something invisible. Something deadly.

He had asked for just one plant, and we had shared its gift freely. Allowed him to harvest it as we tended to our ailing little one. But when we went for the winter star to save our snowling, we were met with horror.

We tore the hidden cavern apart, dug through the soil, overturned every rock, but the man had taken them all.

Just one, he had said.

He had lied.

I blink away the past, cursing myself. I should have known she had come for the plant. She had come to take it, and she had come to leave. Just as the human had before her. Memories and grief bury me in an avalanche of pain. The darkness tries to pull me under and my beast thrashes, tearing at my skin, searching for my light in the darkness.

No, it roars. *She is different. She is mine!*

My hands curl into the ice, anchoring me in the present. The past does not own me. Not anymore.

Now I see just how blind I had been. The gods had not cursed me; they had given me a gift. Rare and precious, like the first breath of spring. Like something I had not dared to hope for. With her eyes the color of its petals, and her fire bright enough to stand against the storm.

She will not break like the snowling. She will not wither like my mate. She survived me. She will survive this.

And Ben?

Ben will not.

The mountain has already begun its work. The storm is rising, the wind shifting like a living thing, curling through the valleys, whispering through the trees. Echoing my heartbreak. My rage.

I close my eyes, feeling the air tremble. The ice shifts beneath my feet, a warning. The land knows. It has already judged them. And when the time comes, I will not whisper.

I will be waiting.

CHAPTER THIRTY-FOUR

This morning, I'm the one waking Sita at first light. We pack in silence, our movements automatic, mechanical. Even our exhaustion feels quieter now, settled into our bones, past the point of complaint.

We eat as we walk, even skipping tea in favor of hitting the trail. Today feels significant. Whatever this journey holds, it's about to end. Because I don't know if I have another climb in me after this. Today has to be the day.

I can't help but wonder if this will be my happily ever after or another epic tragedy. But the mountain doesn't care about stories, only survival. And right now, the grueling trail takes all of my concentration, leaving no room for fear—or hope.

Within a few hours, Sita points out another landmark. The jagged rocks rise like frozen sentinels, watching over the narrow pass ahead.

"The whispering gorge is the passageway to the Migoi's territory. After this, we only need to find the frozen falls which mark the entrance to the cave," she says, then pulls up her hood, motioning for me to do the same. "It will be...loud."

I don't question her strange instructions, especially for something called the whispering gorge; after all she has gotten me this far. I just follow, tugging my scarf tighter as we step between the towering cliffs. As I adjust my hood, something bright catches my eye. A vivid streak of red against the muted landscape.

I kneel, brushing away snow and loose stones until my fingers close around it—a scrap of lace, half-frozen in the ice. My breath catches, recognition sparking in my chest.

"He's leaving me a trail," I murmur, more to myself than to Sita. The thought of him watching over me, guiding me, wanting me to find him, has tears pricking at my eyes.

Sita glances over, brows lifting in curiosity. "The Migoi?"

I nod, holding up the torn lace from the panties I had on the day he rescued me from the avalanche. A laugh bubbles out of me, half delirious with exhaustion, half giddy with hope. Yes, he had carved my name into the rock but this confirms it.

"He knows I'm coming for him. And if he's leaving clues," my voice trails off, excitement rising. "It's like he wants me to find him."

She tilts her head, considering, then offers a faint smile. "Then let's not keep him waiting."

With renewed purpose, we enter the gorge, and the mountain unleashes hell. Wind slams into us, a howling, living thing —not a whisper, but a scream. It shrieks through the narrow passage, funneled between the towering cliffs, a relentless, deafening force that vibrates in my skull. I stagger as the gusts shove at my body, tearing at my clothes, clawing at my exposed skin.

I brace myself, digging my heels into the icy terrain.

The air is filled with a high-pitched wailing, a chorus of voices howling through the stone. The wind carries something ancient, something mournful. It doesn't whisper—it wails.

I don't know what these walls have witnessed. But I know pain when I hear it. My pulse pounds in my ears, matching the rhythm of the wind's shrieks.

A fresh gust hammers into me, nearly shoving me off my feet. I clutch at the rock face, gloved fingers skidding against ice, barely keeping myself upright.

The mountain does not care if I fall. But I care. I will not be stopped.

I grit my teeth, forcing my body forward, step by agonizing step. The wind presses against me, trying to turn me back. I can feel it in every blast of ice against my cheeks, every gust that threatens to knock the breath from my lungs. It is as if the land itself is testing me one last time. Making me prove my worth, my love, my will to save him.

But I will not fail. I will not turn back. My determination is resolute. Because this is nothing compared to the hell that Eryon has suffered. The mountain's wailing is a whisper against the roar of his grief.

I think of him—of the heat in his touch, the quiet weight of his presence, the fire in his voice when he spoke of his pain. I think of the moment he gifted me a name, pulsing with power. I think of the cave, where he stripped me of sight and sound, leaving only sensation and belief.

He had saved me. He had shown me my own strength. And now it's my turn to show him—he is worth saving, too.

So I push forward, every muscle in my body burning with the effort. The wind does not own me. The cold does not own me. Ben does not own me.

I own myself.

And I will give myself freely—to the one who never asked.

The walls of the ravine begin to widen. The howling wind starts to lessen. The force battering my body relents, just the slightest bit. I roar through my teeth, as if to tell the mountain that I have made it, that it has not broken me.

And then—silence. Deafening stillness.

Sita stumbles forward beside me, panting. She clutches my arm, her breath fogging the air. Her voice thin but triumphant, she cries, "We did it!"

I exhale a shaky laugh, the tension bleeding from my shoulders. "When you tell this story, don't call it the whispering gorge. Call it the screaming abyss of questionable life choices."

Her smile widens, and she shakes her head. "Noted."

We press on, snow crunching beneath our boots and the fragile blossom of hope burning in my heart, brighter than ever.

On and on we climb, our pace slowing, each movement heavier than the last. The short days of winter work against us, the dimming light urging us to hurry despite our exhaustion.

We inch around a steep curve, the trail thinning until it's nothing but a jagged ledge, clinging desperately to the mountainside. A misstep here could send us plummeting into the abyss below.

I force my focus to narrow, blocking out the ache in my body, the bone-deep exhaustion. The mountain feels alive as I slide against the rough wall, arms hugging it as I drag my boots along. It exhales icy breath against my cheeks, watching me with jagged edges and testing me with loose rocks.

Despite the thrill of knowing we must be getting closer, the relentless elements are starting to wear us both down. The biting wind snakes its way under collars and sleeves to find any sliver of exposed skin, and my legs ache with every step.

I don't know how many more days we can survive on little sleep, protein bars, tea, and sheer hope. Today has to be the last day. It *will* be the day. There isn't any other choice.

My focus narrows to the extraordinary effort of sliding one foot forward, planting it with care, then dragging the other to meet it. Above us, snow begins to flurry down, dusting our shoulders and obscuring the already treacherous path.

Just when I think the rest of my existence will be nothing

but cold, gray trudging, Sita lets out a sudden whoop of excitement. I force my tired legs to shuffle faster and round the final bend, breath catching at the sight before me.

A frozen waterfall stands before us, towering into the sky, a monument to winter itself. A pillar of frozen water, impossibly blue in the dying light. The ice catches the last remnants of the sun, shimmering with hints of silver, violet, and deep sapphire.

It is the most breathtaking natural structure I have ever seen.

Slipping off my gloves, I reach out, fingers brushing against the ice. Its surface is flawless, cold enough to bite, yet warmth blooms in my chest.

We made it.

As my gaze drifts down the icy column, something small wedged into a tiny fissure catches my eye. I brush it free from the light dusting of falling snow and pull it free.

Sita peers over my shoulder. "Is that a—"

"Soapberry," I whisper.

My throat tightens. My hands tremble as I clutch the tiny offering to my chest, remembering his hands, slick with lather, mapping every inch of my skin. The hot springs, the scent of steam and earth wrapping around us. The gentle pop of the soapberry's skin between my fingers, the way the silky foam had coated my hands as I reached for him. The way he had let me.

His hair, damp and spiked from my fingers raking through it. The tension in his muscles melting beneath my touch as I traced the strong lines of his back. The sound he made when I pressed my thumbs into his shoulders, when I made him surrender to pleasure instead of duty. The slow roll of his breathing as I massaged away centuries of solitude. The way he shuddered when I touched him—not from cold, but from something deeper.

And his eyes. Watching me. Worshipping me as he said, "Let me show you again. Let me show you you are worth saving."

The memory crashes over me like an avalanche. The heat of

his touch, the weight of his promise, the unspoken offering in his hands as he lathered the soap over my body. It had not just been cleansing—it had been a ritual. A vow.

A full-body shiver rolls through me—not from the wind, but from something deeper, something unseen but pressing against me all the same. Now that we are here, every second that passes without him is too long.

My breath catches as the air around me feels charged, thick with something electric. My fingers curl instinctively around the soapberry, gripping it harder than necessary, as if letting go might sever something invisible between us.

Such a simple gift, a single, perfect soapberry. Not lost or discarded, but perfectly placed. Just like us.

I run my thumb over the smooth surface, breath catching in my throat. This is his way of speaking to me, of guiding me, of asking without words. Not just a message or a promise, but a plea.

I exhale, trying to steady myself, but my pulse is erratic, hammering in my throat like a tabla drum. There is no mistaking it. He is watching me. The weight of his presence is as real as the ice beneath my feet, as real as the ache in my body, as real as the desperate, stubborn hope that we made it in time clawing its way up my ribs.

I force out a slow, shaking breath and press the soapberry into my palm, squeezing it tight. He wants me here. There is no doubt in my mind, or in my heart. He is waiting. And this time, I will not let him slip through my fingers.

Sita lets out a soft, triumphant laugh, pulling me back to the present. Suddenly, she throws her arms around me. I hug her back, a surge of warmth overtaking the cold. For a moment, the exhaustion, the hardship, the fear—it all melts away. Only resolve remains. We made it, and now, we are going to save him.

We pull back to smile at each other over our victory, but the moment is shattered by the sound of slow clapping.

CHAPTER THIRTY-FIVE

Dahlia

My blood turns to ice. I whirl around, heart slamming against my ribs.

Ben.

He stands at the edge of the frozen waterfall like a conqueror, boots planted in the snow, his smirk as sharp as a blade. Flanking him, faces sharp with ruthless determination, is his team. And beside them, a man clutching a leash, barely holding back a snarling wolf, its frosted breath curling in the air.

I lock my legs, forcing my body to stay upright as my weak knees threaten to buckle, but the shock lingers in my veins like poison. I was supposed to beat him here. I was supposed to stop this. What if I'm already too late?

"They must have paid him well," Sita murmurs, her voice taut with fury at seeing a local with Ben's group.

It takes me a second to process her words, to register the man standing among Ben's crew. He won't meet our eyes. He knows what he's done.

"Well enough for him to risk the Migoi's wrath," I say, my

voice sharper than the wind. My fingers tighten around the soapberry, grounding myself. "We had a run-in with him before."

My heart bleeds for Eryon. Another betrayal. Another greedy man come to take what is his.

Sita's voice cuts through the tension, seething with a fury that matches the storm that has started raging around us, as if even the mountains are angry. "How could you betray the Migoi who has guarded these mountains for centuries? To turn against him is to break your dharma and dishonor the balance of nature."

"Greed," I say, my voice cold as I pass judgment on the group in front of us. All guilty of the same sin. "Humanity's downfall. Always."

My poor Eryon. Why must this be the price he pays over and over? Why is this his reward for centuries of watching over the mountains and forests, helping wherever he could? Another evil man coming to take what he has painstakingly recultivated?

Rage bubbles up inside me, scorching and relentless. I came here to show Eryon that he is worth saving, too. And damn it, I'm going to save him. I swivel my stare back to Ben, bile rising in my throat at when I'm about to do.

"Ben," I call out, extending my hand toward him in a placating gesture. "I guess it's my downfall, too. You're right. There's no way I could've done this without you. Can you at least get me back into the University? I know how much pull you have there."

I take a few hesitant steps and say, "I'll help you get the plant, but I need access to the future drug—and something to go home to. I know you could never forgive me, and I'm not asking you to. But please, throw me a bone here."

Years of being with this narcissist have taught me how to play him like a fiddle. Pander to his pride, stroke his ego, make him feel like the big man who's doing a favor for poor, helpless

Dolly. I know in my heart that I'm the one who got him everything, but he could never admit it. A true narcissist, through and through.

Sita stands frozen, slack-jawed, her eyes wide in disbelief at the sudden change of heart—one she knows doesn't align with who I am. I have to trust that she will sense my plan and not do anything to give me away.

I turn to her and place the soapberry in her hand. "Here, you might as well take the key to my room back since I won't be needing it anymore."

She cocks her head at me, brows furrowing in confusion as she looks down at what I've pressed into her hand. She hardens her voice and says, "I don't want you back anyway if you're going to join these men."

I feel her fingers curl around mine, a subtle but telling signal, as she silently accepts the "key" from me. She understands.

"Oh, Dolly," Ben croons. "You always were a stupid girl. We're already here. I don't need you. And I don't want you. I couldn't care less that you have nothing to go back to."

He nods at Sita, triumph shining in his eyes. "And now you've got nothing here, either."

He lets out a cruel laugh, but I lean into my facade and push the farce further.

"Ben," I cry, pretending to be heartbroken. "You still need to navigate the cave system. You have no idea what that beast is like. I can help you."

His eyes narrow as he considers my words. Thankfully, all of my field notes were strictly professional, no mention of my relationship with the Yeti, so as far as he knows, what I'm saying is true.

I hesitate, not wanting to overplay my hand but knowing I'm running out of time. I need him to be impulsive, not analytical.

"Ben, I barely escaped with my life. Please, let me help you. I just want to make sure this plant gets turned into medicine. I am the one who needs it because—" My voice breaks, and I swallow hard before I can continue. "I inherited the gene. You have the power to save my life."

I didn't need to act that last part out. It's my truth.

A smile spreads across his face at the crack in my voice, at my desperate plea. His chest swells with self-importance, and I see the gloating aura settle around him. I've won this battle. The war isn't over yet, but this is the first step.

"You may have escaped with your life, but I heard about the price you paid," Ben leers at me, lip curled in disgust.

Rage pulses through my veins. How dare he lecture me on morals when he cheated on me in my own house. I should have done more than break the bastard's nose. I only hope I have a chance to do so now. That thought alone helps me to keep my anger in check and continue this ruse.

"Lucky for you, I'm not a monster. I'm a good *man*. Of course, I'll save your life. The headlines will be incredible. Hell, the PR story will have investors scrambling to fast-track this drug. And my payout. Fine. You lead the way. But make no mistake—I won't hesitate to kill you. This plant is worth more to me than your life ever did."

"Of course, Ben. Thank you," I say, eyes downcast to give the impression of acquiescence—but more importantly, to hide the victory that must be shining in them.

The air changes.

The storm bends, shifting around something larger. Something inevitable. A presence so vast, it makes the mountain feel small. The wolf whimpers as his handler backs away and the other men shift, their breath turning shallow, hands twitching toward their weapons. They don't see him yet. But they feel him.

A deafening roar, fiercer than an avalanche, shakes the earth. The ground trembles beneath my boots, and the air thickens, charged and waiting.

He is here.

The remaining men close ranks, flanking Ben. When their eyes go round, I don't need to turn around to know Eryon has appeared behind me. The very air shimmers with his presence, menace and danger radiating off him in waves to collide against my back.

Like the others who quake in terror, my lizard brain screams at me to run. But the fear licks through my veins like fire and pools low in my belly, desire pulsing in my core as I recall the feel of him against my skin, the heat, the lust. To be this close to him again yet so far away is excruciating.

"Sruhnar," he growls.

I spin to face him, dragging my gaze up his terrifying form, awed at his presence even after we had explored every inch of each other's bodies. He appears larger and more fearsome than ever with his chest heaving and his luminous quicksilver eyes snapping with frozen fire.

When our gazes meet with the force of an avalanche, I see exquisite pain reflected in their depths and realize he must have heard my ruse.

I hold my hands up, "Er—"

"Do not say my name," he snarls, lip curling to reveal his sharp teeth.

Chapter Thirty-Six

"He told you his name?" Sita asks, shocked into speaking.

I glance at her, pulse hammering in my throat. The wind howls through the mountains, whipping loose strands of my hair into my face, but I barely register it.

Sita's dark eyes search mine, and she whispers, "Migoi only tell their mates their names. They have great power. In all the centuries this Migoi has been here, no one knows his name. Except you."

Her whispered words hit like a thunderclap. My knees nearly buckle.

Mate.

The word sinks its teeth into my ribs, clamping down so tight I can't breathe. A roaring fills my ears, but I don't know if it's the wind or my own blood, surging like a storm through my veins. My body knows something before my mind does—knows in the way my stomach drops, in the way my fingers tingle with something electric, in the way my heart clenches so tightly it may burst.

The wind doesn't howl anymore. The mountain doesn't exist. There is only this truth.

I am in love with a Yeti.

And he—

He loved me first.

A terrible, aching clarity settles over me. I think back to the soapberry, placed at the base of the frozen waterfall like an offering. The scrap of lace he left in the snow, a thread of red in the white expanse, a trail meant only for me. The mark he carved into stone, his silent call to me across the mountain.

Eryon didn't need to leave me clues. But he did because he wanted me to find him.

And that means despite his fury, despite the pain in his voice when he forbade me to say his name—he still wants me here.

I am his mate. I choose Eryon, and the realization steals the breath from my lungs.

He's furious. I can feel it, thrumming in the air like the coming storm. But beneath the rage, beneath the tension coiled in his massive frame like a wound too deep to close, I feel something else.

Something fragile. Something raw.

I know he witnessed our journey, saw me battle the whispering gorge, watched as I braved the screaming wind and the snow and the mountain. And I know, deep in my bones, that if we had been in true danger, he would have come. But this—this is different. This is *my* fight. It is my turn to show him that he is worth saving, too.

I will be the white knight. I'll save the day, and then I can explain everything—my subterfuge, my deception, my desperation. Then, we can forget the rest of the world.

Even if staying here with him means my death, I'd rather die by his side than live without him. Let it be here in his arms, swallowed by his warmth, buried in his scent, lost in the quiet sanctuary of his cave.

Let me be his.

A shuddering breath escapes me, curling in the frozen air. My heart pounds, steady, insistent. I would finally be living for myself—a life on my terms, driven by my own choices. And if love is the sum of those choices, then so be it.

I deserve Eryon. My heart beats his name like a mantra, fueling me with a fierce determination. My gaze snaps back to him, willing him to understand. Desperately trying to communicate with him by my eyes alone.

I try to piece together a solution, shifting the invisible chessboard in my mind, searching for the elusive strategy that will save us. But the odds are daunting. Ahead of me stands one very enraged Yeti, and behind me looms one very dangerous man. The space between them feels like a no-man's-land, and I am the one caught in the crossfire.

There are no good moves. No safe exits. Someone is going to lose, and I will make sure that it is not going to be Eryon.

A loud click breaks the silence, and I spin back to Ben to see him holding a gun, aimed straight at Eryon. The stakes have just been upped. The fading light glinting wickedly off the metal slams into me like a physical blow.

"I was hoping you would lure him out. I can't imagine what the payout will be for this monster plus the plant. You won't be so fierce when you're locked in a cage, *snowman*," Ben sneers.

No.

Not again. Not another loss. Not another wound carved into Eryon's soul. Not this time.

A sharp inhale cuts through my lungs, too shallow, too tight. I see everything at once—Sita, frozen in horror. Eryon, body coiled, muscles flexing, teeth bared. Ben's finger tightening on the trigger.

A lifetime of fieldwork has trained me to observe first, to analyze, to think—but this isn't that kind of moment. Because

I'm not Dahlia, the scientist anymore. I am Sruhnar, and I am going to protect my mate.

I don't think. Instead, I react on pure primitive instinct.

Time fractures. I see Sita's mouth open in a scream, but all I hear is the determined beat of my own heart, pushing out the blood I need to save him. I don't feel the burn in my legs as I throw myself forward, snow crunching, gravel kicking up in my wake. I don't heed the wind howling around us, the mountains crying their warnings.

The only thing that exists is that gun. This moment. This choice.

I push faster. Each movement is unstoppable. I am already marked for death; let Eryon have a second chance.

In slow motion, I see the minute motion of Ben's finger pulling the trigger followed by the recoil. I should be scared, terrified of being shot, but instead, all I feel is a deep sense of calm in achieving what I had set out to do. For even if I die, Eryon will know that he is worth saving. There is no greater purpose for my life that I could have chosen.

I brace myself for the impact of the bullet, but there is no deafening crack, no explosion of pain. Instead, a sharp sting pierces my shoulder. I look down, but instead of the blood I expect to see blooming from a gunshot wound, I find a dart.

I try to reach for it, but my arm won't listen. Instead, it falls limply to my side as a wave of syrupy warmth floods my veins, sticky and slow. My legs buckle, and I crash hard onto my knees, the impact rattling up my spine. Then the ice rushes up to meet me. My head hits with a solid crack, and stars dance in my vision. I am completely paralyzed. Helpless to do anything except watch.

I feel everything—the shock of the cold ground pressed against my cheek, the icy wind whipping snow against my face. My lungs seize. I try to breathe, but the air is too thick. The weight in my limbs spreads until I am as heavy as stone.

I can't see Eryon anymore, but I know he's there. I can feel him, just beyond the dark closing in. I wish I could call out to him. Just once. I wish I could tell him this was my choice. That I would choose him every time.

A shadow moves over me, and for a brief second, hope flares in my chest that I will at least get to see him once more. But I truly am cursed, because instead Ben's ugly mug floods my vision.

If I had the strength, I would be furious that his is the last face I see instead of my mate's. But my mind is too tired for even that.

For a second, something flickers across his face that looks like regret. As if he can't believe he pulled the trigger. As if, for one fleeting moment, he remembers who I used to be.

The girl who gave up everything for him. The girl who pushed his work forward, made him look brilliant, built his success at the cost of her own. The girl who let herself shrink so he could shine. The one who would have done anything to stand by his side.

But that girl is gone.

In her place, a woman lies paralyzed in the snow. And if he mourns her at all, it isn't for my sake. It's for the control he lost. The power he will never hold over me again.

His jaw tightens, and the moment evaporates like a cloud of breath in the cold. There is no remorse. Only greed. The truth pierces my foggy thoughts—I was always disposable to him.

Somewhere behind me, Eryon moves. I cannot see him, but I feel it in the way the air shifts and the pressure changes. A presence so vast it warps the space around him. Unstoppable. Inevitable.

The storm has broken—and Eryon is the avalanche.

A roar tears through the air. Not just a sound, but a reckoning. It crashes against the mountains, rolling through the cliffs, shaking the trees down to their roots. Snow tumbles in thick sheets from the ledges above, a force of nature set loose.

It reverberates through my bones and rattles in my chest, a sound so powerful it feels like a touch, his touch. A sound that is not just rage but promise.

You will not take her from me.

A roar that does not just judge, but condemns. That does not bargain, does not plead, does not leave room for mercy. A deep guttural promise of not just destruction, but death. The scales of nature will be balanced.

Ben stumbles back, face as pale as the surrounding snow. His bravado falters for the first time—he looks afraid.

I force my lips to move, my breath shallow, my strength draining from me like melting snow. My voice is barely a whisper, but I make sure Ben hears it. I *need* him to hear it.

Before the darkness claims me, with the very last iota of strength I have left, I gasp, "You're the only monster here, Ben."

CHAPTER THIRTY-SEVEN

She betrayed me.

The words are poison in my veins, a sickness that burns through my chest. I watch her lie, about me, about us and everything we had. I see her step toward the man who tried to steal what was mine. I witness her speak false words, hold out her hands to *him*—hands that once clutched at me, traced my skin, trembled in my grip as she came undone.

And now—she is his.

A tearing, splitting sensation rips through my chest. I cannot breathe. This must be what she felt under that damned avalanche. There is no air without her. No light, without her. Only darkness and death.

The storm howls in my ears, wind shrieking through the ravine. I do not know if it is the land's fury or my own. Perhaps they are one and the same. The world narrows to a knife's edge. Snow churns around us, a vortex of white and shadow like the maelstrom of my heart.

The pain erupts out of me in a primal scream that threatens

to bring down the mountain itself. She turns to me, those damned blue-violet eyes reminding me of everything I've lost, again. I see her lips move, forming around the gift I foolishly offered. Not just the sounds that make my name, but myself, my very soul.

My name on her lips had once been sacred, but now it is a curse I cannot bear to hear again. I will not let her speak it.

I stop her, but instead of shame or regret, instead of the fear that should be flashing in her eyes, instead I see acceptance. Resolve. A steely determination that has her eyes blazing brighter than the stars. A look that has the smallest voice inside of me daring to whisper, maybe I am wrong.

Because I have seen this look in the eyes of a mate before. And the only thing strong enough for this level of commitment in the face of loss, is love.

Before I can listen to the quiet whisper, before I can let hope think about blossoming in this land of ice and snow, a click draws both of our attention, spinning us back to face the one they call Ben.

He holds a gun raised directly towards me, his finger tightly curled around the trigger. His eyes are as dead as his heart. Before I can move, before I can sweep my Winter Star behind the shield of my body, she proves that small voice right and runs towards the looming danger.

Her legs churn, snow kicking up in her wake as she launches herself directly into the path between me and death.

No.

NO!

The shot cracks through the air. The storm stills as the mountain holds its breath with me. The whole world waits in silence as Dahlia's shoulder takes the impact and she slams to her knees before her body falls. And so do the stars. The very earth stops spinning. Not even a single snowflake dares to break the stillness of the moment.

Too late, I understand.

Her words had never been a betrayal. They had been a sacrifice. A deception. She was never his. She was never theirs. She was always mine.

And now—she is dying for it.

The earth roars.

No, it's me. It detonates from my chest, the fury of centuries unleashed. It is not a sound meant for human ears. It is the voice of the wild, of the storm, of the earth itself crying out in wrath.

The ground beneath me cracks. The cliffs tremble. Snow cascades from the ledges above, the mountain itself answering my rage.

I am moving though I do not remember choosing to move. My body surges forward, but she is already still. Silent. Gone is the flush from her beautiful face, gone is the light from her eyes. This great loss demands justice, and I will rain down the punishment and revel in it.

The world stops in the space between my heartbeats. The space where she will live for all eternity, but only one beat more is all the longer any of them will live before I tear this world apart. Starting with them.

The first man barely has time to scream as I hit him like a landslide, claws rending flesh, bone, sinew. Red sprays hot against the snow, steaming in the cold. His weapon clatters uselessly to the ground. His body crumples, and something in me twists.

She did this for me.

I grab the next man by the throat, lifting him from the ground as he claws at my wrist. His eyes bulge. His mouth gapes, gasping for air that will not come.

This is for the words she choked on to keep me safe.

I squeeze. His neck gives way with a wet crunch, and I toss him aside like he is nothing more than kindling. Another turns, raising his rifle. My heart beats a staccato rhythm of guilt.

I should have been faster. Moved faster. Understood faster.

I rip the gun from his hands and with it the arms from his body. He barely has time to register the pain before I send him sprawling over the cliff's edge, the mountain swallowing his screams.

Her hands had trembled when she gave the soapberry to Sita.

I see it now—her plan, her quiet defiance. The beast inside me demands more sacrifice, more carnage. More revenge. But there will never be enough blood to sacrifice in her name.

I grab another by the waist, lifting him overhead. His bones snap like dry branches as I bend him backward until his spine breaks. I plow through them like the great Northern winds. Fierce. Relentless.

She trusted me to protect her.

The others run, or at least, they try. One man scrambles backward on the ice, clawing at the snow, eyes wide with the kind of terror that turns men into prey. I descend upon him like the storm itself, my foot pressing down until his ribs crack beneath my weight.

He gasps, pleading. As if that would save him. But it is his mistake, because the only voice I want to hear, need to hear right now, is silenced. I seize him by the leg and swing. His body slams into rock, bones shattering on impact. Once. Twice. A final, sickening crack. I let what remains of him fall to the ground in a useless heap.

She fought for me. And I doubted her.

A snarl cuts through the air, sharp and furious. The wolf with its teeth bared, hackles raised, has returned. I whirl to face it, growling back, my own hackles raised and claws extended. I am one with my beast. The wolf whimpers in response, tucks its tail, and bolts back into the trees.

I spin in a circle, looking for my next target, but only one remains.

Ben.

He stands frozen, his gun shaking in his grip, ragged breath misting the frozen air. I am on him before he can think to run. His scream is cut short as I lift him from the ground. He flails, kicking at empty air, his boots scraping uselessly against my chest.

I stare into his eyes. I want him to understand. I want him to see. All the men like him. All the destruction. All the greed. All the pain.

He will be the last. I will make sure of it.

I tighten my grip. He gurgles, his face turning red, then purple. His heartbeat hammers against my palm, frantic. I could crush him. Snap his spine. Tear him apart.

But that is too kind.

I step to the very edge of the mountain, my feet steady and sure, never tearing my eyes from his as they begin to slowly turn red from the pressure. I let him dangle, let his terror bloom like the rarest flower.

The storm resumes in earnest around us, the mountain crying out for vengeance. The cliffs above groan as snow shifts, fractures deepening, the land itself demanding justice.

Then—I roar. A sound so raw, so deafening, it shatters the ice beneath our feet. I do not care. Let the mountain take me as well. I am ready to meet my Winter Star in whatever lies beyond this world.

Ben shakes, pupils blown wide. His mouth moves, but no words can escape the crushing grip I have on his throat.

Good. He deserves no last words. He chokes out a faint gurgle, desperately trying to move air into his lungs while his fingers scrabble at my wrist, clawing for purchase, for mercy.

Mercy.

I think of Dahlia, lying in the snow. Her body breaking to

protect me. I think of the fear in her eyes—not of me, but for me. I think of what I almost let myself believe.

He made me doubt her. He made me hesitate. He made me see her as something weak, something selfish—when she was always the strongest of us.

I snarl, tightening my grip, and feel something snap beneath my fingers.

Ben chokes, a strangled, pitiful sound. His lips move, attempting to form words—a desperate plea from a desperate man.

I do not care.

I lift him higher. Hold him there. Let him know he is nothing. He has always been nothing so I will return him to it. I pull back and hurl him into the sky. For a moment, he flies. Arms flailing. Finally able to breathe, he lets out an agonized, hoarse scream.

Then—he falls. The abyss takes him. The last echo of his cry stretches out, fading, until it is swallowed by the earth. The mountain's call for sacrifice, my call for vengeance, my Sruhnar's blood debt has been satisfied.

When silence reigns once more, I stop and take a shuddering breath. My chest constricts, my heart scarcely able to beat in a chest that has caved in on itself. The bloodlust still thrums in my veins, but something colder grips me now. Darker.

All-consuming grief. A companion I had hoped never to see again.

I turn to look upon her one last time where she lies in the snow. My Dahlia is movement and light and laughter. And now, she is still. So still.

The world shifts—no more fury, no more vengeance. Just—silence.

I drop to my knees. I reach for her, already dreading the stiffness, the cold, the absence of my light. My hand trembles as I press it against her chest, waiting for nothing. But there—there is something. A heartbeat. Slow. Weak. But there. My heart stutters as my mind tries to comprehend. Can it be?

I sweep her up into my arms, and then I see it. A dart sticking in her shoulder, not a bullet. Such a small insignificant thing. And yet, it could have taken everything from me. It was meant for me, but she took it instead.

I thought her strong. I thought her unbreakable. But in this moment, she is so *small* beneath my hands. So fragile...so human.

I almost lost her.

And for the first time in centuries, I am afraid. Afraid to hope. Afraid to breathe. Afraid that if I do, she will slip away. I pray—to the Creator, mother moon, to the gods of the old world and the new, to any power that will listen.

Please. Let her live. Take my life if you must, but let her live.

Carefully, I stand, cradling her against my chest, shielding her from the wind. She is a small, fragile, breakable thing in my monstrous hands. And though she is even colder than when I pulled her from that avalanche, I feel a whisper of her breath against my skin. Weak, but real.

A tremor runs through me. Relief pulses with terror, merging into a pain I do not know how to hold. I press my forehead to hers, desperate, pleading, willing my very lifeforce into hers.

"Take everything I have, Sruhnar. Take my warmth, my fire, my heart." I clutch her tighter. "I am here, my Winter Star. My mate. Come back to me."

CHAPTER THIRTY-EIGHT

DAHLIA

Time passes by in a series of polaroid pictures. Snapshots of light and movement. The worried faces of Sita and Eryon. Being enveloped in heat and soft fur. The most delicious drink I've ever tasted poured into my mouth.

And then—nothing.

Perhaps this is what death is. Simply nothing. If I'm dead, I may as well catch up on my rest, free from the howling wind and the cold scrabbling at me like skeleton fingers. But I doubt I would need sleep if I were truly gone, which means—I'm alive.

My eyes snap open on a sharp inhale, the scent of deep earth washing over me, warm and familiar. A faint undercurrent of snow and pine tears at my heart.

Eryon.

I blink, the darkness taking shape into shadows cast by the banked embers of a fire. I flex my fingers and wiggle my toes, checking in with my body. My limbs respond easily, but something feels—different. Not just better, but more.

I stretch like a cat, rolling my shoulders, and the movement is glorious. The furs piled on me slide off as I sit up, leaving my bare skin exposed to the cool air of the cave. I reach for my shoulder, searching for some trace of injury—some lingering pain from where Ben shot me—but my skin is smooth, untouched. Not even a pinprick.

I swing my legs over the edge of the bed and stand. Nothing hurts. No aches, no soreness. If anything, I feel stronger. Energized. My muscles hum with power, my lungs expand as if breathing in the world for the first time.

What the hell was I shot with? If that is what is making me feel this way, I kinda want more.

Padding toward the fire, I stretch my hands toward the heat, basking in the cozy warmth. I listen for any sign of Eryon, but all I hear is the cave itself—deep and quiet, like a living thing at rest.

My growling stomach breaks the silence just as I spot my pack leaning against the wall. I pull it toward me, hunger gnawing at my stomach. I root around inside, digging to the bottom to search for anything edible. My fingers close around something unfamiliar.

I pull it out to find a bundle of moss and bark, bound with delicate vine. My stomach tightens, unease prickling up my spine. This wasn't here before. I know every item in my pack, every last thing I brought with me.

I sink to my knees next to the fire and unwrap it slowly, reverently, as if touching something sacred. As if I already somehow know its contents are beyond precious. The moment I see the petals nestled in the carefully crafted container, my breath catches.

The *Silene vitalis*.

He must have placed it in the bottom of my pack for me to find later before he sent me away. Wrapped with such care it breaks my heart, its petals remain pristine, shimmering faintly even in the dim light of the fire's coals. He gave it to me. A whole intact plant, roots and all.

Even in his heartbreak, he was still trying to save me.

A lump forms in my throat, hot and suffocating, as I clutch the bundle to my chest. He cast me out, heartbroken over the old traumas and fears of being used and duped. He told me to leave. But even in his pain, he ensured I would live. He let me go, even though it must have killed him.

Ben had said my life was worth nothing to him, despite all the years I had devoted to him. But Eryon had shown me, with this one gesture, that my life meant *everything*. That I was worth saving, yet again.

The weight of it crushes my chest, the meaning behind his actions sinking into the well of my soul like a stone. He'd chosen his duty over me. But even then, he still saved me.

I clutch the flower to my chest, rising swiftly to my feet. I have to find him. I need to tell him—everything. I don't hesitate. I run. Thank the gods I hadn't taken the time to empty my pack back at the guesthouse because then I wouldn't be here with him. My Eryon—my mate?

The thought nearly stops me in my tracks. I want to call out his name but hesitate after he told me not to. As I run, I ponder Sita's words. Since he told me his name, does that mean I am his mate?

Do I want to be?

The answer slams into me with the force of an avalanche.

Yes. YES. I want this. Want him. More than I've ever wanted anything.

The tunnels blur past me, my feet moving instinctively, carrying me through the twisting cave system toward the heart of the mountain. I should be exhausted. I should be weak. Instead, I feel faster than I've ever been. My body moves with a newfound strength, my heartbeat steady, my lungs eager.

Eryon.

The name beats in my chest with every step. At last, I reach the secret garden. The lush oasis unfolds before me, bathed in moonlight. The stars shimmer overhead, a vast expanse of silver and midnight blue, reflected in the rippling waters of the hot spring.

I slow, my breath coming in steady pulls as I make my way to the flower's home. Kneeling in the soft earth, I take a shaking breath and press my fingers to the soil. This is it. The reason I came here. The key to saving my life.

I clutch the delicate petals, my heart hammering as I ponder the weight of my decision, weigh the balance of fate. For years, I have fought to prove my worth. To Ben. To the world. To myself. I have scraped and struggled, desperate to be something more— to be needed, to be valued. Loved. But standing here, in this sacred place, I realize—I was chasing the wrong future.

Not anymore.

I don't need a lab. I don't need a legacy. The truth isn't a whisper. It's an avalanche. It crashes over me, unstoppable, undeniable. I love him. More than my career. More than I love myself. More than my own life.

I *need* him.

If I take this flower now and leave, I might live. But leaving is betrayal. And living without him is not life. It would be nothing more than shadows and darkness. He is my light.

Tears burn my eyes as I stare down at the flower, at the shimmering violet-blue nestled in my palms like an answered prayer. Then, with a shaking breath, I force my fingers to unclench.

Here it stays, and here I'll stay if he will have me. For forever long I have.

With careful hands, I nestle the fragile roots back into the soil, smoothing the earth over them. Standing, I take a step back, smiling proudly at the way the plant looks like it had never been disturbed. Sure, the plants are promising, but here is where they belong. Not in a lab, stolen from their home and protector.

The air shifts. A whisper of breath skates over the back of my neck. A presence I have felt before, the day I came to this mountain and felt him watching me. Waiting.

Now, as the air stirs, and the weight of his gaze settles over me, I know—he was always meant to find me.

I turn slowly, heart pounding, and there he is.

Eryon stands before me, his massive frame silhouetted by the moonlight, his silver eyes blazing. I am both dreading and anticipating this moment in equal parts. Does he understand why I said what I did? Does he still care for me? Will he allow me to stay?

Before I can weigh the thoughts, he whispers my name, *his* name for me, "Sruhnar."

His voice is thick, strained, filled with something more than just longing. His silver eyes flicker, roaming over me, as if memorizing every inch—afraid I might vanish if he looks away.

The way he rolls the *r* reverberates deep in my belly. He is standing so close I could reach out and touch him, can feel his breath coasting over my flesh, smell the crisp scent of snow and pine that clings to him.

My lips part on my inhale, trying to breathe in his very essence. I want to explain everything, clarify every word he witnessed, but he doesn't allow me the chance.

He closes the distance in one swift motion, his hands fisting in my hair, his mouth claiming mine.

I pour my explanation, my apology, my hopes and desires into every touch of our lips which says more than my mere words ever could. My legs wrap around him as my hands sink deep into the thick fur across his chest, my fingertips seeking the unique velvet texture of his skin.

His scorching kiss tells me that all is forgiven. Every thrust and retreat of his tongue as it dances over mine tells me that balance has been restored.

"Mate me," I gasp against his lips between kisses, feral with desire. "I want you at your wildest. I am not afraid."

He slides me slowly down his body and sets me gently on my feet. He takes my face in his hands, locking eyes with me and declares, "I will be more beast than man. It will be raw, primal. This will not be any gentle lovemaking, no plant to ease the way. It will be a claiming. And once I claim you, I cannot, will not, let you go."

I square my shoulders and nod once, my voice firm with my resolve as I say, "I don't want you to let me go. I want to claim you just as much as you want to claim me. I don't care what you are, as long as you are mine. Just as I was always meant to be yours. I want you—every part of you, wild and untamed."

His lips curl into a wicked grin, his silver eyes dark with something primal. He drops his hands and takes a step back. Then another.

His body doesn't just grow, it transforms. Expands into something massive, untamed. His fur thickens like a living storm, claws unsheathing like curved blades. The transformation is startling. Any trace of the man behind the beast is gone. The creature that stands before me is pure Migoi.

His roar splits the night, shaking the stone beneath my feet. The sound of a predator. A command. A warning.

A thrill licks up my spine.

His silver eyes lock onto mine—not a man, not a beast. Only —my mate. He drops his head back and roars, "Run."

Chapter Thirty-Nine

Dahlia

Fear slams into my stomach like a lead weight, dragging at my limbs until instinct kicks in, screaming at me to do what he commanded.

I spin and bolt, darting into the nearest tunnel. I have no idea where I am going in this rabbit warren of crisscrossing caves. I don't think—I can't think—I just keep moving, feet pounding against the uneven ground as though the devil himself is chasing me.

But Eryon isn't the devil. He's something far worse. He is a god of winter. A harbinger of hunger and the hunt. And I am the willing sacrifice.

My breath comes fast and uneven, my pulse thundering in my ears. My feet slip over loose rocks, but I recover—too fast, too precise. My body is stronger than it should be, my muscles burning but not faltering. Strength pulses through my veins, something wild, something new. For a flickering second, the thought crosses my mind—could I truly outrun him?

The tunnel splits ahead. The left slopes upward, a faint

breeze curling through the passage. I veer that way, lungs pulling in air as I chase the promise of open space, of escape. The incline steals my breath, my calves tightening, but I don't stop. My ragged breaths drown out all sound as I push onward, until—

Eryon

I feel my form growing, larger even than the beast's mantle. Change shivers over my skin, not just elongating my thick white fur but standing it on end.

My claws unsheathe, sharpening to their full lethal points. My vision sharpens, cutting through the darkness as if the mountain itself bends to my sight—every rock, every shift of shadow clear as day.

I hear her.

The frantic pound of her heart. The raw scrape of bare feet against stone. Breath, shallow and uneven, caught between instinct and exhilaration. She runs—fast, reckless. Blind. She doesn't know these tunnels. But I do.

Her scent trails behind her like a lure made only for me— sunshine and spring, fire and defiance, undercut by something richer. Something deeper.

Her desire. It curls in the air, potent and intoxicating, filling my lungs until my body thrums with the need to claim her.

The beast inside me scrabbles at my skin, wild and insistent, demanding I tear through the dark after her and take what is mine. The same beast that raged when I saw her collapse, her skin as pale as the surrounding snow. The same beast that nearly lost her.

Only with the sheer will borne of centuries do I restrain myself. I let her run. Not in fear. Not in desperation.

The first time she ran, it was to save me. To shield me from death, even when it should have been me protecting her. That moment—the sight of her falling, the breath torn from her lungs—will haunt me until the end of my days.

But now—now she flees in promise, in surrender. And this time, I will catch her.

She has laid her claim on me. Asked me to lay mine on her. Spoken the words, but more importantly, proven them with her actions.

Actions I hope never to see repeated. She has given up everything for me. She has chosen not just me, but *us*. Never again will I doubt her. Never again will I let fear cloud what I already knew from the moment I saw her—she is *mine*.

Heat floods my veins, primal and absolute. My cock throbs at the delay, the restraint nearly unbearable, but the longer I wait, the sweeter the moment will be when I catch her. This time, I will not doubt. I will not hesitate.

She has chosen me. Not as a last resort. Not out of desperation. But because she is mine as surely as I am hers.

I can almost see her as she races through the tunnels, tuned into her exact location. Keeping myself from running to her becomes more than I can bear, and at last—I unleash my beast to pounce upon her like that damned avalanche I pulled her from.

Only unlike the temporary snow, I will consume her like the mountain. Unmoving, unshakable, endless as time.

Finally, I can wait no more, and my legs spring into action, carrying me towards my Winter Star, my mate.

The moment I unleash myself, the cave walls blur around me. My muscles propel me forward with the full force of the beast I have held in check for centuries, closing the distance between us in mere heartbeats.

I do not run.

I hunt.

The tunnel walls flash past. The scent of her is stronger now, sharper with exertion, rich with anticipation. She knows I am coming. She believes she is running toward safety. She does not yet realize she is running straight into my arms.

I let her think, just for a moment, that she could escape me. But she cannot because she is already mine. She always was. But tonight, I will carve that truth into her soul. Brand my claim into her flesh.

I tear through the tunnels, faster than breath, faster than thought. Faster than fate itself.

The path she has chosen ends ahead, a cavern of shimmering crystal and moonlit stone. The perfect backdrop to her beauty.

I move faster. The air pulses with my presence, with the raw, electric energy of the hunt reaching its climax. I see her now, just ahead—her muscles coiled as she spins, realizing her mistake. The tunnel has betrayed her.

There is nowhere left to run.

I slow just enough to drink in the sight of her. She is wild and perfect, chest rising and falling with exertion, skin flushed with heat. Her curls are a halo of tangled fire, her wide eyes burning not with fear—but with hunger.

For me.

She cannot yet see me, but I see every inch of her. She senses my approach, a slow, wicked smile curving her lips. She stands her ground, hands fisting at her sides, pupils blown wide. Her scent thickens, laced with the primal understanding of what is about to happen.

Dahlia

A burst of silver light unfurls before me as I stumble into a cavern that looks as if it has swallowed the night sky. The walls are lined with jagged crystals, catching the dim moonlight from a narrow crack in the ceiling, refracting it into a thousand fractured constellations.

I pause, mesmerized, my chest heaving.

The air shifts. A ripple of energy—electric, charged—pulses through the cave, shivering over my skin.

The beautiful distraction is my downfall; air whooshes out of my lungs as a strong arm wraps around my middle and snatches me from where I stand. A startled scream leaves my lips before a hand clamps down over my mouth as his scent surrounds me, snow and pine and mine.

Harsh panting in my ear turns to a satisfied groan as he growls out, "Mate."

I sink my teeth into the fleshy palm covering my mouth, startling him enough to drop me to my feet. I take off back the way I came, away from the beautiful crystals. I am feeling smug at my escape until a hand wraps itself in my hair streaming behind me. I'm brought up short, pain prickling delightfully across my scalp as fear pools in my belly.

Eryon

I let her run. Let her think she's escaping. The thrill of the chase sings in my blood, coils in my muscles, but I don't lunge—yet.

Her scent is a beacon, blazing through the darkness, guiding me toward her. She smells of fire and spring, of sunshine and *mine.*

Her hair, loose and streaming behind her, is a gift. I seize it, wrapping the wild curls around my fist, and pull.

A sharp gasp, a stumbled step—then she's mine again.

She fights me, her small body bucking like a feral thing, but I trap her beneath me, pressed against the earth, helpless and perfect. I fist a hand in her hair, tilting her head, baring her throat. I lower my face, inhaling deeply.

The beast in me snarls in triumph, savoring the feel of her pinned and breathless beneath me. Soft where I am hard. Fragile where I am unbreakable. She is so small against me. But not weak. Never weak. She bares her teeth at me, fierce and defiant.

I love her for it.

I will break her anyway.

She whimpers, thighs pressing together, her scent thickening. She likes this. She *wants* this. A growl rumbles deep in my chest, primal and approving.

DAHLIA

One moment, I'm on my feet. The next, he has me pinned beneath him, pressed against the earth, his heat enveloping me. Panic and need coil tight in my stomach, battling for dominance. My instincts scream at me to fight. But another, deeper instinct, one far older, urges me toward beautiful surrender.

"Eryon—" I gasp, but his growl cuts me off.

"You ran." His voice is deep, guttural. Not human.

"I—"

"You ran," he interrupts me again.

It isn't a question. It's a declaration. A challenge. A dark thrill pulses through me. My fingers curl into the earth as I admit, "I ran."

We both know he isn't talking about this moment, but the moment I ran to save him. A sound rumbles from his chest, something primal and pleased. His hand fists in my hair, tugging my head back, exposing my throat.

Dragging his nose along the long line of my neck, he growls so low I can scarcely make out the words, "You saved me. You *chose* me."

ERYON

My lips crash against hers, claiming, consuming, setting fire to everything between us. She arches into me, her body molding against mine like she was made for this. My claws drag down her sides, not to harm, but to feel. To mark.

She is small against me, fragile—but not breakable. She has proven that.

She does not beg. She does not surrender. She bares her teeth against my mouth and takes as much as she gives. My perfect, reckless mate. My Sruhnar.

The beast in me is barely contained, the need to rut, to take, to brand her from the inside out pulsing through every fiber of my being. But something deeper, something older, steadies my hands.

She is alive. Warm. Strong. Mine.

She fought for me, risked everything for me. And now, here she is, wrapped around me, kissing me like she belongs to me— because she does.

The weight of it crashes over me, something heavier than lust.

Gratitude.

I almost lost this. I almost lost her. And if I had—there would be no world left to stand upon.

My hold tightens as I press my forehead to hers, breathing her in, my voice a raw, guttural whisper. "I will never let you go again."

"And I will never leave you," she shudders against me, her nails digging into my back, her lips trembling against mine as she whispers the word that is my undoing, "mate."

DAHLIA

Eryon flips me onto my hands and knees. The earth is cool beneath my palms, a stark contrast to the heat of his body as he cages me in, trapping me exactly where he wants me. Where I want to be.

A hiss escapes my mouth as he curls his massive form over me, trapping me between his large body and the earth. A satisfied growl rumbles from his chest as he subdues his prey. I had longed for this, to be taken by him in his full Migoi form.

I wanted the experience of pure primal claiming but now that I'm trapped, his hard cock pressed between us, I'm not so sure. Before I can think it through, my body reacts—bucking wildly, trying to throw him off my back, but it's futile. I can't so much as budge the creature wrapped around me.

He brings his nose to my hair, scenting me. As his breath cascades over my ear and neck, shivers race across my shoulder and down my spine, leaving goosebumps in its wake.

I turn my head, desperate to catch a glimpse of those luminous eyes I love so much. Instead, I am rewarded with a snarl and a lick up the side of my face.

One large hand palms the back of my head, forcing it down to the ground to keep me pinned. A cry leaves my lips as the glorious weight of him disappears from my back. It turns to a gasp when he wrenches my hips up into the air. Great, snuffling breaths trace down my spine and over my ass. I hear a sharp inhale followed by a satisfied moan, my only warning before he devours me.

ERYON

Her body fits against mine too well, curves molding to my heat, yielding even as she trembles. Her pulse flutters beneath my lips. Her scent, thick with need, coils around me, drugging me. And when I part her thighs, when I press my mouth against her inner core, dripping with need—she screams.

I am going to consume her like a wild fire. She asked for my wildest. She will have it. And by the time I am done—she will never doubt who she belongs to again.

DAHLIA

I am drowning again. Drowning in heat, in sensation, in him. His tongue is sin and fire, claiming every part of me. He feasts on me like a starving creature, dragging pleasure from my body until I am shaking beneath him.

He laps at my pussy, my ass, my cheeks, devouring me. The building sensations are a direct counterpoint to the harsh earth digging into my hands and knees. My head and body are pinned, immobile.

His great tongue probes at my entrance, slipping inside of me. A cry rips from my throat as his mouth finds my core, licking, sucking, claiming. His tongue is impossibly long, hot, and thick, sliding inside me in deep, delving strokes.

I buck against him, my body writhing in his grasp, desperate for more, for everything, for him.

He gives me no reprieve. His fingers stroke over my clit, teasing, punishing, owning.

I sob his name, my body breaking apart beneath his mouth, drowning in pleasure. I whimper, pressing back, needing more—needing everything.

And then—he's gone.

A broken sob escapes me at the devastating loss. I whimper, thrusting my hips back against empty air, desperate for his touch.

"Oh, please," I beg, wanting the warm heat to return to my dripping core. "Please."

A dark chuckle rumbles behind me.

"Please what?" he snarls.

"Please, do that again," I whimper.

ERYON

She begs so prettily. I need to hear more of her cries, more of her need for me. I want to hear her choose me again, choose us, over and over. The need will never be sated.

"Do what?" I demand, barely able to form the words through the haze of lust boiling in my veins, the red threatening to consume my vision.

I see her warring with embarrassment, but her needs win out. "Please put your tongue inside me again."

I need to fill every part of her, taste every inch of her decadent skin. Lay claim to all of her. Instead of returning my tongue to plunge into her sex, I explore the rest of her body tasting all of her, claiming all of her.

I map every texture, every soft hollow, every decadent curve until her taste is all I know. Until I've branded her into my tongue and my touch into her skin. I wait to meet her needs until she is a whimpering, quivering mass of desire under my touch.

A startled scream quickly morphs into a moan as I finally return to her core to drive my tongue deep inside of her, carefully sheathing my claws and moving a hand up to her entrance to fill her up completely.

When she begins to clench and pulse around my finger and tongue, I work another finger into her tight heat.

She lets out a hiss at the intrusion, but I know I need to prepare her to take me as much as I can. I revel in every moan, every whimper until I find the rhythm that makes her sing, touch the spots that make her ripple and clench around me.

I learn my mate inside and out. Pleasuring her is a gift, and it is one I look forward to perfecting. My tongue grows more insistent as her arousal drips from my hand. I pulse it deeper, finding the spot inside of her tight channel that makes her cry out.

When her hips thrust back into me, I work one more finger in, wringing a torrent of incomprehensible moans and cries that echo like music through the cavern.

My movements reach a fevered pitch along with her cries, my restraint hangs by a thread, but I want, no I *need*, to hear her consumed by pleasure. I rub small circles with my thumb over her sensitive bundle of nerves to push her over the edge and she falls like a landslide. Sublime, consuming, devastating.

My control frays, unspooling at the edges. I line up my throbbing erection, already dripping in anticipation, with her entrance. The moment stretches impossibly heavy in between the beats of my heart.

I coat myself in her arousal, hardening impossibly further at the shine that proves her choice. I want to hear her plead, hear her sob my name as I take her—but she is mine. And I will not simply take. I will *claim*.

I sink my aching member just inside her welcoming, hot channel, and she clenches around me, already trying to pull me inside of her. But I wait for a heavy beat, living in the moment of anticipation. The last second of before, knowing every moment after this we will be mated.

The thought has me unable to hold back any longer, the beast within finally clawing its way through my resolve, punching my hips forward to lay claim. The first thrust is brutal, despite my preparations, stretching her around me, stealing the breath from both our lungs.

She gasps. I snarl.

And then—I ruin her.

The cavern echoes with the sounds of our mating—rough, primal, unrestrained. There is no hesitation, no holding back. She asked for my wildest and she will have it. And by the time I am done, she will never doubt who she belongs to again.

She shudders and lets out a low moan as her body welcomes me, stretches around me. Perfect, tight, *mine*.

I don't start slow. I fuck her open. The cavern shakes with the force of our mating. The sound of skin slapping, the wet, obscene drag of my cock inside her, her cries, my growls. A perfect symphony of sound and heat and primal claiming. The sound of us.

DAHLIA

I am undone.

This is what I had wanted. For him to mate me in his full beast form, no holding back. I spread my knees wider and brace myself on my arms. No amount of foreplay could have prepared me for the onslaught that is Eryon in full beast form.

Every inch of him stretches me to the breaking point, burning and blissful and so, so much. He grips my hips, holding me still, forcing me to take all of him.

Every nerve ignites, pleasure streaking through my body like wildfire. I sob his name, shaking, overwhelmed, as he pumps his hips, long strokes that explore every inch inside my tight heat.

He feels twice as large as the last time. Thicker. Longer. Every pulsating vein, every ridge is an exquisite texture sliding over my sensitized nerve endings. My own harsh pants echo in my ears.

He bottoms out against my cervix, but I know I still haven't taken all of him. He wraps his arms around my body and holds me suspended in front of him, managing to caress my breasts with one hand while the other applies pressure to my belly and clit.

All I can do is take his cock as he pushes in further after every retreat. I feel my stomach moving with his member, and pleasure begins to swell within me. His shaggy soft hair envelops me, his body curled around mine.

I imagine when we must look like—a great beast rutting into a helpless female—and the taboo thought pushes me further into dark decadence. Pure animalistic pleasure.

Everything blurs into sensation and heat. I can feel him warm even more around me and within me, the large veins that line his impressive cock pulsing, enlarging. Sweat drips off my body just as the arousal drips from between my thighs. The caves echo with our shared cries of pleasure.

"Mine," he growls against my neck, his grip tightening on my hips.

"Yes," I whisper, voice raw and wrecked.

He pulls back, then slams forward, driving me across the cave floor, filling me, wrecking me. Small pinpricks of pain flare on my knees as they drag over the rough stone, a small pebble lodged beneath, but they are no more than an afterthought as I'm consumed by Eryon.

"Say it." His voice is rough, desperate.

I know he needs this. Needs *me*.

And I? I need him.

Writhing and clawing at the ground, I gasp, "Eryon, I'm yours. Always."

I cannot stop the whine that falls from my lips as he abruptly pulls out of me, only to moan in surrender as he flips me over and thrusts impossibly deeper. With his great arms wrapped around me, all I feel is Eryon.

He holds me so tight to his body I don't even touch the cold stone floor. Those silver eyes that haunted me across continents stare into mine with the brilliance of a million galaxies, luminous in the darkness. Each long thrust drags against every nerve ending that is on fire. Each slam of his hips into mine rubs his thick textured curls over my clit in a delicious counter point.

A low growl starts, vibrating from his chest against my skin. It picks up in volume until his whole body is consumed with it, vibrating against me. I am surrounded and filled by his heat, his touch. His love. I feel it in every movement, every breath, every beat of my heart. And I know, I am ready.

On instinct, I let my head fall back, exposing my throat in both offer and surrender. I hold his stare and watch as his body shudders. His rhythm falters. I watch the icy grey of his eyes turn to molten quicksilver.

And then—he *breaks*.

ERYON

She gives herself to me, completely, irrevocably. When she drops her head to expose the creamy column of her throat to me, I come undone.

She is everything. The spring to my eternal winter. The sunrise in my endless night. My salvation. My mate.

As I am overwhelmed with love, with her, my knot grows and pulses, locking us together, ensuring my seed stays deep where it belongs. Branding my claim into her flesh. I sink my sharp teeth deep into my lip until copper floods my mouth, then quickly seal my mouth around her neck and bite down, mingling her lifeblood with mine to marry our souls, sealing the bond, and claiming her as mine for eternity.

She convulses around me and screams my name, her body milking mine, her pleasure wringing me dry. I spill inside her, filling her with everything I have, everything I am. I do not let her go. I will never let her go. Wave after hot wave pulses into her, liquid fire.

My mate. My Winter Star.

As the last of our mingled cries fade, I roll onto my back, cradling her close as our bodies remain joined.

She is soft and pliant, still trembling from the force of our mating with aftershocks that run through her body like tiny earthquakes. A deep peace sinks into my soul at the weight of her in my arms, the curve of her small body against mine. I press my lips to her hair, inhaling deeply.

My mate. My *forever*.

DAHLIA

I burrow into his fur and warmth, filled with his seed and sealed with his knot. His scent is everywhere—pine, winter, mine. My skin is coated in him, his seed locked deep, his bite still throbbing at my throat. I press my fingers to his mark, feeling the slow, steady thrum of our bond beneath my skin. I will wear him proudly for the rest of my life.

"Eryon," I whisper into his velvet skin.

"Mhm," he mumbles in reply.

"The tea you gave me—," I start, but he lays his finger across my lips, silencing my question before I can voice it.

He gently pushes my shoulders up so that I am straddling him, staring down at his great silver eyes reflecting the crystal cavern back at me like the night sky.

"I knew you were my mate from the first time I saw you looking for that plant. The way you were bent over, that sweet ass on display for me," he quips as he grabs a double handful of that same body part and chuckles.

Voice turning serious, he says, "Then the sun caught your

hair and lit your curls up like the most beautiful sunset, and all I could think about was sinking my hands deep into your hair and sliding my cock between your lips."

I feel him begin to harden again inside of me, my insides turning molten as he slowly slides his hands up over my curves to bury them deep in my hair.

His voice turns soft but insistent, and he says, "But when I saw your eyes, shimmering like the petals of the winter star in the moonlight, I knew you were a gift from the gods of creation, and I loved you from that moment."

I bite my lip as tears prick the back of my eyes at his confession of the heart.

"The flower was always meant to be yours." He thrusts inside of me, reflecting the intensity of his words as he continues. "So yes, I hid it in your bag even when it broke my heart to send you away."

Another powerful stroke fills me, pulling a gasp from my lips as he declares, "I was a fool. A hurt one, but a fool nonetheless. So, when you swept back into my life like the North winds and then tried to sacrifice yourself for me, you're damn right I poured its healing elixir down your throat to save your life."

His hips pick up a punishing pace, thrusting up into me as he stares deep into my soul. He gives a small shake of my head as his hands tremble with intensity

"I will never—" *thrust* "—never be separated from you again."

It's all I can do to keep my eyes open and focused on his great silver ones.

"You are my mate, Sruhnar."

I know this, but to hear the declaration fall from his lips with such intensity, such reverence, has the tears that threatened moments ago spilling over.

"And nothing, not even death, will take you from me."

His words slam into me, raw and absolute, carving themselves into the long lines of my bones. I cling to him, my body shaking, my heart splitting wide open.

I don't just hear his vow—I feel it. I believe it.

I detonate around him, overflowing with his love and the intensity of knowing—I love him just as fiercely.

EPILOGUE

DAHLIA

Months have passed since I left the outside world. I have embraced my wild side, and thanks to the *Silene vitalis*, I am healthier than ever. My days are filled with laughter and love that usually leads to raw, animalistic sex. For the first time in my life, I am wanted and accepted for who I am, and it feels like coming home.

I'm in the hot springs, watching the night sky as I wait for Eryon to return from gathering the offerings that are left for him, that often includes letters from Sita. Tonight, I eagerly await him not for news of the outside world, which I care less and less about as time passes, but to give him my own news.

At last, he returns, dropping a large basket at the head of the spring and sinking in next to me. He gathers me in his arms and situates us on the stone bench. I relax back against him, moaning softly at the way he reaches around to cup my breasts. The increased sensitivity has me panting. The full moon makes it way past the edge of the stone roof, flooding the alcove with silvery light.

"Eryon," I say.

"Mm," he replies as he nuzzles my neck.

"The moon cycle has come and gone," I say, seeing if he will pick up on my hint.

"So, it has, my sweet Winter Star," he says as he kisses along my shoulder.

I take one of his large hands from my breast and guide it down to rest on my belly. He freezes for the space of several heartbeats, then spins me around to face him.

"Sruhnar?" His voice is full of hope, excitement shining in his eyes.

I cup his face in my hands and nod. "A snowling. Or at least, a half snowling."

He drops his forehead to mine, his breaths short and tight. When he lifts his head and meets my eyes again, tears are streaming down his face. "You are worth any price, my Winter Star, my Sruhnar."

Eighteen long months have passed. Sita even visited a few times, but there is no lore she knows of involving Migoi babies, and we didn't want to have her researching or asking around so as not to raise any suspicions.

Eryon seemed to remember his last mate being pregnant for quite a while but that was many years ago. He simply reminds me that the child will need to carry the strength of centuries and the patience of the seasons.

I eat well and sleep when I want and regularly consume the *Silene vitalis* tea. Eryon had redoubled his efforts to make sure that we had a bumper crop and had set about preserving it in a variety of forms as a safeguard.

We have shelves stocked with all parts of the plant in dried form, powdered, whole leaf, made into teas, and even, with some items supplied by Sita, tinctures and salves. At the far end of one of the tunnel systems we even have some in what I call "the freezer." A convenient storage area set into a section of permafrost.

It was as if he had funneled all of his anxieties over the pregnancy into extreme preparation for the only thing he could to ensure my health, and possibly the snowling's.

Despite no known history of a Yeti-human baby, I continue to be healthier than ever despite my rapidly growing abdomen. I should at least have had back pain or the pelvic pressure I'd heard other women complain about. But I feel shockingly well.

A sudden urge for fresh air has me getting out of bed. I slowly make my way up through the tunnels, my fingers trailing over the newest drawings—the ones of Eryon and me, the beginning of our story.

I step into the alcove, or the back porch, as I've come to call it. It's safe to be out here alone, and even though I love our home in the caves, sometimes I crave not just the warmth here but the open skies above. Eryon would be frantic if I left the caves on my own in the middle of the night.

As I walk out into my favorite place on earth, even the *Silene vitalis* seems to glow a little brighter under the full moon tonight. The moonlight and stars bathe this lush slice of heaven in a hundred shades of magnificent silver.

For the first time, my belly feels uncomfortably tight. I trace the enormous curve with both hands, whispering softly, "Little snowling, your daddy and I can't wait to meet you. Whenever you are done growing and can arrive safely, we will be waiting."

I don't want to pressure the little one into coming early. I surrendered myself as soon as I suspected I was pregnant to this miracle, deciding to enjoy every day to the fullest. Living with Eryon had taught me to respect the cycles of nature and find comfort in the calm quiet of moments like this.

While he had prepared more *Silene Vitalis* than could ever be consumed, I had read through a few books Sita had dropped off on wilderness medicine and childbirth. We had prepared a small kit with birth supplies for things like cutting the cord and expanded our supplies to cover most minor emergencies a child could get into.

I thought we were as ready as possible, but as my belly tightens again, pulling a small gasp from my lips, I start to panic at the overwhelming possibilities of what could go horribly wrong alone on the mountain. A soft breeze carries the scent of snow and pine to me, and I take a deep calming breath of it.

I make the conscious decision that I will not be afraid, and as Eryon comes up behind me and wraps his strong arms around me, I tap into his strength and surrender myself to this cycle, too. My belly tightens again under his hand, and he gasps.

"Sruhnar?" he asks, full of hope.

"I think it's time. Help me into the water and then please go grab the kit."

He guides me into the spring and helps me to sit up on the natural stone bench. The hot water feels amazing as it supports the weight of my belly and runs over my skin in a warm embrace.

I try different positions as I start to become uncomfortable, and when Eryon returns, it's to find me on my hands and knees. I rest my head on the bank, the ground soft beneath my face and the ground smelling sweet.

I am elated to be welcoming this little one into the most beautiful and magical space on this earth. The night gives way to dawn while the contractions pick up in both speed and intensity. I have no idea how long labor lasts with a snowling, but much like my pregnancy, it feels to be a very long time.

Eryon is attentive, feeding me little bits of food, offering sweet water to drink, and massaging my back. Just as the dawn breaks and golden light chases away the silvery shadows, the pain peaks. I feel a snap like a rubber band followed by gushing fluid.

What I thought was pain before is nothing compared to the contractions that come with my water breaking. I can sense the shift, as if my body is now getting down to serious business.

Instinctively, I squat in front of Eryon, telling him to sit in front of me. I pull his knees up and use them to balance my weight, breathing deep until I am overwhelmed with the strong urge to push.

I push and I push while Eryon encourages me to do whatever feels right. But it doesn't feel right. A second of clear focus washes over me, and I realize something is off. I'm not making any headway despite all the pushing.

"Eryon, listen to me. I need to get this baby out, and I don't feel like it's coming down correctly. I'm going to get on my hands and knees, so you'll need to get behind me and help catch the baby."

"Sruhnar, my Winter Star. I have complete faith in you. I will do whatever you wish. Just tell me what you need from me." His voice is calm and steady as he helps me onto my hands and knees.

I know I made the right call as something shifts and the urge to push becomes even stronger. With a primal scream, I bear down with all my strength and finally feel my baby crowning. I cry in relief, waiting for the next contraction to push again.

Eryon talks me through everything he is feeling and seeing, his voice breaking with emotion as our little snowling slides into his hands. I sag back to recline on the bank as he passes me the little bundle, and I cradle it to my chest, looking down in awe at the baby in my arms.

He drops his forehead to mine, and we bask in the moment that we become a family. He helps me recline against him as I bring the baby to my breast, my breath rushing out as it latches.

"Oh. I wasn't expecting that. What a hungry little thing," I say in wonder as I gently trace my finger over a perfectly round cheek covered in downy white fuzz. A smile splits my face at the bright violet-blue eyes that blink up at me. My mother's eyes.

"Hungry little *girl*," he corrects, an answering smile splitting his face.

"I feel some more contractions, I think the nursing is triggering the placenta to release," I say, falling back on the books I've read.

I breathe through a few of the contractions, enamored with the little girl who's popped off my breast to stare in wonder at the world around her.

I'm just starting to worry that something is wrong with as strong as the pain is getting when I feel the overwhelming urge to push again. I pull my legs up and give in to it.

Eryon helps hold my tired legs as I continue to strain. "I don't think this is just the placenta. Quick, get ready," I pant out between pushes. No questions asked, he quickly places his hands between my legs, and with the next push, he catches a second snowling.

We stare at each other in shock. Whereas the first little girl is snow white like her daddy, this little fluff ball is silvery grey, an almost blue tint to the soft downy coat.

"A son," he murmurs. He is quiet for a moment as he holds the second baby up in the light of dawn.

"Eryon?" I say softly.

He places our son at my other breast with reverence, his hands—appearing even larger as they cradle the tiny heads—resting protectively on each of them. Bowing his head, he exhales a breath that seems to carry the weight of his gratitude and awe.

He murmurs what sounds like a prayer in an ancient language, and after a long beat, meets my eyes. "I never thought to hold a snowling again. And now we have not just one, but two snowlings. *Two.* I will never be able to thank you for this gift, Sruhnar. Thank you, my Winter Star."

He holds us close, this impossible, perfect family, as dawn spills golden light over the mountain. His arms are a shield, a promise, a vow.

I came here seeking a cure. Seeking survival.

Instead, I found eternity.

AFTERWORD

Welcome to Yeti Season. Feral. Fluffy. Fiercely devoted. Ready for more?

If you want the original short and spicy novella that inspired Winter Star, Check out *Yeti or Knot* on Amazon.

For more cinnamon roll monster romance, don't miss *Chosen by the Yeti*—new heroine, new world, same swoony Yeti monster energy. Can you find the link between these worlds? Continue Yeti season today!

Acknowledgments

Thank you to my emotional support editing team, Beth Hudson, Ink, my PA and all around champion, Amanda, my alpha & beta teams (Amanda, Bree, Nicole, Lauren), my ARC & street teams, and the monster queen herself, Biblio Barbie, for all of her support and encouragement. To my family and friends, thank you for your love and patience as I talked about Yetis for months and frequently disappeared.

Thank *you*, my darling readers, for getting lost in the frost with me.

And finally, thank you to my mother for my love of reading. I put a piece of her into every story I write, that she may live on forever.

Follow me @CassandraElizzabeth and visit cassandraelizzabeth.com to subscribe to my newsletter, get updates on upcoming books, and join my reader community.

If you enjoyed this story, please consider leaving a review—it means everything to indie authors.

Remember, *YOU* are the light.

Namaste,
Cassandra

About the Author

Cassandra Elizzabeth writes love stories that bleed—dark romance, monsters, and heroines who don't just survive, but rewrite the stories meant to destroy them. Her work blends gothic atmosphere, raw emotion, and the dangerous beauty of love that refuses to die.

She is the author of the *Immortal Redemption* series and several monster romances. Cassandra proudly identifies as a disabled and rare disease author. As a gene carrier for a fully penetrant form of a terminal disease, she writes on borrowed time—and makes every word count.

Through her stories, she explores legacy, longing, obsession, and the defiant hope that even the darkest love can still heal. When she's not writing, she's chasing her twins, fighting for rare disease awareness, or tending her garden full of strange and beautiful flowers—always searching for the ones that bloom in the dark.

www.ingramcontent.com/pod-product-compliance
Lightning Source LLC
Chambersburg PA
CBHW071350300726
48976CB00006B/1827